A LIFE WITHOUT WATER

Cover design by Okay Creations
Book layout by Lori Colbeck

ISBN-13: 978-1-950348-20-6

A LIFE WITHOUT WATER

MARCI BOLDEN

PINK SAND
PRESS

For Hanna and Maxine -
I love you bigger than the sun, and the moon, and the stars.

ONE

CAROL DENMAN BLINKED. The long and slow kind that gave the brain a moment to process unexpected information. When she lifted her lids, her assistant still stood on the other side of her desk. Tiana's near-black eyes filled with a million questions. The rich umber skin above her nose crinkled as she drew her brows together.

The words she'd spoken lingered in the air between them.

There was a man standing outside Carol's office asking to see her. Not just any man. Her *ex-husband*.

"You were married before Tobias?"

Tiana's voice was low enough that no one outside the office could possibly hear, but to Carol's ears, the words sounded as if they had been announced through a bullhorn. The question spun her tightly held emotions out of control. The skin above her brow prickled with the first signs of nervous sweat. Clenching her fists, digging white acrylic tips into her palm, she took a breath to calm herself before the telltale sign of anxiety—bright red creeping up her pale neck until it settled over her face—could start.

She blinked again. This time the rapid, mind-clearing kind. She dislodged the knot in her throat before finding her voice. "Yes. A long time ago." *A lifetime ago.* "Did he say what he wants?"

"No." Confusion faded to what appeared to be concern. "He looks nervous. Should I tell him to leave or...I can call security."

Security was a seventy-three-year-old overweight retired police officer who was far more invested in completing the *Houston Chronicle*'s crossword puzzle than he ever was in doing his job. Carol suspected even if she did need help, old Charlie Turner would call 911 and offer crowd control long before he'd intervene with some kind of physical altercation in her office. Not that she was worried about what her ex would do to her.

Just the opposite.

She was more concerned she'd grab the sterling silver scissors from her desk drawer and shove them repeatedly into his chest.

Outside her window, early summer sunlight reflected in a blinding starburst off the man-made pond where geese liked to gather as they migrated. This time of year the water was smooth. Still. Deceptively calm. As she stared at the water, memories of her life with John flashed through her mind like an old 8-mm film on a loop.

Laughter, singing, playing.

Screaming. Crying. Begging.

Tiana's quiet voice cut into Carol's thoughts. "Should I tell him to leave?"

"Um... No." *God, I'm going to regret this.* "It's fine. Show him in."

"Are you—"

She cut Tiana off with a resolute nod. "Show him in."

Tiana hesitated before disappearing through the glass-paneled door. Though the three panes had been frosted to afford Carol some privacy, movement was evident on the other side. She felt her stomach knot, knowing Tiana was speaking to John, inviting him in to see the woman who'd disappeared from his life so long ago. Carol inhaled as much oxygen as her lungs would hold, then exhaled through parted lips in an attempt to regain her emotional footing.

She inhaled.

Exhaled.

Pushed the emotions down.

A set of knocks—a rhythm she recognized from decades ago—fell on her door. *Knock-knock. Knock.* He'd used that same beat to draw her attention to him from their first date, when he'd shown up with a handful of wildflowers he'd denied picking from the side of the road, until the night she snuck out of his life while he was sleeping.

Her entire body tensed at the sound. So familiar. So...*haunting.*

Then there he was. Her past in the flesh. Standing before her, looking as uneasy as she felt. She'd spent years rebuilding herself after leaving him and even more years quieting the discontent he'd sown deep into her soul. As she met his gaze, that old feeling washed through her like a tsunami. Her impeccably composed life fell apart and, as always, she had little control over whatever storm John was about to bring crashing down on her.

How many times had he told her she needed to calm down and relax? Live in the moment; worry about the rest later. She'd never mastered those particular attributes that had always come naturally to him. However, even with his laid-back attitude toward life, crow's feet had cut deep lines around his eyes and pronounced parentheses curved around his mouth, making him look much older than his—how old was he now?—fifty-six years. Gray peppered his brown hair, especially around his temples. His shoulders stooped slightly, as if he carried the weight of the world. Or years of guilt.

She stared, unmoving in her chair. Her heavy heart held her down like an anchor in a wild sea of rage.

What did he expect her to do?

Smile? She couldn't.

Hug him? She *wouldn't*.

After staring in deafening silence for several long seconds, John gave her a lopsided grin that was as familiar as his knock. She used to find the half-hearted smile charming. She used to find a lot of things about this man charming.

By the time she left him, she couldn't even find something she liked.

"Hey, you." His voice, as it always had, settled over her like a warm blanket. Only now that blanket seemed to be made of fiberglass. His deep baritone felt like a thousand invisible splinters embedding into her skin. "It's been a while, huh?"

"Twenty-four years." Her voice came out hoarse. Cracked. Broken. She gestured to a chair on the other side of her desk. "Sit."

His feet seemed to be as glued to the floor as her body was to her chair.

"Or stand. Whatever suits you." Gathering the papers she'd been studying before his arrival gave her a legitimate reason not to look at him longer than she already had. The pages didn't need to be stacked in perfect alignment, but she tapped them on her desk—one side, then the other, and back again—until they were. She didn't realize he'd sunk into the chair until he slid a Snickers candy bar across her desk.

There it was. The peace offering. The lame gift that always paled in comparison to the offense for which he was trying to make amends.

He gave her that smile again. "That used to be your favorite."

It'd been years since she'd eaten a Snickers. She'd changed her bad eating habits long ago. The candy was far too sweet for her now. Even so, she set the bar aside with the papers. "Thank you." Her gratitude sounded as empty as it felt.

"You go by Carol now," he pointed out. "You, uh... You always hated being called that. You said it sounded too old."

"Well, I'm older."

His tilted smile returned. "Aren't we all?"

"No," she said coolly. "Not all of us."

His face sagged for a few seconds, and then he continued as if she hadn't intentionally gut-punched him. "You got remarried."

"Yes."

"Did you have kids?"

Tapping into the Ice Queen façade he'd often accused her of, she froze her heart from the inside out, which had always been her go-to defense where John was concerned. "No."

He glanced around her office—the commercialized space with cherry-colored bookshelves that held medical dictionaries and binders of federal guidelines, a desk polished every night by the custodial team none of the executives ever saw, and framed degrees that were supposed to relay her competence for sitting in the sterile environment. "Look at this place. You've done good for yourself, kiddo."

"I'm not a kid, John. I am a grown woman who's made a life for herself despite the damage you caused."

He pressed his lips together as if to stop himself from rebutting.

Oh, how easily she fell into another of her old defense tactics, rebuffing any attempt he made at civility in case he was drawing her in for the kill. "Sorry, that just came out."

"No, it's okay. I blindsided you by showing up. Seeing me can't be easy for you."

Carol looked out to the water. "It's June. June is difficult."

"Her birthday is tomorrow."

She cut her gaze to him. "I know."

Staring at his hands, he toyed with a gold band on his left ring finger. Carol hadn't cared enough to ask if he'd remarried, but clearly he had. If his sudden appearance hadn't shaken her so deeply, she might have inquired about his new life. Asked what kind of poor broken soul he'd found after she'd finally gained the courage to leave him. Asked if he manipulated his new wife as much as he used to manipulate her.

John stopped playing with his wedding ring and heaved out a big breath. "I want to see her."

Carol didn't respond. Didn't move. She should have known why he was there the moment Tiana announced his unexpected visit.

Lifting his gaze to hers, he seemed to beg with his eyes. His expression triggered memories of the many times in the past she'd seen that exact same silent plea on his sad face.

She'd become immune to his puppy-eyed looks long before leaving him.

"Please. I'm her father."

Her lips trembled until she pressed them together. When she spoke, the tremble moved to her voice, making her words quiver. "I know who you are."

"Please, Caroline...Carol. I want to see her for her birthday. Then I promise I'll leave."

She focused out the window, back at the water, pushing away the memories that always seemed to be trying to drag her backward. Part of her wanted to tell him to burn in hell, but he was right. He was Katie's father. He had a right to see her on her birthday. His request wasn't unreasonable, but damned if she didn't want to tell him to go back under whatever rock he'd slithered from.

After a moment, she pushed a button on her desk phone. "Tiana, I need to leave. Reschedule anything I have this afternoon, please."

John didn't say another word as she gathered her things, simply following her out of her office. Once in the elevator, he leaned against the faux-wood-paneled wall, skimming her over, top to bottom, with the kind of candor that used to amuse her. She wasn't amused now. She knew exactly what he was thinking. He was judging her appearance and all the other changes she'd made since walking away from him.

Her once long sandy-brown hair was layered at shoulder length with golden highlights to hide the encroaching grays. Pediatric scrubs had been replaced by tailored suits and too-high-to-be-practical heels. Instead of an oversized purse stuffed with tissues and snacks, she carried a Tumi briefcase filled with documents and a laptop that rarely left her sight.

She no longer accepted a few extra pounds because she was too busy to do anything about them. She worked out for at least an hour every morning to keep her figure lean.

She wasn't Caroline Bowman any longer.

She was Carol Denman.

And Carol Denman wasn't too worn down to return his blatant stares. Carol Denman wasn't too fed up with his lies, denials, and manipulations to handle whatever he planned to toss her way. She'd had a long time to recover from his antics and was more than prepared to hold her own.

Returning his deliberate gawking, her earlier assessment stood. He looked like hell. The wrinkles in his suit spoke to the cheap material and the fake leather on his shoes had worn long before the soles. The dark stain on his collar, probably coffee, was faded enough for her to know it'd been washed and set in. While she'd taken a huge step forward in her life without him holding her back, he seemed to be stuck in the same rut where she'd left him.

She embraced the sense of superiority he'd always accused her of harboring. His penetrating stares used to intimidate her. Oh, how she'd hated feeling judged—by anyone, but most especially by John. Her former self bent over backward to please him, even when that meant undermining her own self-worth. Now she was impervious to his judgment of her. Now she had the confidence to see he had been right. She *was* better than him. "Go ahead," she said impassively. "Let's have it."

"What?"

"Whatever smart-ass comment you're cooking up."

He shrugged as if he had no idea what she was insinuating. "I was thinking that you look nice."

She didn't believe him. John always had a thinly veiled jab ready to casually kick her feet out from under her. Raising a brow, she let him know she didn't buy his innocence.

"That outfit must have cost a few pennies."

Ah, there it is. She smirked, making it clear his dig had missed the mark. "Yeah. A few. Still a cop?"

"Detective."

"Life goal achieved. Congratulations. Where?"

"Dayton."

"Never left, then."

The twitch that played on his lips and the twinkle in his eye gave away the underlying intent of his words before he even said them—he was about to go for the kill. She braced herself for the next round.

"*I* never felt the need to run away."

Tilting her head, she smiled like an angel. "You never felt much of anything, thanks to Anheuser-Busch."

Instead of responding, he looked up at the floor indicator. She knew how his cop brain worked. How he was processing her reaction bit by bit, tucking away the information to pick apart later. His comment about her outfit had rolled off. His jab about her leaving had been rebuffed. The old approach at knocking her off balance was failing. He was analyzing the situation, putting every nuance of her voice into the right box to better prepare for his next assault.

As the elevator bumped to a stop, Carol pushed herself upright and walked out before John. The click of her shoes echoing through the tiled lobby as she led him from the building was the only sound between them. His silence, she suspected, was due to him trying to figure out what had happened to the woman he'd married.

Outside, the humid summer air enveloped her, pressed down on her, and made her feel as if she were...*drowning.* Or maybe that was the presence of her ex-husband sucking the air from her personal space.

She didn't look at him as he stepped beside her and kept her pace as she strode down the sidewalk toward the parking lot. "You can follow me."

"I took a cab."

Of course he'd taken a cab. Driving himself would have made things too easy. She pressed a button on her keyring and a silver Lexus SUV chirped to life. She set her bag in the back and climbed in behind the steering wheel. "*Don't,*" she warned when he reached for the air conditioner controls the moment she turned the ignition. "The air will take a few minutes to cool down. Be patient."

He lifted his hands in surrender. "I'm not used to this heat. This humidity is smothering." As she eased out of her reserved parking spot, he sank back against the tan leather seat. "Nice car."

She let his comment fall unanswered, unsure if the compliment was sincere. The old John, the one she used to know, assumed anyone who drove expensive cars and wore fancy suits had to be some kind of a swindler. The only honest people, as far as he was concerned, were cops and nurses—an amendment he made only after she had earned her nursing degree.

He redirected the conversation when she didn't engage. "Last I heard you were in St. Louis. How did you end up in Houston?"

"Last you heard? I didn't keep in touch with anyone after I left. How did you hear anything about me?"

"Well, you did send me divorce papers. From St. Louis."

A memory of sitting in a rundown law office while decisively signing her name on those papers flashed through her mind. "So I did. My husband's job brought us here about fifteen years ago."

"What does he do?"

"He worked in environmental sciences for a gas company."

"And now?"

She tightened her hands around the leather-encased steering wheel as her answer echoed around her mind. "And now he's dead."

Her words stung her more than she suspected they surprised John. Though Tobias had been gone eight months, there were still times she poured two cups of coffee before her heart clenched in pain as she remembered he wouldn't be joining her for breakfast. She still reached for him in the morning, lifting her head to listen for sounds that gave away his whereabouts when she found his side of the bed empty. She still picked up her phone and started to text him whenever she might be late getting home. Every time, she felt the harsh slap of reality across her soul. He wasn't having breakfast. He wasn't in the house. He wouldn't receive that text. The man she had needed more than the air she breathed was gone.

"I'm sorry." John sounded sincere.

The car started to cool, but the tension made the atmosphere as unbearable as the afternoon heat had. The proximity to the Gulf of Mexico could make summer afternoons in Houston feel unforgiving. John wiped his hand across his forehead before dragging his palm down his thigh.

Though she had grown used to the temperature and humidity, she remembered how stifling it had felt when she and Tobias had first relocated. Suppressing the urge to let her ex swelter unnecessarily, she turned the temperature down a few degrees.

She didn't owe John an explanation, but the words tumbled out of her as the air filtering from the vent cooled. "He was hit by a truck while on his morning run. It was foggy. The guy didn't see him in time."

"How did you meet him?"

"When I went back to school."

"Medical school?"

She licked her lips. "I went back for medical science. We had a class together." Warmth filled her chest at the memory and a smile eased the tension in her jaw. "Sometimes I had to go to class straight from work. One day this snotty twenty-something made a comment about how I smelled like vomit and bleach. Tobias's mother was a nurse, so he took great offense. He put her in her place, then asked me out to dinner. He was trying to be nice, but we had a great time. We were fairly inseparable after that."

"Sounds familiar. We were inseparable for a while, too."

The absurdity of his observation caused a soft laugh to escape her. "My relationship with Tobias was *nothing* like what I had with you."

Despite her warning not to touch anything, he turned a vent to blow into his face. "So what do you do with your *medical science* degree? Because you sure as hell aren't seeing patients dressed like that."

She returned the vent to its original position, which she'd angled for optimal cooling of the entire cab, not just the passenger seat. "I work for a pharmaceutical company keeping it FDA compliant."

"Working for Big Pharma, huh? That's noble."

She glanced over in time to catch him roll his eyes. Though she had a million ways to defend her job, she chose not to. He'd never understand that she could help people without being hands-on. In his mind, executive positions were a sham created by rich people to keep them rich.

"How are your parents?" she asked to distract him.

"Gone. Mom thirteen years ago; Dad eleven. Both had cancer."

"I'm sorry. They were always good to me."

"Mom was heartbroken when you left. You were like a daughter to her."

Carol's chest grew heavy remembering the petite woman who had always greeted her with gentle hugs. John's mother had taken Carol under her wing, taking time to teach her things about life her mother never had. "Leaving wasn't easy, but it was best to cut ties. She would have tried to change my mind."

"They missed you. They hated how things ended with us. So did I. Just so you know."

"I think we all hated how things ended, John."

Silence hung in the air for a long moment before he muttered, "You know what I mean."

She did know what he meant. Disappearing in the middle of the night and sending divorce papers from hundreds of miles away had been the chickenshit way out, but it was the only way she would have found the courage to leave. "We weren't going to recover. Not after everything that happened."

"I know."

"I did what I had to do."

"Yeah. And your parents?"

"Dad died of a heart attack Thanksgiving Day a few years ago. Mom sold the house and moved to Florida with her sister."

"Sorry for your loss."

Glancing in the side mirror, she eased into the center lane before admitting, "We barely spoke after I moved."

"I'm not surprised."

She focused on maneuvering through mid-afternoon traffic as quiet settled between them. Carol tried to fight the memories, but John had opened the floodgate she'd kept hermetically sealed for years. Flicking her eyes his way, taking in his profile, she could almost feel herself being propelled back in time.

———

Caroline lifted her gaze to the police officer. He offered her a lopsided grin in response. They'd been exchanging flirty looks at the coffee shop for two weeks. She smiled as she returned her attention to the books sprawled out across the table.

Her heart jumped in her chest when he finally made a move. The anticipation had been building, a slow burn that had risen to the point of consuming her. She thought of little else, which was not like her. Her focus tended to be firmly on the plan she had made for herself. She had her life plotted out, and a girlish infatuation with a cop hadn't factored into it. Which, for some reason, made him that much more appealing.

He spun the chair across from her, straddling the seat as he rested his arms on the back. The brazenness of his action should have sent her running, but she was intrigued. His confidence was like a cloud that surrounded her, impeding her from seeing the warning signs that were flashing neon lights around him. "Have a drink with me."

She couldn't stop her grin from widening, but she kept her eyes on her books. "No."

"Dinner?"

"No."

"Coffee? I know you like coffee."

"No."

He sighed with exaggerated disappointment, as if she had been rejecting his advances for months instead of moments. She finally gave in and looked at him. Damn, he was even more handsome close up. His dark hair was unkempt, only adding to his attractiveness. His eyes were blue, like hers. The color was light at first yet seemed to darken as she stared. She now understood why people were fascinated by the ever-changing shades of her irises. Looking into his eyes was hypnotic.

She managed to tear her gaze away and look at the notes in front of her. "I'm studying for finals."

Nabbing one of her books from the pile, he flipped through a few pages. "What's your major?"

"Pre-med."

"Gonna be a doctor?"

"A pediatrician."

Dropping her book on the table, he heaved a dramatic sigh. "Oh, that's too bad."

That wasn't the response she usually received. Most people were in awe of her choice. "Why's that?"

That goofy grin formed on his lips again. "Doesn't seem right to ask a pediatrician to play doctor with me."

She creased her brow at his bad joke, but couldn't help but giggle in a way that sounded more like the girls she'd despised in high school than her studious self. "As if I would anyway. I don't even know you."

His smile sent a thrill through every nerve in her body. Boys didn't smile at her like that—like they wanted more from her than answers to a test or help with a paper. Boys didn't notice girls like her. However, this man had, and Caroline's heart was doing crazy things in her chest.

He winked, as if he hadn't done enough damage to her insides already. "You're right. We should fix that. Go out with me." He lifted his hands. "I'm a cop. You'll be perfectly safe."

Somehow, she doubted that—she was already in danger. She didn't know a lot about men, or dating, or...lust, but looking into his eyes made her stomach roll over and her body tingle in ways she didn't understand.

"I'm John," he said, extending his hand.

She hesitated before slipping her palm into his, sensing that she would be sealing her doom the moment she touched him. "Caroline."

He opened his mouth, but she lifted her free hand to stop him. "No, I was not *named after a Neil Diamond song. No, I do not like that song. No, you may not sing it to me. Ever."*

"Me sing Neil Diamond?" He chuckled. "That'll never happen."

"Thank you."

"Meet me here tomorrow night at seven, Sweet Caroline."

She started to chastise him, but he smiled and winked, and the words left her.

"Leave the books at school."

She didn't respond as he stood and spun the chair back

around the right way. He walked away, as smugly as she'd ever seen a man walk. As he left, she debated what she should do. He was clearly going to break her heart, but there really was no deliberation to be had. She'd show up. She'd known it the second he'd asked. She'd heard sparks could fly between two people, but she'd never experienced it. Never even really believed it until the first time she'd glanced up and found John watching her. She'd instantly felt alive and a million red flags went up in her mind.

She ignored each and every one. There was something about him she couldn't resist. She'd smiled and held his gaze and willingly walked into the web he'd spent the last two weeks spinning for her. A trap she feared she wasn't woman enough to handle.

———

Twenty minutes later, Carol pulled up to a large iron gate. She waited for the inevitable lecture, but John sat silent as she slid a fob from where it was attached to her visor. He didn't say a word as she stretched to hold it to the scanner. However, as the gates opened, he apparently couldn't hold his tongue any longer.

"You know—"

"If you're about to spew statistics about crime inside gated communities," she said, "you can shut your mouth. This has been a perfectly safe place to live for the last fifteen years."

He pressed his lips together, remaining speechless. Carol steered through the neighborhood she and Tobias had selected specifically for the children they'd never have. She pulled into the driveway of the three-bedroom red brick house that had become a one-bedroom mausoleum with an upstairs office and a shrine to the past. The large windows on the front offered plenty of natural light, but she'd rarely opened the blinds since Tobias's death.

Seeing her neighbors going about their lives as if her world hadn't been completely upended eight months ago was too painful. Watching life continue without Tobias was so gut-clenchingly unbearable, she tended to hide from the reminders that life did indeed go on.

The garage door rose when she pressed a button on her rearview mirror and she parked her SUV next to Tobias's sleek black BMW 760Li. John didn't say a word as he stood, looking over the sedan, but Carol suspected he was thinking how unfair it was that a guy who studied the environment got a car like that while "hardworking Joes" could barely make ends meet.

She silently dared him to make a comment, *just one*, about her husband. He didn't. He met her at Tobias's bumper and followed her through the garage.

"You should lock this," John said when she opened the door between the garage and her kitchen without using a key.

Ignoring his suggestion, she set her briefcase on the counter on her way to the fridge. "Something to drink? I don't have much. Orange juice. Water. Milk." She read the date on the nearly empty half-gallon jug. "Scratch the milk. This is probably cheese by now."

"I'm okay. Thanks." He shoved his hands in his pockets and scanned the living room while she set the jug in the sink to deal with later.

Following his gaze, she tried to see her living area through his eyes and imagined he saw the pristine white sofas and glass-topped coffee table as sterile and unwelcoming. If she were honest, she did too, on some level, but that was how she liked things. Clean. Orderly. Uncluttered. Even so, she rarely spent time downstairs anymore. Most evenings, she walked in and filled a glass of wine, and then carried it to her office upstairs, where she worked until she went to bed.

Avoiding the rest of the house made it easier to pretend Tobias was working late or holed up in his home office. Maybe having dinner with friends. Or visiting his mother. Anywhere that didn't involve a casket and a hole in the ground. She'd considered selling the house several times, but she could still feel Tobias here, and she wasn't ready to leave him behind. She'd already left too much behind in her lifetime.

"Is this your husband?"

She hadn't noticed John leave the kitchen. Seeing him in her living room holding a photo of the last anniversary she and Tobias had spent together felt like a betrayal to her husband. John's sudden reappearance in her life seemed like an invasion. He had no right to see that photo, to peer into the life she'd made without him. She crossed the room, took the frame from him, and put it back in its place, adjusting the angle until the photo sat in its proper position.

"He's Black," John said, as if he couldn't make sense of what he'd seen.

Scowling at him, she said, "Your keen observations must be the envy of the entire police department."

"I didn't mean it like that."

"Of course not. Nobody *ever* means it like that, John."

"It's only that—"

She lifted her brow, waiting for him to try and climb out

of the hole he'd dug himself into. When he pressed his lips together instead of trying to explain himself, she eased her defensive posture. "Tobias was brilliant and successful. He was kind and understanding. I could not have asked for a more loving and supportive marriage than that man gave to me. But, yes, let's focus on his race because that's what's really important."

John lifted his hands in surrender. "Okay, I deserved that. I'm sorry. You look happy in this picture, Caroline."

"I was. My husband made me *very* happy."

"I'm glad. I'm sorry for your loss."

The irritation that had been choking her since he had shown up at her office started threatening what little control she had left. Counting to five in her mind, she tried to calm herself. The exercise didn't help. Her brain and body remained on high alert, agitated as hell at his presence, at his intrusion, but mostly at his ignorant observation about Tobias. "Let's get this over with so you can go."

He stopped staring at the photo and met Carol's gaze. In that moment, with his suit jacket rumpled, his hair longer than most men his age would wear it, and a touch of insecurity in his eyes, she saw him for the irresponsible man-child she'd married thirty-plus years ago. Her heart did a little flutter—not like it had the day he'd picked her up for their first date, but like that of someone about to face some long-held fear.

Somewhere in the back of her mind, she'd known this day would come. The day she had to face the past she'd spent so much time running from. From the moment John had resurfaced, she'd unwittingly been strapped into a roller coaster. The slow climb was over. She was about to reach the highest point and tumble into a downward spiral. All she could do was hold on and hope it was over soon.

"Where is she?" His voice was no more than a whisper and contained a tremor of fear Carol found at odds with the foolhardy man she remembered him to be.

"Upstairs." Somehow Carol found the strength to take a step. Then another. Every stair she conquered exhausted her. The weight of the past constrained her, making every movement toward the second floor nearly impossible.

Reaching the first door on the right—the one she rarely found the courage to open—she gripped the knob. Her heart raced. Pounded. Slammed painfully against her ribcage.

She wasn't sure why. Her daughter was in there. Waiting. Always waiting. For some reason, her stomach rolled as she turned the handle. Sweat broke out on her brow. The last time she and John had stood together as parents had been during the worst time of her life. Those memories clawed at the back of her mind, demanding to be set free after years of being locked away like the monsters they were.

Swallowing her fear, she pushed the door open and lowered her face as John stood motionless beside her. "Come downstairs when you're done."

He grabbed her hand and murmured her name. The desperation she saw in his eyes was the same she'd seen all those years ago and caused her lungs to restrict until breathing became impossible.

"I'm sorry," he whispered now, as he had then. "I know it doesn't make a damn bit of difference, but I am *so* sorry, Caroline."

Her eyes began to burn. Her vision blurred. She blinked back her tears, but the sheen distorted his face. Gasping, she jerked her hand from his. "Do what you need to do. Then leave."

He nodded and stepped into the room. She didn't want to watch, but she couldn't stop staring at his slumped shoulders as he crossed the room. For the briefest moment, he stood in silence before a sob ripped from his chest as he dropped to his knees in front of the pink-and-silver urn that held their daughter.

TWO

THE ANNIVERSARY of Katie's death hit Carol especially hard this year. Tomorrow would have been her thirtieth birthday. She'd be a grown woman. She'd have a career. A family.

Carol should have been a grandmother. She should have a family to visit, to hear their laughter and share their stories. She should have had a lifetime of memories with her daughter. Instead, she had nothing more than a tiny front tooth, an old stuffed bear, and a box of knickknacks she couldn't bring herself to throw away.

And an urn full of ashes.

She forced the echo of the doctor's words from her mind before they could take hold and make her remember the feeling of her child's lifeless body in her arms. She opened a bottle of wine and filled a stemless glass, wishing she had something stronger than Pinot Grigio to numb the stabbing pain in her chest. Her second glass went down nearly as fast as the first. By the third, she was calm enough to carry the drink to the sliding glass doors and stare at the flower garden that filled her backyard with vibrant colors.

Tobias had the grass stripped out after they'd accepted they would never need room for children to play. Instead of a swing set and sandbox, he filled the area with delphiniums, lilies of the Nile, salvias, and more varieties of blooming hosta than she could name. A stone path flared into an oval with a small wrought-iron table and two chairs that reminded her of a café in Paris they'd visited the summer before he'd died.

He'd practiced speaking French as she sipped her coffee and ate a pastry. For the most part she'd held in her giggles, but every now and then his forced accent was bad enough that a laugh rose from her.

He had taken great pride in tending to his garden. Now, Carol paid someone to maintain the plants. Even without his touch, the flowers flourished. They grew. Carol hadn't. Somehow, she'd found the strength to move on after Katie's death, but Tobias's passing had stunted her. She hadn't taken a single step forward. Everything was the same. Her life was the same. Only emptier.

Maybe she simply didn't have the same resolve to survive she'd had twenty-four years ago. Maybe the constant sense of loss had finally won. First Katie. Then the children she and Tobias were never able to have. And then Tobias.

So much loss. So much misery to carry.

Heavy footfalls on the stairs drew her attention. Forcing herself to turn toward John, she cleared the emotional clog from her throat. "There's wine if you want."

He kept his red-rimmed eyes downcast. "I, uh, I've been sober nine years now."

She was surprised he'd finally admitted he had a drinking problem. He'd always denied he was a functioning alcoholic. He blamed his need to drink on the stress of being a cop. He blamed *everything* on the stress of being a cop.

"I've had a bit too much," she said, setting her glass aside. "Let me call you a cab."

"Caroline, I—"

She turned, anger causing her to clench her teeth so tightly her jaw ached. "I don't want to hear how sorry you are. I don't want to hear your stupid excuses or your bullshit justifications. I want you to leave, and I don't ever want to see you again."

"You won't. But I'm taking her with me."

Gripping her wine glass, she swayed at the impact of his statement. Feeling as if he had kicked the world from beneath her, stunned and off-balance, she narrowed her eyes. "Excuse me?"

He lowered his focus, and hers followed. He had Katie's urn cradled in his left hand. Carol started to fully comprehend what was happening.

Lifting her steely gaze to his, her voice quivered as she asked, "Are you trying to steal my daughter's ashes?"

John brought the container to his chest, embracing it as he had Katie when she was a baby sleeping with her little head on his shoulder. "You've had her for twenty-four years. It's my turn."

Bile rose and burned her esophagus. "*Your* turn?"

John licked his lips. "Do you remember how we were going on vacation that summer? Our first real family vacation. We were going to take a road trip across the country. Katie was excited to see all the places we'd read about in her books. She couldn't wait to see Mount Rushmore and the ocean. Yellowstone. She had such a long list of things, there was no way we could see them all in one trip. Remember?"

Carol didn't want to remember the promises they weren't able to fulfill to their little girl, but she was slammed by a memory of Katie curled in her lap as they looked through one of the many science and nature books John's parents had bought to nurture Katie's curiosity. Carol shook the memory loose before it could overcome her.

His bloodshot eyes filled, and a sad smile touched his lips. "We thought we had time, didn't we?"

"We *should* have had time," she squeezed out through her teeth. "We *would* have if it weren't for you."

"I know," he said in resignation. "There isn't a day that goes by that I don't relive it. The way you screamed when you found her—"

"Stop!" Closing her eyes, she turned her face away. That moment snuck up on her far too often without her being reminded. For twenty-four years, the scene had spontaneously popped into her thoughts and knocked her to her knees without warning. The most ordinary thing could bring her to a screeching halt as her heart sank and her stomach knotted. She'd be going about her life, and then a voice in the back of her mind would whisper, *"Katie's dead."*

As if she could forget.

Facing him again, she embraced her anger to keep the sorrow at bay. He'd taken Katie from her. He'd robbed her of the life she was meant to have—the only child she'd ever had. Now he wanted to take the only thing she had left—Katie's ashes?

Hell no.

"Put her down and leave," Carol said, her voice cold and unwavering.

"I'm taking her," he said. "I'm going to show her all the things I didn't get to before she died."

"Before you *killed* her."

He didn't respond to her accusation. She wasn't sure how she'd expected him to react, but he took the verbal hit without denial or his usual excuses.

"Give her to me." Closing the distance between them, she held her hand out. "John. Give her to me."

"So she can sit on a table? Hidden away like a secret you don't want anyone to know."

"Excuse me?"

"When's the last time you were in that room? When's the last time you sat with her? Talked to her? The dust on her urn..."

"I don't need to sit in that room to talk to Katie. I talk to my daughter every single day. A layer of dust doesn't give you the right to take her away from me."

Straightening his back, he rose to his full height. "She's my daughter, too. I'm going to take her to all the places she wanted to see."

"Go to those places. See whatever you need to. Katie stays *here*."

He cradled the urn in silent defiance.

A bitter laugh erupted from her. "Oh my God, John. Are you really going to make me call the police and turn you in for stealing my child's remains?"

"She was my child, too. I want my time with her."

Clenching her fists, she silently counted to five, willing herself to remain calm. "Despite you showing up unannounced, I let you come to my home. I let you stay as long as you wanted. I've been more than reasonable."

"More than reasonable?" It was his turn to laugh, a sound that was rife with resentment and anger. "If you had *ever* been reasonable, I wouldn't have had to hunt you down like a fugitive on the run, *Carol.* You disappeared with *my* daughter's urn in the middle of the night."

The cork on her fury popped. Years of bottled-up rage erupted as she closed the gap between them. Jabbing her index finger into his chest, shoving hard enough that he hunched back in response, she screamed, "You're the reason she's in an urn, John!" She poked him again. Harder. "You did this! *You!* If you'd ever been any kind of father, she'd still be alive."

Hurt found his eyes and softened his glower. *Good.* She wanted to hurt him. To break him. Make him feel all the pain he'd caused her for too damned long. She removed her finger from his chest only to point at the glass-and-metal table next to him. "Put the urn down, or so help me God, you'll be in one too."

"Caroline—"

"*Don't* call me that."

Lowering his gaze, he gave a measured exhale. "I didn't come here to cause you more pain. I thought, somehow, you would have found a way to forgive me by now. I'm sorry. I'm sorry I upset you, and I'm sorry I hurt you. But I *am* taking her." He turned for the door.

She hurried around him, blocking his way. "Put her down, John."

"No. I need to do this. I need to say goodbye to her. The way we planned."

The way they had planned was to stop at all the places Katie had wanted to see—mountains, monuments, oceans—and leave a piece of her behind. They'd sprinkle her ashes across the country little by little, letting go bit by bit as they went. Each stop was intended to be another chance to ease the pain of their loss. Except Carol couldn't let her go. She couldn't follow through. She couldn't spend one more moment with the man she blamed for the death of her child.

So she'd left and taken Katie with her.

She'd be damned now if she'd let John take her away. Grabbing his arm as he stepped around her, she jerked him to a stop. "I said no."

He yanked away from her grip and kept moving, but she wasn't the pushover he remembered. She wasn't the docile girl he'd married. She wasn't the naive young mother who had convinced herself he'd never let anything bad happen to their little girl. She was strong now. She was a childless mother with nothing to lose but the last bit of her daughter that remained.

Pressing her palms into his back, she pushed with all her might, knocking him off balance. John took several stumbling steps before turning to face her, mouth open and eyes widened with obvious consternation. She took advantage of his confusion and grabbed for Katie. He pulled the urn from her reach. Lurching again, she wrapped her palms around the cold metal jar.

He gripped one of her wrists and tried to pull her hand away. His eyes were full of sorrow, but that didn't soften her hatred for him. Not the slightest. Instead, his show of sympathy enraged her. How dare he look at her with such pity as he tried to take Katie from her *again*?

Balling her fist, Carol pulled her arm back and crashed her knuckles into his nose. She expected him to take several steps back, to cover his face, probably even to curse at her.

She didn't expect his eyes to roll back as he collapsed into an unmoving lump at her feet.

Her stomach dropped to meet him as panic rolled through her. She loomed over him, not certain what to do. "John?" she called hesitantly. She nudged him with the almond-shaped tip of her black pump. "John?" She kneeled down and pressed her fingertips to his neck. Once she was confident he wasn't dead, she eased Katie from his limp hand and hugged the urn to her chest.

What an idiot. Trying to steal Katie's ashes?

Carol started for the stairs but changed her mind and crossed the living room to Tobias's office. He had taken over the downstairs office years ago. The window looked right into their neighbor's backyard with an oversized playground and in-ground pool where the kids loved to run and jump. Even with the blinds closed, their screams filtered into the room in a childish crescendo, clawing at her heart in a way only Tobias seemed to understand.

The safe behind his solid oak desk had plenty of room to keep Katie out of John's reach. She tapped a few numbers into the keypad and opened the fireproof door before setting Katie's urn inside. The etching was a bit worn on one side from years of running her fingers over the letters, making some of them difficult to read, but she had the words memorized.

KATHRYN ELIZABETH BOWMAN
BORN JUNE 5, 1989

Died June 22, 1995

Once her daughter was secure from being...*ash*-napped... Carol returned to the living room and stood over her ex-husband. She could call the police. She was well within her right to defend herself and her daughter. Pressing charges against him didn't appeal to her. All she wanted was for him to be gone. Now that he couldn't take Katie, she expected he'd storm away as he tended to do when he'd lost a fight.

She was wrapping an icepack from the freezer in a towel when John moaned. She crossed the room and stood over him until he came around.

He blinked at her several times, as if getting his bearings. "Hell of a right hook you got there, kid." Putting his hand to his nose, he gingerly moved the cartilage from one side to the other.

"Broken?"

"No."

Squatting down, she rested her forearms on her knees as he struggled to sit. "I'm sorry. I didn't mean to hit you, and I certainly didn't mean to knock you out."

He searched around him for a few moments, patted the plush gray-and-white diamond-patterned area rug, and then sighed when he confirmed she'd taken the urn.

"I told you, you aren't taking her away from me."

"Message received. Where'd you learn to hit like that?"

She held the icepack out to him. "Houston's a big city. Tobias wanted to make sure I could take care of myself."

"He was a boxer?"

"No. Maybe I could be," she said with a smile. Gripping his elbow, she helped him stand and cross the room, where she eased him onto a barstool. She offered the icepack again. "Do you want this?"

"No. I'm okay."

"You sure?"

"Yeah."

"I'll call you a cab, then." She tossed the icepack on the counter.

"Caroline—" he called as she reached for her briefcase.

"Carol." Meeting his gaze, she stared him down to get her point across. "My name is *Carol*. I have been *Carol* for twenty-four years. Caroline..." Tears stabbed at the back of her eyes. "Caroline died with Katie, John. I'm Carol now."

"I didn't come here to—"

"Steal her remains?"

"To fight." His tone was firm but tired, like he'd spent such a long time preparing for this conversation that he was too exhausted to actually have it. "I don't want to fight with you. I wanted to make peace. With her. With you. With myself. It's been a long time." He put his hand to his chest and patted the wrinkled white button-down covering his heart. "I need some peace."

She knew that feeling all too well, but he wouldn't find absolution here. Not from her. She had tried to let go of the past, of the hurt, of the blame, but seeing him brought all that old hurt to the surface. She'd never let any of it go; she'd simply stuffed all those feelings and her former name into an urn with her daughter's remains.

"When I got here," he said, "I couldn't leave without her."

"You *are* leaving without her."

He nodded. "Before I go, you're going to hear me out."

The anger that had started to ease spiked again. "*John.*"

Florets of red bloomed across his cheeks as he stared her down. That blush used to be a warning to her to back down. He was losing his well-maintained grip on his temper. This time, she dug her heels in and braced herself for the battle ahead. He jabbed his finger onto the white-and-gray granite countertop, much as she'd done to his chest when accusing him of killing their child. "You owe me five minutes. You owe *us* five minutes."

"I don't owe you anything."

"We were parents. *Her* parents." A sheen filled his eyes.

A less angry woman might have softened, but Carol added another layer of ice to her heart, making sure he couldn't pierce her armor. John leaned back and clasped his hands, pushing his breath out between his lips in an apparent attempt at calming himself. He never would have done that two and a half decades ago. Carol had always been the one who caved. She had been the one who accepted losing the fight just to stop the emotional bloodbath.

"Let me say this while I can," he said. "Then I'll leave and, I swear, you'll never have to see me again."

Carol sank onto a barstool at the other end of the long slab of granite. She gripped the edge, as if she could somehow absorb some of its unwavering strength. "I'm not rehashing that day. I will not relive a moment of her death to appease you."

His mouth dipped into a frown, but he nodded and took a moment before speaking. "I can still hear her laugh, you know? Sometimes I come home at night, and I swear I hear her call from her bedroom. 'Daddy, come kiss me *guh-night*.' Remember how she said *guh-night*?"

Flashes of the rundown ranch she'd left behind filled her mind. "You still live in our house?"

"I thought about selling it a million times," he said after a stretched silence, "but I never could bring myself to do it."

"It's hard to let go," she said, thinking of her own struggles.

"I...I had a rough patch after you left. Between losing you and Katie, I had a hard time working. They put me on paid leave, but...I guess it's no big surprise that I drank my check instead of paying bills." He didn't meet her gaze. He was clearly ashamed of the failure he was confessing. "The bank threatened to take the house, but Mom and Dad helped me until I could pull my head out of my ass. Which, as you might recall, was no small feat for me. They paid the mortgage off because they didn't want to lose Katie's home any more than I did."

The small two-bedroom starter home had been ragged when they had moved in. Over the six years she'd lived there, she had painted the walls and scrubbed the linoleum clean, but the aged house never sparkled like the house she shared with Tobias.

The day she and John walked through the small space with a real estate agent, John had jumped at the chance to buy the house. Carol had a rock in the bottom of her stomach. The house needed work, but they couldn't afford a nicer neighborhood on their paltry budget. He had a long list of projects he could do to fix up the house. She'd known then he wouldn't follow through. He rarely did. She couldn't really imagine how broken-down it must be after all these years. John hadn't been much on maintenance back then. His father did more than he should have for his grown son and daughter-in-law. She wondered who'd taken over after Mark died, since she doubted John had changed that much.

"I don't blame you for leaving," John said, bringing her back to their conversation. "I don't blame you for hating me. I don't blame you for never looking back. I wasn't strong enough to walk away from the past. I tried. I did. The memories always pulled me back. I loved you. I wasn't good to you. I see that now. It *is* my fault that Katie's gone. I need you to understand how incredibly sorry I am."

Her emotions knotted in her throat, making it a challenge to squeeze the words out. "Sorry can't change anything, John. I wish it could, but my little girl is dead."

"I know," he said so softly she wasn't sure she hadn't imagined it. "And I take full responsibility for that. I do. It took some time to break the habit of making excuses for myself, but now that I have, I know it's my fault Katie's gone." He choked out the last words and sniffed. "All I can do now is ask for forgiveness."

"I can't," she whispered. "I can't forgive you. I wish I could. I've tried. I can't."

After a moment, he nodded. "That's okay. I don't deserve your forgiveness. Doesn't hurt to ask, though, right?" He offered a weak smile as he stood, but he didn't head for the door. He moved around the stools separating them, stopping directly in front of Carol. He looked her over, this time without the judgment in his eyes. This time he took her in as if trying to memorize her. "I'm very happy that you had a good life. Despite me." Leaning down, he kissed her head. "*Guh-night*, Mommy," he said as Katie had done many times before Carol had left to work the third shift at the hospital. "We love you."

The words broke her. She closed her eyes and buried her face in her palms. Her shoulders shook as Katie's voice echoed through her mind. She didn't know how long she sat, sobbing, but when she lifted her face, John was gone.

———

Carol had finished the wine. *All* the wine. She'd sat in the kitchen, staring at the urn she'd retrieved from the safe, drinking until she couldn't even walk up the stairs. She'd collapsed on the sofa, cursing her stupidity as the room spun beneath her. She knew better. Her limit was two glasses. She'd surpassed that *before* John left. The rest went down just as fast and with just as little success at stopping the floodgate against the tears and memories from opening.

Her eyes burned and her sinuses felt as if she'd poured cement into them. She hadn't stopped crying until she passed out. The sound of her cell phone shrieking was like a hot poker searing through her brain. She reached for the phone that always charged on the nightstand beside her bed. Instead, she knocked over the empty bottle that sat on the clear glass-top coffee table Tobias had imported from Italy eight years ago.

If he were alive, he'd have hissed at the sound of glass scratching over glass as she righted the bottle. He wouldn't have said a word, but a sharp gasp would have been followed by a sigh of relief that the table hadn't shattered. She'd told him having a glass table was a ridiculous idea, but he'd fallen in love with the style, and she'd fallen in love with his excitement as they'd stood in a shop in Tuscany.

The memory flew from her mind like a bullet when her

phone rang again. She blinked, realizing the sound was coming from the briefcase that still sat on the kitchen counter, and pushed herself to stand. Her head felt so heavy as she wobbled that she nearly fell back. Her stomach rolled, and she swallowed hard, taking a quick assessment of her body. The third shrill ring brought her back to reality.

Checking the time on the smartwatch encircling her wrist as she moved, she had to force her eyes to focus to see where the digital hands were pointing.

Six thirty a.m.

She picked up her shaky pace. The last time she'd gotten a call this early in the morning, Tobias had been hit by a truck.

Her heart dropped at the number on the screen. It was a local call so it couldn't be about her mother in Florida. Or about Tobias's family in St. Louis. There was no one else left. Still, panic gripped her heart. "Hello?"

"This is Houston Methodist. Is this Carol Denman?"

God, please. Not another one of these calls. She couldn't take another of these calls. "Yes," she barely managed.

"Ma'am, Johnathan Bowman gave us your name as a point of contact. Do you know him?"

"Yes." Sinking onto the barstool she'd occupied the night before, she rubbed her fingertips against her closed eyelids. If she didn't know better, she'd have thought someone had filled them with sand while she'd been sleeping. Her eyes were dry, and the lids felt grainy against them. "Is he okay?"

"He's been admitted and is asking for you."

She darted her focus to where she'd knocked him out cold the night before. *Oh, God.* "Ad-admitted? What's wrong?"

"I'm sorry, ma'am. All I know is that he's asking for you."

"What room?"

"Three twelve. You're welcome to—"

Ending the call, she cut off the invitation to visit her ex-husband. Her gaze again moved to the spot where he'd been unconscious. Oh, crap. What had she done?

She slid off the stool, rushed to the couch, and slipped her feet into the heels that she'd kicked off at some point before passing out. Though appearances were usually at the top of her list—she used to tell Tobias she couldn't *act* like she had herself together if she didn't *look* like she had herself together—Carol grabbed her briefcase and hurried out the door without as much as a glance in a mirror.

The morning traffic hadn't started and the trip to the hospital was fairly quick. Her clicking heels echoed in her ears as she went straight to the elevator. As much as she hated John, she hadn't meant to hurt him. Would never intentionally hurt him.

Okay, maybe she thought about bashing his face in from time to time. And maybe punching him had felt *really* good. But she hadn't meant to hurt him.

The elevator stopped on the third floor, and she dashed by the nurses' desk looking for signs to point her to room 312. In the corridor, the sounds of beeping machines and hushed voices surrounded her. Slowing, she listened to the sounds. Smelled the disinfectant. Felt death envelop her.

Her body tensed as her stomach constricted and she brought a hand to her mouth to tamper the urge to vomit. This wasn't a reaction to her overindulgence in wine. Her surroundings were more than she could handle. Reaching out until her palm rested on the cold wall, she closed her eyes and remained in control. The racing of her heart sent blood throbbing in her ears. After several inhalations, she opened her eyes, but she was no longer in the Houston Methodist corridor.

———

Caroline stood in the emergency room at Miami Valley Hospital in Dayton staring at the door Katie had disappeared through. A man straddled her little body, counting as he pressed down on her chest while two other paramedics ran with the gurney, rushing her to a waiting doctor.

As a pediatric nurse, she knew death. She knew death far too well. She'd seen death indiscriminately claim children. This one. That one. Cancer. A bike wreck. A tumble down the stairs. Death couldn't take Katie. Katie couldn't die. Katie wouldn't die. No. She'd be okay. She had to be okay.

Death would lose this time. This one time. Please, God, let death lose this time.

After what seemed to be hours, Dr. Goodman came through the swinging doors. She had worked with him before. She knew him. Katie was in good hands with him. He never gave up on his patients. He would fight for her little girl until there was no fight left.

But as she looked into his eyes, she knew.

Oh, no. No. Not Katie. Not my Katie.

"Don't," she'd whispered. "Please don't say it."

"I'm sorry. We did all we could."

Arms wrapped around her as she screamed and her knees gave out. She thought they belonged to John, but she wasn't sure. She'd never know for certain. Someone caught her before she hit the cracked linoleum, but they couldn't stop the sound erupting from her chest. She screamed until her throat was raw.

She didn't stop until a nurse stuck a needle in her arm and injected a sedative to calm her. She'd done that to other mothers before. The ones who had become hysterical and couldn't control themselves. Mothers whose children had died. Mothers who had lost everything.

She was one of those women now. The newest member of an elite club no woman ever wanted to join.

Eventually, she calmed. Went numb. Not from the shot, but from the shock as she and John were led to the small room where Katie was stretched on a bed. Her little lips had turned dark purple from lack of oxygen. Caroline was reminded of how the dye in the grape popsicles Katie liked left her lips looking much the same color.

Brushing her hand over Katie's hair, she blinked, forcing her tears back. "Wake up, baby," she whispered, knowing she wouldn't. "Look at Mommy. Katie. Please. Look at me."

She didn't. She never would again.

A sob swelled in Caroline's chest, and she scooped Katie into her arms. Hugging her tight, memorizing the feel of her baby limp in her arms, inhaling the chemical scent that clung to her hair, kissing the forehead that was far too cold.

"Ma'am," a woman said gently, pulling Carol from the memory. "Are you okay?"

She glanced around, taking in the hospital. She swallowed before nodding. Only she wasn't okay. The acid in her stomach threatened to burn its way up her throat. "Yes. I'm fine."

"Can I get you some water?"

"No," she muttered. "I'm okay."

"You look a little pale. Should we find you a seat?"

"No. Really. I'm okay. Thank you."

The woman seemed hesitant to leave. "Come to the nurses' station if you need anything."

"I will."

The nurse walked away, and Carol forced what remained of the memory from her mind. She wasn't going to think about that day. Not now. Not ever again.

She found John's room and tiptoed to the bed. He appeared fine. Like he was sleeping. He was breathing on his own. The IV in his arm was hooked to a bag of simple saline, steadily dripping into his vein. Nothing seemed to indicate what was wrong with him.

Easing into a chair next to the bed, she inched the uncomfortable metal frame closer. He looked younger now that he was resting. The crease between his brow had become permanent, though less pronounced than when he'd been staring at her the day before. With his piercing blue eyes closed, his presence wasn't nearly as intrusive on her soul. She could sit back and see him, really see him, and let the sharp edge of her anger dull. Not completely—enough to not hate him with the passion of a thousand burning suns. Maybe nine hundred and ninety-nine.

She smirked at her assessment. That sounded to her like something John would have said years ago. She hated when parts of him snuck up on her, as they tended to from time to time over the last twenty years. She supposed that was inevitable after sharing her life with him for so long. Did parts of her stick to him? Did he ever think something and then realize it was her voice creeping up into his mind?

She bit her lip hard—the way she did when she didn't want her emotions to get out of her control—not willing to acknowledge that there could still be parts of Caroline alive inside the darkest depths of her, hiding in the corners of her mind as if they'd been waiting for John to shine light on them. She'd worked hard to put that part of herself to rest. That part was weak and scared and easily persuaded to go against her own instincts.

She rubbed her thumb over the surface of her nail, distracted by a small chip in the acrylic overlay. Scratching at it with her thumbnail, she debated whether she should stay until John woke up or leave a note on the bedside table to let him know she'd checked on him. By the time she decided she needed to stay at least long enough to speak to his doctor, Carol had picked a perfectly good oval-tipped French manicure off two fingernails.

She needed John's physician to tell her that John was okay; then she'd leave. She had a life, after all. A schedule to keep. Work to be done. The meetings that had been canceled the previous afternoon had been rescheduled. Cancelling a second time would be completely unprofessional. She sure as hell couldn't go into the office wearing the same suit as the day before. The thought made her consider that she hadn't even checked herself before leaving the house. She moved gingerly toward the bathroom to soften the sound of her damned high heels. Flipping the light on, she cursed as the florescent bulb flickered before illuminating the room in a whitewash that stole the color from her face.

Using her fingers, she did her best to comb through the strands that were lying in various directions, overlapping in places they shouldn't. By the time she was done, most were back in place. Her face was still sticky from sleep, so she ran the water until the temperature was cool enough to shock the remaining sleep from her system, but warm enough not to be painful. She splashed water over her face several times before patting herself dry with a towel.

Tossing the bleached terrycloth onto the counter, she frowned at her reflection. She still looked out of sorts. Out of control. Emotional. That was the word. She looked *emotional*. The observation struck a nerve deep inside her and she physically flinched before turning away from the mirror. She was standing directly outside the bathroom when the door leading to the hallway opened. The man who entered wasn't wearing the typical white coat, but he did have a stethoscope draped around his neck.

"Carol Denman, I presume?" He extended his hand as the door silently closed behind him. "I'm Dr. Collins. Johnathan's admitting physician. How are you holding up?"

She shook his hand out of obligation, but had no interest in being social at the moment. "How is John?" she asked, keeping her voice soft to match his so neither disturbed the patient.

He gestured toward the bed but didn't break eye contact with her. "He's resting now, as you can see. What can you tell me about his medical history?"

"Not much. I...I don't know him well. What can *you* tell me about his current medical condition?"

Silence.

Damn it. Pressing her lips together, she glanced at the

bed. Bad news. Definitely bad news. Whatever had sent John to the hospital was more serious than a punch to the face. Somehow, that didn't alleviate her concerns as much as she'd hoped.

"Has he mentioned his health to you?" Collins asked.

"No. Before he showed up at my office yesterday, I hadn't seen him in over twenty years."

"Do you have any idea if he's been ill?"

"He didn't say." Yet somehow that made his unexpected visit more logical. John did very little without reason and strong motivation. If he were ill, that would likely prompt him to seek out the peace he'd told her he needed.

"Do you know who we can contact to find out?" Dr. Collins asked, disrupting her thoughts. "I'd really like to review his medical records to treat him properly."

She shrugged. "He's a detective in Dayton, Ohio, but I don't know much more than that."

"Okay." He looked to where John was still sleeping. "I'll get someone on making a few calls for me to see if we can find out more. You're welcome to stay as long as you like, but please don't disturb him. I want him to get as much rest as possible until I have more information."

"Of course."

The doctor left her standing where she'd been when he entered, and she swallowed hard as she turned her focus back to John. His cell phone was on the bedside table. After only a moment of internal debate, she picked it up. Running her finger over the screen caused a number pad to come up. Password protected. She didn't even think twice before punching in Katie's birthday—0605.

The phone unlocked. John was nothing if not predictable.

She opened his contacts list and scrolled through the names, searching for one that was familiar. Ah. Bert Janowski. He'd been John's partner when she'd met him. She and Bert had been friendly enough. He might remember her, which would make the conversation a bit less awkward. She hoped.

After pressing the little phone icon next to his name, she waited for the call to connect.

"Whadda ya want, ya bastard?" a gravelly voice on the other end of the line demanded.

"Bert? You may not remember me. I'm John's ex-wife."

"Caroline?"

She grinned. Hearing that name come from John was like a match lighting her nerves afire, but Bert saying the name she hadn't used in years had a sentimental feeling to it. She hadn't lied when she told John that Caroline, and all that she'd hated about the person she was then, died with Katie. The few people whom she still talked to from her past, her mother included, had agreed to call her Carol. She needed, for her own sanity, to cut all ties with the past, and Caroline. For some reason, her given name on Bert's lips didn't sting as much. "Yes. It's Caroline." God, she couldn't remember the last time she'd said that name aloud.

"Holy hell. How are you, girl?"

She faced the bed. "I'm good, but something's happened to John. He's in the hospital—he's okay—but the doctor needs his medical records. Do you happen to know whom I should tell him to call?"

A heavy sigh sounded through the phone. "I don't know who his doctor is, but he goes to a clinic by the department. I can get the name and text it to you."

"That would be great. Thank you. What about his wife?"

"Wife? No, John never got remarried."

Looking at the wedding ring on his hand, she started to protest, but then she recognized the simple band as his half of the set they had bought before they'd exchanged vows. It was an exact replica of hers. She'd tossed hers out two decades ago. John's was still on his finger.

"You're with him, then?" Bert asked.

She hesitated. "He gave the hospital my name. They called me. I'm only here until they can sort this out. I'm not staying."

"He's sick, Caroline. Real sick. As soon as he found out, he made it his mission to find you. He wanted to make peace with you before...you know...the end."

Her heart seemed to stop beating for a moment. "The end? What's wrong with him?"

"He started acting strange a few months ago. He'd get real agitated or forget something that he shouldn't forget. The captain made him go to the doctor. He didn't want to, but we were all getting worried, you know. As soon as he got his test results, he started talking about you and how he had to find you—"

"*Bert*. What's wrong with him?"

"He's got a tumor. In his brain. There isn't anything they can do about it."

Her breath caught. Well. That explained a lot about the last eighteen hours.

THREE

IF THE SMELL of the hospital took Carol back to Katie's death, hearing the machines reminded her of Tobias's. He'd died by the time she'd gotten to him. Not technically. The machines kept him alive until she could fly his family in to say goodbye. But he was already gone. As a nurse, she'd been around death enough to know the moment she'd walked into the room that he'd never recover.

She didn't have that sense about John. John would wake up. He'd say her name.

The last time she heard Tobias say her name was when he'd tried to nudge her from bed to go running with him. She'd rolled over, pulled the covers up, and told him to go without her—she wanted a few more minutes of sleep. She hadn't even opened her eyes to look at him one last time. He had kissed her head through the blankets, swatted her behind, and told her she was lazy. Then he was gone.

Forever.

Walking into his hospital room, she'd instantly known

he'd never wake up. He'd never say her name again. As she knew John would.

She shouldn't have been here. She didn't *need* to be here. She'd called Tiana and let her know she'd be late, but she should have gone to the office. She turned from the window, ready to leave, only to find John watching her. This close to escaping. Swallowing hard, she gave him a smile, though she wasn't sure if it was to cover the fact that she was about to leave or to offer him some kind of comforting reassurance.

"Welcome back," she said.

He dragged his hand over his face. "How long was I out?"

She sat in the chair next to his bed. "A couple hours, I think."

He closed his eyes and exhaled. "Feels like it's been days."

"I called Bert. He's going to talk to someone in HR to find out who your emergency contact is and see about getting your medical records, but now that you're awake, you can tell the doctor whom to talk to."

"He can talk to you."

"I'm not your family."

"You're the closest thing I have left."

She didn't want to have this talk when he looked vulnerable and she would inevitably start to feel sorry for him, but her questions were unavoidable. She'd known it the moment she realized the ring on his finger was the one she'd put there over thirty years ago. "John. We're divorced. We've been divorced for a long time. I'm not your family anymore."

"You're Katie's mother. That makes us family. No piece of paper can change that."

She bit her lip and rolled the plump flesh between her

teeth for a few moments before asking, "Why are you wearing that ring?"

"Because you put it there."

"*Why* are you wearing *that* ring?"

"Can I have some water?"

The man was as evasive as ever. Why deal with a problem when he could deflect? She pushed herself up, filled a plastic cup about halfway, and held it out to him.

His hand trembled as he reached out and struggled to lift his head.

Damn it.

She didn't want to nurse him. Didn't want to show him the compassion he deserved given his condition. Even so, she cradled the back of his head and lifted it for him to sip from the cup she pressed to his lips.

"Thanks." He fell back against the flat pillow.

She returned to her seat and put the water aside. "I'm married to someone else."

"You were."

Carol jolted at the sting of his words. Oh. The audacity it had to have taken for him to point out that she was widowed, but then again, he was being his usual uncouth self. "I *am.* Tobias's death doesn't change who he is to me. He is my *husband.* I am *his* wife. Nothing will ever change that."

John shook his head. "I'm not delusional, okay?"

"No? Then why are you wearing a wedding ring twenty-four years *after* our divorce was finalized?"

"This ring"—he lifted his left hand to show her—"is all I have left of us, Caroline. Those were the happiest days of my life. I'm going to hang on to them. Whether you want me to or not."

Holding back her knee-jerk response took all her resolve. She wasn't going to argue with a man stuck in a hospital bed. "Bert says you have a tumor?"

His forehead creased, as if he were angry she'd been told. "Glioblastoma." He tapped the front left part of his skull. "Got a nasty little sucker growing right here."

Carol didn't flinch outwardly, but she shut down for a moment on the inside, long enough to process the outcome. That wasn't the kind of diagnosis anyone wanted to hear. Without proper treatment, that single word was a death sentence. The months leading up to the end could be some of the most painful of a person's life. Seizures. Headaches. Erratic behavior.

"I'm sorry," she said, running her thumb over her picked-at fingernail.

"I'm not." He held his fingers less than an inch apart. "I'm this close to seeing our girl again."

"I doubt that will comfort the ones you leave behind, John."

He dropped his hand onto his lap. "I didn't mean to upset you yesterday. I got it in my head that I needed to see her before I died. When I got there, I...I acted like an idiot. I never should have tried to leave with her. I'll be gone soon. I had no right to try to take her from you before I go."

"I shouldn't have hit you. If I'd known—"

"Don't beat yourself up." He grinned. "Or me. Don't beat anyone up."

A laugh escaped her at his unexpected humor. As much as she hated John, she couldn't deny that he'd always been able to make her laugh. "I should get your doctor."

He grabbed her hand before she could leave his side.

"Will you stay? I need someone to translate what he says into something I can understand."

Carol looked at his hand on hers. How many times in her life had he grabbed her like that? The don't-leave-me hold. The don't-walk-out look in his eyes. The plucking her heartstrings to please understand one more time. Jesus, this was all too familiar. Steeling herself against his emotional manipulation, she said, "You should have a friend or family member with you. Tell me whom to call. I'll stay until someone else can get here."

Disappointment clouded what little hope had shone in his eyes, and he released her hand. "No. That's okay. Don't worry about it. Thanks for checking in. You should...get back to living your life."

Oh, yes, another familiar tactic. The cold-shoulder dismissal because she didn't cave. Like a washing machine— all he had to do was push a button to start the same old cycle.

She hesitated as long as it took to remind herself that he wasn't her responsibility and she wasn't falling back into this game with him. "If you need help getting someone here—"

"Someone at the department will take care of me. Don't worry about it." His eyes softened, and he sounded sincere when he said, "I'm glad I got to see you one more time, Caroline. I wish...I wish I hadn't made such a mess of things."

"I'll get your doctor."

Carol still looked like hell with her hangover and crumpled business suit, but as she approached the nurses' station, she reminded herself that her strained appearance was nothing the hospital staff didn't see on a daily basis. "Could you please let Dr. Collins know Johnathan Bowman is awake?"

The woman pecking on her keyboard didn't bother glancing up. "Of course."

After thanking the nurse, Carol headed toward the elevators and pushed the button to summon a car to leave John and his problems behind her. In the past. That was where he belonged. Her life was in the present. A life she'd created without the emotional blackmail of a drunk who was terrified of living alone. She'd never had to cover for Tobias. She'd never had to lie to their family and friends about why he missed a function or why she was late or why she'd been crying.

She had left that life far behind her, and she'd be damned if she'd let him drag her back into it. No. No, she was not Caroline any longer, and John was Caroline's problem. Not Carol's.

Glioblastoma.

The word hit her, and she had to close her eyes.

If Katie were still alive, she'd have spent her thirtieth birthday knowing it was likely the last one she'd ever have with her father. She would have sat by his side, holding his hand and reassuring him as she soaked in every moment she could. They probably would have talked about the good times they'd shared, laughing so they didn't cry.

For Carol, this was the one day a year when she could think of Katie in a hospital and not think about her death. She could think back on a memory with John and not hate him. He'd been exuberant to become a father. He'd been more than proud. When the doctor announced they had a daughter, John cried. He'd actually held Katie and cried, and Carol was so overcome with love for him that all his previous improprieties faded away. All those nights he'd spent drinking instead of being at home preparing the nursery were forgiven. All the times he'd spent money that should have gone to bills at the pub were forgotten. All the bad faded away, and in that moment she'd loved him more than she could have ever imagined possible.

Watching him hold their baby, seeing the pure love on his face, had shown her all she needed to know about him—he did have the ability to love someone more than he loved himself. He could have been an amazing husband and father.

From the day they'd met, he'd had a way about him that made her believe he could be better than he was. That day, even after all he'd put her through, she could see the awe on his face as he held Katie. The wonderment in his eyes was something she'd never forget.

Carol couldn't come up with a single scenario where she and John would still be married, but she knew if Katie were there, she would have been as well. For Katie. Because that was what mothers did—or should do. They set aside any bad feelings harbored toward their exes to be there for the kids.

If Katie were alive, Carol would have been there for her daughter. She should be there now. *For Katie.*

"Ma'am?" a voice called from a million miles away.

Carol blinked until she could focus on the man standing inside the elevator with his palm pressed against the sliding door.

"Going down?" he asked.

She opened her mouth, then snapped it shut and shook her head. He lifted his brow, giving her one last chance. When she didn't step into the car, he pulled his hand back and let the door close.

Swallowing, Carol turned down the corridor toward

John's room. "This is some birthday, baby girl," she whispered. She had no doubt in her mind that John would make her regret this. But she'd do it.

For Katie.

He lifted his face when she stepped into his room. Hope sparked in his eyes again. That look was too familiar. The feeling was too familiar. She'd caved in again. He'd won again. He always seemed to win.

"I'm only staying until someone else can get here," she warned. If she didn't stand her ground from the start, he'd chip away at it until she didn't have any fight left in her. She'd allowed him to do that to Caroline more times than she could remember; she wasn't about to let him do it to Carol. Holding out his phone, she waited for him to take it. "Call someone."

"I...I don't know anybody who can afford to fly down here on a whim."

Don't cave, Carol. Don't let him twist you around. "I'll pay for the ticket. I'll make the arrangements. I'll do whatever is needed, John. I need you to have someone here who can help you through this."

He didn't make a move to comply with her request. He looked at her, clearly hurt. As if he hadn't used her soft heart as a weapon against her a thousand times in the past. "If you don't want to be here, why'd you come back?"

"It's her birthday. Her father shouldn't be alone in a hospital on her birthday."

"Do you remember—"

"I don't want to remember," she snapped, refusing to give her ex-husband even a moment to get inside her head. "I'm here for Katie. Because she'd be here if she could. Nothing's changed.

I will not reminisce with the man who took my child from me. I am sorry that you are sick. I wouldn't wish this on anyone, but it is not fair that you expect me to take care of you. I will be here until someone else can arrive, but I will not be made to feel responsible for your well-being. Not after all this time."

The quiet that fell between them was filled with emotional grenades—a thousand things she wanted to say, old resentments and accusations that wanted to force themselves to the surface, anger and blame that had waited too damned long to be unleashed. She had her fingers on the pins, ready to pull and throw the bombs if he dared to push her on this. If he dared to make her feel guilty for not wanting to be dragged back into the hell he always brought with him.

"Look who's up," Dr. Collins said, walking in. He hesitated, as if sensing the tension between them, but recovered quickly. "Um, I need to talk to you about your condition, John. Do you want Carol to stay?"

Carol entwined her fingers and squeezed, fighting the urge to throw her hands up and walk away from the entire situation, as her ex-husband confirmed the doctor could openly disclose medical information in front of her. Dr. Collins made a note in John's chart, verified Carol's name "for the record," and scribbled some more.

He was stalling. She knew this technique. She'd seen it plenty of times before. Bad news was coming.

An eternity ticked away before he looked at John. "I received a copy of your medical records from your regular physician. I'm sorry about your prognosis."

"Has the timeline changed?" John asked.

"I can't really say without more extensive testing. An MRI, a CT scan..."

"I don't want more tests."

She tilted her head to look at John. "There could be changes in the tumor—"

"So what if there are?" John snapped. "There's nothing they can do about it. Is there?" He shrugged when she opened her mouth.

"Will his prognosis be different?"

"No," Dr. Collins said. "Based on what I saw in your medical records, I agree with the original prognosis. Given the severity of the seizure you had last night, I'd say you've started the downhill slide. We can make you more comfortable for the time you have left."

"More comfortable?"

"On a scale of one to ten, how bad are your headaches? How often?"

John sank back into the bed instead of answering.

"They will continue to get worse as your condition deteriorates," Dr. Collins said. "Your seizures, like the one that landed you here, will continue to get worse. All your symptoms will continue to get worse. Let me run a few tests. Maybe there is something the other doctor missed. Maybe we can help you here. Make things a little less painful."

Defiance, like that of a teenager, lit on his face. "That'd be nice, but I'll be traveling."

Carol frowned. "For God's sake, John. You're not making that trip. Not now."

He looked at her with all the stubbornness he'd had the day she'd told him they were too young to get married. He hadn't taken no for an answer then, and he obviously was determined not to take no for an answer now. "I'm going. You were right. I don't need her with me to say my goodbyes, but I'm still going."

"You can't drive," she said.

"Carol is right. You absolutely cannot drive," Dr. Collins agreed.

"I know that. I have bus tickets. Houston was my first stop. To see you."

She shook her head as she fell back in her chair. Yup. He was already making her regret not stepping into that elevator. The doctor stared at her, but she simply shrugged. This wasn't her problem.

"John," Dr. Collins said. "I don't think you appreciate the severity of your condition."

"My headaches aren't going to go away. My seizures are going to get worse. Then I'll die. Did I miss something?"

"You don't need to be in hospice yet—"

"I'm not going into hospice."

She sat forward again. "*John*."

"*Caroline*," he barked. Scowling at the doctor, he used the same clipped tone. "Her name is Caroline. *Car-o-line*. Not Carol."

She rolled her eyes. "Oh my God."

"I'm not dying in a hospital."

"Hospice will come to your home," Dr. Collins said.

He looked at Carol as if to confirm what he'd already decided. "I'm saying goodbye to our daughter. The way we planned."

Dr. Collins turned to her for an explanation.

"Our daughter passed away a long time ago. We planned on spreading her ashes in several locations, but we divorced before that happened." She turned her focus to the patient. "And it isn't happening now."

John grabbed her hand and continued as if she hadn't even spoken. "Come with me. You're a nurse. She's a nurse," he told Collins with all the pride that used to fill his voice when he introduced her to his fellow police officers. "She can help me."

"I was a pediatric nurse twenty-four years ago."

"You still know how to hand out pills, don't you?"

"I strongly advise against this," Dr. Collins said. "Your condition is going to deteriorate. What we don't know is how rapidly."

"I'm going," John said to Carol. "I'm going, and neither of you can stop me."

Shaking her head, she looked at the doctor. "I'd love to say this is the tumor talking, but he's always been this stupid."

———

Despite her intention to work half a day, Carol didn't make it into the office. By the time she left the hospital, she was emotionally and physically exhausted. John still had the ability to siphon every ounce of patience from her being. He was going to take a bus to all the places he wanted to visit. A bus! In his condition.

Idiot.

Sitting cross-legged on the floor in Katie's room, she stared at the framed photo of her snuggling with her little girl. Katie's pigtails had natural curls at the ends that Carol had loved toying with. She'd stick her fingers in the twists and lightly tug, watching them bounce back into shape. She'd do that over and over as they were reading or talking about whatever held Katie's interest at the moment.

By the time she stopped, her hands would smell faintly of the strawberry shampoo she used on Katie's hair. Closing her eyes, she inhaled as the scent filled her memory. Strawberry shampoo and grape popsicles. That was what Katie smelled like in Carol's memory. Even now, she couldn't catch a whiff of either of those things without automatically looking for her daughter. Moments would pass before she'd remember that Katie couldn't possibly be there. The smells came from other women's children. Her child was gone.

———

Katie sat at the kitchen table with an oversized crayon in her hand and all her books about national parks spread before her. Too short to reach the floor, she swung her feet, causing a rhythmic thump-thump *each time the heel of one of her bright red rain boots hit the support beam of the table. John's mother had bought them when Katie suddenly became scared of storms. They were supposed to be a reminder that with the thunder came rain, and rain made big puddles to jump in. However, Katie loved the boots so much, she refused to wear anything else, including her tennis shoes. Caroline had told her the boots were for outside, but as usual, John contradicted her and gave Katie permission to wear them indoors. Now Katie refused to take them off other than to bathe and sleep.*

"Daddy says we can go to Mount Hushmore, too."

"Rushmore," Caroline corrected. She stifled the urge to rein in Katie's plans. There was no way they could afford this trip.

When John and Katie had started talking about exploring, she'd agreed it would be fun. But every day the list of places John promised to take Katie grew. He didn't seem to understand that meant the budget for the trip would grow, too.

Once again, he was filling Katie's head with promises they couldn't possibly keep. He was always doing that, and then Caroline had to be the bad guy and tell their daughter no.

Sliding a cheese sandwich and half an apple on the table for Katie, she sat next to her little girl and read the list. She tugged a curl before rubbing her hand up and down Katie's back. "That's quite a trip you have planned there."

Katie set her crayon down and wrapped her tiny fingers around the sandwich. "Daddy says we can go wherever I want. How far is the ocean?"

"Too far, kitty cat."

She stopped kicking her feet and looked up at Caroline, disappointment making her mouth sag. "But Daddy said—"

"I know what Daddy said." She leaned over and kissed Katie's head, burying her nose to smell her hair. "We'll do our best to see everything, but maybe we can save some things to see next summer, hmm?"

Voices from outside drew her attention. Her smile faded as she peered out the sliding glass door. John and his father were sweating in the late May afternoon. Katie's birthday was still a few weeks away, but the moment she'd told his parents she wanted a swimming pool this summer, they'd run out and bought one.

She frowned when John yelled for his dad to turn the hose on. The frame was built—because his parents couldn't simply buy a kiddie pool; they had to buy Katie a full-sized monster that took up most of the backyard.

She swallowed hard and ran her hand over Katie's hair again. "We have to have rules for the pool, kitty cat."

"I know. Grandma told me." She had put the sandwich back down and was now misspelling ocean. O-s-h-u-n. "No swimming without a grown-up."

"Katie, look at me, please."

Bright blue eyes focused on Caroline.

"Just like you can't go to the park by yourself or ride your bike down the street by yourself, you can't go into the pool by yourself."

"I know, Mommy. Grandma told me."

Katie returned her attention to the list of places she wanted to see, and Caroline returned hers to the activity in the backyard.

"Mommy," Katie called.

Caroline lifted her brows in question.

"How do you spell Grand Canyon?"

She put her hand on Katie's head. "Oh, sweetheart." Instead of dashing her baby's happiness with a dose of reality, she spelled the words.

The smile on Katie's face got even wider. She bounced out of her chair, threw her arms around Caroline's neck, and hugged her tight. "This is going to be the best trip ever, Mommy."

She kissed Katie's head. "Sure is, kiddo."

———

"Oh, kitty cat," Carol whispered as she brushed her fingers over the words etched in Katie's urn. "I don't know how to do this."

Unfortunately, she was practiced at getting through situations she didn't know how to. Putting herself into autopilot mode, she pushed herself up and dragged her fingers under her eyes to dry her tears.

She was good at autopilot. Autopilot had gotten her through losing Katie, leaving John, and burying Tobias. Autopilot had gotten her through the past eight months. Tonight, it got her to the tiny grocery store that only sold local foods, to the hospital parking lot, and all the way to John's room. She knocked on his door as she pushed it open, allowing herself to reconnect with her actions because autopilot only went so far before someone noticed. When people noticed, they grew concerned. That was another thing Carol had learned a long time ago.

John looked up and froze, obviously surprised to see her. His smile was slow to spread, but he was clearly pleased she'd come back.

"Did you eat?" she asked.

"A little."

"I usually do this alone, but..." She reached into the bag she'd brought and pulled out a small cake. "Since you're here, I think we should celebrate her birthday together, don't you?"

"Yeah. We should."

She pried the top off the container, then handed him a plastic fork. Sitting on the edge of his bed, she stared at the little round cake covered in white icing and pink fondant roses, but didn't dig in. Neither did he.

"What?" she asked when he continued to stare at her.

"I...I didn't expect to see you again."

She gnawed at the inside for her lip, debating what to say to him. "I feel like she's telling me something," Carol whispered. "Like she brought you here to force me to face her loss. Maybe you're right. It's been twenty-four years, John. It's time to let go."

"Will you go with me?"

"Do you have any idea how much it hurts me to see you?"

"Because of Katie."

"Because of *everything*. I'm sorry you're sick. *I'm sorry*. But I'm not going to fall into your trap again."

"What trap, Caroline?" He closed his eyes. "Carol. I'm not setting a trap."

"You are. My God, you show up out of nowhere. The day before her birthday. Don't tell me you didn't choose right now, this moment, because you knew I'd be off balance."

He pointed to his head. "I didn't choose the timing."

"You couldn't wait a few more days?"

He set his fork down. "I deserve to see her on her birthday."

"A phone call would have been nice. A little warning to allow me time to brace myself."

He cut his gaze to her, his stare full of accusation. "Would you have let me see her?"

She didn't know. She couldn't answer that honestly. She'd like to think that she would have been a big enough person to grant his wish. Maybe she wouldn't have been there, but she would have made arrangements for someone to be at her home to let John in. She probably wouldn't have wanted to see him, but she was certain she would have allowed him to see Katie if he'd asked. She shrugged in response. "I guess we'll never know because, like always, you did whatever you wanted without taking anyone else into consideration."

He looked away. "I've changed."

"No, John, you haven't. You're still just as manipulative as you've always been."

He returned his glare to her. "I'm going to be dead in a few months. Have some compassion, huh?"

"I wouldn't be here if I didn't."

"Really?" Cocking his brow at her, he smirked in that way he always did before throwing a few cruel words her direction. "Because I'm pretty sure if I touched you right now, I'd get frostbite."

She tilted her head and stuck her bottom lip out at him, taunting him with her exaggerated pout. "Oh, nothing breaks my heart more than my asshole of an ex-husband thinking I'm frigid." She transitioned her mocking face to a stone-cold glare in the blink of an eye. "You want to know why I was so damned cold to you, John?" Leaning closer, she held his gaze to get her point across. "Because I learned a long time ago that you see warmth and kindness as weakness, and when you see weakness, you go straight for the kill."

He snorted a half-laugh as he rolled his eyes. "Jesus, Caroline. You still know how to be dramatic."

"And you still know how to be a conniving bastard." She put the cake on the tray hovering over his bed and stood. Walking to the window, she stared out at the city lights. "I hate this. I hate how you make me feel. How you've always made me feel."

"And how's that?" he asked flatly.

She spun on her heel, arms crossed defensively over her chest, to face him. "Not once, not in twenty years, did I ever question Tobias's motives. Not once did I question how I should react or respond to something he said, wondering what he was trying to get out of me. I have always had to analyze *every* word that comes out of your mouth. Our relationship has always been a high-stakes chess game. One wrong move and I'm cornered by your lies and deceit with no way out."

"I'm different now!"

"Are you? Are you *really*?"

"Yes! That was the alcohol, Caroline. That was me being young and stupid and inexperienced. And scared." He turned his head a touch and once again displayed his sad eyes for her. "I was always scared of losing you. You were so much better than me. You deserved more than I could ever give you."

"There." She pointed at him accusingly. "Right there it is. *Feel sorry for me, Caroline. I'm broken, Caroline. Only you can fix me, Caroline.* That's it, John. That's the move right there."

"It's the truth. You were better than me."

"Oh, boo-hoo. You *chose* to be less than you could be."

"Because I chose to be a cop?"

"Because you chose to be a drunk." She stared him down, waiting for him to deny the allegation. He didn't. She relaxed a bit. "I never begrudged your career choice, John. I begrudged how you used it as an excuse to be a shitty husband and father."

He focused on the hands he'd clenched in his lap. The muscles in his jaw worked, but she wasn't sure if he was clenching his jaw to bite back the words he wanted to say or if he was trying not to swallow the dose of reality she'd dumped on him.

She pressed on since he was no longer fighting back. "And you can save your song and dance about how you have nobody else to help you through this but me. One word,

John, and there'd be a hundred cops across the country lined up to make sure you got to make this trip. You don't need me, and you know it."

He let his shoulders sag, as if all the strength had left him. "I'm not saying goodbye to Katie with strangers. You're her mother. My wife."

"*Ex*-wife."

He met her gaze again. He didn't look angry and defensive now. He looked sad but determined. "We're a family, Caroline. That means something to me."

That used to mean something to her, too. That was how she justified staying with him longer than any sane person would have. They were family. Family didn't give up. Family didn't leave. But she should have left. She should have left long before he had a chance to cost Katie her life.

Carol inhaled a long, slow breath as she mentally steeled herself against his assault on her defenses. "You're using our daughter to twist me around."

"I'm not," he said, lowering his voice, as if intentionally keeping any edge from his words that could possibly set her off again. "I want..." He blinked as his eyes dampened. "Christ, Caroline. I lost everything, too. I lost my daughter *and* my wife. Now I'm standing at death's door looking back on my life, and I hate what I see. I hate the man I was and everything I put you through. I want to make peace with myself before I die, but I can't do that without making peace with you first. That's all I'm asking."

She stared him down, gauging how much honesty she could find in his words. She couldn't even begin to count how many times she'd let him convince her to do his bidding. He was too good at playing her emotions. She was the guitar, he was the player. And play her he did. Over and over again. "I don't trust you," she whispered.

"You have no reason to. But I have no reason to lie to you now." He held his hands up, gesturing to the hospital room. "What could I possibly be trying to get from you, Caroline?"

Exhaling slowly, she broke down his request in her mind and couldn't find an ulterior motive. Accepting that John Bowman didn't have a hidden agenda seemed to be asking for a target to be put on her head. Even so, she nodded. "Okay. Here's the deal. I'll go with you. We'll say goodbye to her like we planned. Then I'll take you home where someone, I don't care who, will be waiting to take care of you. You will not try to manipulate me into giving you more than that. Do you understand?"

"Yes. Thank you, Caroline." He held his hand out. She hesitated before taking it. Just like when he'd introduced himself years ago, the moment he squeezed her hand and smiled, she felt like she'd sealed her fate.

———

The following morning found Carol standing much as she had the night before—in front of the hospital window with her arms crossed. This morning, however, Dr. Collins was standing next to her with a look of pure distress on his face.

"I have to say again how much I disagree with what you're doing," he said. "John? Are you listening?"

John sat on the edge of his hospital bed buttoning his shirt. His fingers trembled, but he was able to function well enough that Carol could stamp down the urge to help.

"Of course he's not listening," she said with an unintentional irritation in her tone. "He never does."

John finished dressing and then looked at her, an excited smile curling his lips. She wondered if he'd been given more than the necessary dose of painkiller. "I still have the list of all the places we were gonna go." He slid off the bed and held on to the edge as he swayed slightly. "*The* list. The one Katie made." He dug in his pocket as he crossed the small hospital room.

She didn't need to see the list. She'd memorized it in the days they'd spent waiting for Katie's ashes to be returned to them. The paper with oversized messy handwriting in red crayon, most of the places misspelled, had still been hanging on the fridge when Carol had sneaked out of the house she could no longer breathe in. The sense of Katie's death was suffocating in that house. If she didn't escape, she would have died, too.

She held up her hand like a cop directing traffic, determined to stop him before he got any closer. "I don't want to see it."

He pulled the yellowed paper out and unfolded the list, showing it to her anyway. She turned away before she had to face another bit of the past she wasn't ready to. Even so, her mind filled with a flash of Katie eating a sandwich and kicking her red boots against the table over and over.

"Look at this, Dr. Collins. Look at all the places she wanted to go. She was young, but she wanted to do so much. She wanted to be an explorer, didn't she, Caroline?" He looked at the list when no one else seemed interested. Running his fingers over the paper, he smiled. "She was going to be an explorer."

"Are you sure you want to do this?" Dr. Collins asked her as John refolded the paper.

No, she didn't want to do this. She didn't want to commit herself to John for the next few weeks. She didn't want to spread Katie's ashes. She sure as hell didn't want to watch one more person die. She didn't say that. Instead, she sighed. "Did someone call in his prescriptions to the pharmacy I requested?"

"Yes." Turning the clipboard in his hands to lay it flat against his stomach, he seemed to concede and apparently no longer felt the need to fidget. "I don't know that he'll survive this trip."

"Well, I guess we'll get as far as we can and deal with his health when we have to."

Sympathy filled his eyes. "This is going to take a huge toll on you, too. Do you understand that? He can get around now, but that could change with *one* seizure. In a matter of minutes, his health and mobility could change."

She didn't need his help understanding what a risk she was taking, and she certainly didn't appreciate him pointing out what a disaster this was going to be. Even if John was healthy enough to make it to the end of their journey, the emotional impact of this trip was going to hit her hard. She was about to do what she'd managed to avoid for twenty-four years; she was about to face Katie's death and let her go. Tobias had tried to force this issue for two decades. Leave it to John to throw her in head first. He'd always had a way, good or bad, of making her face things she somehow managed to ignore.

Goddamn him anyway.

Pinching the bridge of her nose, she stifled the

exasperation threatening to surface. She hadn't slept a wink the night before, trying to figure out why the hell she'd agreed to this stupid trip. Guilt? Shame? Or because maybe she'd needed someone—*John*—to put a foot in her ass and make her take this step all along. She'd never be ready to put her daughter to rest, but John was right when he said saying goodbye to her with strangers wasn't right. Tobias never knew Katie, had never held her or loved her like John had. He could have been there, helping Carol through the process, but he wouldn't have been going through the process himself, and somehow that hadn't felt right.

Maybe Carol had been waiting for John to find her all this time, so she could do this as well.

Dropping her hand, she met Dr. Collins's concerned gaze with one of her own. "I know that. I do. We never mourned as parents. I left him before we had a chance. He seems to need that to make peace with her death. No matter how badly things ended between us, he deserves some peace, don't you think? Honestly, maybe I need that, too."

He put his hand to her arm and gave her a reassuring squeeze. "If it gets to be too much, you really must find a hospital and have him admitted. Whether he wants it or not. There's only so much you can do for him."

"Yeah," she said, looking at her ex-husband again. "I know."

———

"I thought you'd be sleeping," John said from the doorway of Carol's home office.

She glanced at the corner of her laptop screen to check

the time. Almost midnight. "I'm headed that way soon. Why are you still up? Feeling okay?"

"Nervous." He shrugged as if he didn't understand his professed uneasiness. "I've been thinking about this trip for a long time. I can't believe we're leaving tomorrow."

"Yeah." Spinning her high-backed office chair, she grabbed a stack of papers. "I printed off the directions. I know that's old-school, but I don't like relying on technology, especially once we get out west. Connection with the outside world is hit-or-miss in some areas." She flipped through the pages. "Eighty-six hours of drive time. That probably breaks down to about twelve days with stops." She stared at him, making certain he heard her next words. "You need to find someone to help you before we get to Dayton, John. I'm dropping you off and coming home."

He stared at her for several heartbeats before nodding.

"I'm not trying to be a jerk."

"I know. You've already done more than I expected. It'll be nice to make this trip in your fancy camper instead of a bus. Can you believe I came this close to death without knowing Mercedes made motorhomes?"

Carol chuckled as he broke the seriousness of the moment. "Good thing you found me when you did." She glanced at a photo on her desk. She was pressed against Tobias's side with the Rocky Mountains in the background. Turning the frame to show John the image, she said, "This was our first trip in the motorhome. We went to Denver for a marathon. Tobias didn't like to sit still. We were always on the go. The RV has been in storage since he died. It needs to get back on the road."

"I'm sorry about what I said."

She lifted her brows in question. He'd said so many untoward things since reappearing in her life, she couldn't possibly pinpoint which one he was apologizing for.

"You know..." Red flushed his cheeks. "Pointing out you'd married a Black man. That was stupid. I'm glad you found someone to take care of you."

Her heart did the funny flip that it always seemed to do when someone noted the difference between her and Tobias's ethnicities. That usually led to confrontation of some kind or another, and a long talk between them about how society was still unevolved in certain ways. "We were married for two years before my parents acknowledged him as part of the family. Mom used to call me up and tell me about nice boys she could introduce me to if only I'd go home. Drove me crazy."

"What changed her mind?"

Her eyes swam out of focus as she toyed with the clip on the stack of directions she'd printed. "We were going to have a baby. She loved the idea of being a grandmother again, but I told her if she couldn't accept my husband, she couldn't accept his child. Dad never came around, but Mom did. I miscarried in my second trimester."

"I'm sorry." Sitting in the chair across from her, he picked up the photo. "What does she think of you driving me across the country?"

She forced out a flat laugh. "Oh. I didn't tell her. It's better that she doesn't know. I told her I'd be at a work conference for the next two weeks and not to expect to hear from me. She wasn't surprised. You know how I am; I tend to bury myself in work."

He continued to stare at the picture, rubbing his thumb

over the glass and, if she had to guess, the image of her smiling face. "It's paid off. Not many companies would give someone a month off with no notice."

"I didn't take much time after Tobias's funeral. HR wasn't thrilled with my choice to go back to work. They're counting this as bereavement leave. This probably isn't what they had in mind, though."

He put the photo down. "No. I'd guess not."

She reached for the frame, turning it just so. "I reserved a spot at an RV park in Amarillo for tomorrow night. It'll be a long, hard day, but there isn't much once we get into West Texas. I don't want to get caught out there with no plan for where to stay."

"We have an RV," he said lightly as he sank back in the chair. "We can hole up and sleep whenever we need to."

"Yes, however, for safety's sake, I'd prefer to be in a secure location. Besides, they have real showers and bathrooms. That may seem like a small thing to you, but as the one who will be responsible for the tanks, I'd really like to keep the motorhome bathroom usage to a minimum."

"We can pee outside. Become one with nature."

"*Or* use rest areas and RV parks. We should get to bed," she said as she shut down her laptop. She ignored John's gaze as she put her computer and daily planner into her briefcase along with the map and RV park reservation information.

"Are you taking that?"

"Yes."

"On vacation?"

She snapped her case closed. "No offense, but I don't consider chaperoning your death march much of a vacation. I'm pretty confident I'll welcome the distraction." Hefting the strap over her shoulder, she gestured for the door. "Go to bed. I'd like to be on the road no later than seven."

He rose to his feet but didn't make a move toward the door. Instead he stood, holding her gaze. "I really am glad you're doing this. You need to say goodbye to her, too, Caroline. Whether you want to or not."

"Go to bed, John," she muttered. Once he'd left the room, she looked back at the photo of her and her husband and said a silent prayer asking Tobias to help her through the coming days.

FOUR

CAROL WOKE UP LATE. *Of course* she woke up late. She rushed through a shower and dressed before trotting down the stairs, stopping when she found John at the back door staring out at Tobias's garden, leisurely sipping his coffee as if she hadn't explained their plans in great detail.

She looked from his bag sitting by the door to the half-full coffee pot and back to his relaxed stance. "How long have you been up?"

Facing her, he gave her a warm smile, apparently oblivious to her irritation. "Since about five. I'm still on Eastern time."

She scowled at him. She'd told him they had a long day ahead. She'd told him she wanted to be on the road by seven. But he'd still let her oversleep.

Jackass.

At least she'd packed the RV and fueled up the night before. The motorhome would be ready to roll as soon as they hopped in. She filled her travel mug with the coffee left in the pot John had fixed, rinsed the carafe, and grabbed her purse.

"We don't have to rush," he said, lifting his bag while she double-checked the house alarm.

She shoved him out the door before the alarm could set. "It's about nine hours to Amarillo. Add in lunch, gas stops, and bathroom breaks, and we're going to be closer to twelve. We have to check in to the park by eight. Any later and it will be getting too dark to hook up the RV. And... What the hell are you smirking at?"

"You haven't changed a bit. You have shorter hair, fancier clothes, a nicer car, and an expensive RV, but you're still wound tighter than a girdle at a pie-eating contest."

She frowned at him. "Get in the RV, John."

As she waited for him to settle in, she ran down her mental checklist, making sure she packed everything they could possibly need. "Did you get your meds?"

He adjusted the seat. "Yes."

She pulled the printed itinerary out of her briefcase. "Did you take them this morning?"

He buckled in. "Yes."

Putting the papers in the console between them, she tucked her briefcase behind her seat. "Did you eat? You're not supposed to take those on an empty stomach."

"Yes, Mother."

She resisted the urge to respond, but did ask, "Did you clean up after yourself? I don't want ants when I get back."

"I washed my dishes and put them away."

"And you have your pills within easy reach in case we can't stop when you need them?" After reaching for her seatbelt, she had to try three times before she managed to get the thin metal into the slot.

He jiggled the pouch she'd bought when she picked up his new prescriptions. She turned the ignition, at which point he reached for the radio.

"*Don't*," she warned, as she'd done when they'd gotten into her SUV a few days before. "Don't touch anything."

"For two weeks? I'm not allowed to touch *anything* for two weeks?"

"We aren't even out of the driveway yet, John. You don't need to mess with things."

"Just wanted a little music."

"What the hell am I doing?" she asked under her breath as she put the RV in reverse. Checking the rearview camera on the touchscreen, she started to back out of the driveway, then stomped on the brake, causing them both to jerk forward. "Oh, God!"

"What?" John demanded as she looked at him, her eyes wide.

"Where's Katie?"

He glanced around for a moment, barely hiding the grin on his lips. "There goes our *Parents of the Year* award."

"Shut up," she warned.

As she threw the gearshift into park and unbuckled her seatbelt, John let the laugh he'd clearly been fighting fill the motorhome. Scowling, she shoved the door open.

This was going to be a very long two weeks.

———

Carol climbed back into the motorhome after attaching all the hoses and double-checking the connections. John lay curled on his side on the queen-size bed in the back of the RV. Every mile she drove seemed to add to the headache that had started pounding in his head as they'd emerged from Fort Worth. He'd rubbed his neck, squeezed his head, tried to sleep in the passenger seat, and then he'd given in and taken several pills. When those started wearing off far too soon, he decided to try to sleep the pain off in the bed. Though she didn't like that he was suffering, she was glad he'd put some space between them.

Their time in the RV had bounced between tense silence and bickering over directions. Or the temperature of the AC. Or the music. She'd clenched her teeth so many times she was surprised she hadn't ground them to the gums yet.

She couldn't count how many times she'd silently chastised herself for agreeing to this trip. They were only one day in. Even so, she put her irritation aside and tiptoed to the bed in the back of the RV.

"How are you doing?" she asked, intentionally keeping her voice soft.

John slammed his hand down on the mattress. "For God's sake, Caroline. How many times are you going to ask me that?"

She inhaled sharply at his unexpected attack. "Excuse the hell out of me for pretending to be concerned."

He lifted his head off the pillow. "I'm the same. Okay?"

She lifted her hands in surrender, but rotated her jaw with the anger she couldn't quite hide. "Do you want to try to eat?"

"Just get me another pill."

"It's not time yet."

He chuckled flatly. "What's the worst that can happen? I'll OD?"

She stood staring for several seconds before moving to the passenger seat, where he'd tucked the pouch of medications into the glove box. She grabbed a bottle of water from the fridge and threw them beside him on the bed. She knew he was in pain, and she even felt bad for him, but not enough to continue tolerating him snapping at her. "Take them all," she suggested. "Put us both out of our misery."

He muttered something as she stepped outside the RV but she chose to ignore him. Jerking the storage compartment open, she pulled out the bag she'd filled with gym clothes. Heading for the park's rec center, she followed the sign to the ladies' room and changed into running pants and a tank top. Still frustrated, she climbed on the treadmill, once again wondering why the hell she was putting herself through this.

She started slow, but by the time she'd replayed the entire day through her mind, she was jogging at a fast clip. Before meeting Tobias, the only running she'd done was in hospital corridors. When they'd met, he'd been on a full football scholarship because his speed and agility was like a secret weapon for the home team.

His biggest challenge in life, he'd once told her, was getting her to start exercising with him. She'd only done that because with their crazy schedules, it seemed to be the only time they could spend together. She'd have chased that man to the moon to spend time with him. She never would have gotten in shape if not for him. Though the list of things she'd never have done if not for Tobias was long. He'd pushed her.

He'd challenged her in the best possible ways. He'd made her a better person. A *complete* person.

Well, as complete as she could have ever been without Katie. Even so. She would give it all back to him if she could have had her little girl. That brought her thoughts back to John. The complete opposite of Tobias.

Tobias wanted to see Carol grow; John feared Caroline would surpass him.

Tobias encouraged Carol to be strong; John needed Caroline to be weak.

Tobias lifted her every day; John did his best to hold her back.

It took years for her to realize John hadn't done those things out of malice. He really was scared, like he'd told her in the hospital room. He'd been insecure. A frightened man-child who couldn't stand the thought of his wife being more successful, making more money, and dreaming of having more than he could give her.

It hadn't been easy for her to comprehend that he hadn't intentionally tried to sabotage her goals. Time and distance from him had helped. Seeing him through the lens of time had eased some of her anger. She started to understand that he had been flawed beyond repair long before she'd met him. His ego was as precious to him as anything. Having a woman —more specifically his wife—outperform him was a ding he couldn't handle.

If she hadn't gotten pregnant with Katie, she would have outshone him eventually, and he would have found a fault in her to justify walking away and saving his pride. If it weren't for Katie, they never would have stayed together. They never would have gotten married.

And John never would have been able to hold her back.

———

Caroline's stomach tightened with anxiety when the timer went off. Her vision blurred with unshed tears as she lifted the stick. This was the second home pregnancy test she'd taken. Both were positive.

Damn it.

Yes, she was an adult. Yes, she was in college. Yes, her parents were still going to freak.

And John. What was he going to think?

Who was she kidding? He'd be thrilled. Most of the guys on the police force were starting families. But most of the guys on the police force were married.

John was five years older. He was about to turn twenty-seven and was settling in for the life he wanted.

She had bigger plans. Plans her mother told her would get sidetracked if she stayed in a relationship with an older man. She was close to finishing her undergraduate degree and had already started looking at medical schools. She didn't need her mom to tell her that medical school would be off the table with a baby on the way.

While her parents had encouraged her to look far and wide at the best schools, dating John had changed her mind. She wanted to stay local, so they could be together. She had so many brochures from schools in and around Dayton, she couldn't keep them straight anymore.

Well. She could stop obsessing about that now.

Tossing the test aside, she put her palms to her flat stomach. She could figure this out. She could do this. She needed to change course. That was all. She would complete her nursing program for now and would look at finishing medical school later. After the baby was born and she and John could put some money aside. She'd simply postpone things. This was not the end of her plans.

Just...a detour.

She glanced at her watch. John wouldn't be off duty for another two hours. Instead of sitting there counting down the minutes, she went to visit an advisor. She could finish her degree right before the baby was born.

With John on the police department and her working at a hospital, they could align their shifts and wouldn't have to pay for daycare, which would save them money and allow her to get back on track to getting her medical degree sooner. It could be done. It wouldn't be easy, but she could make it happen.

Confident in her plan, she headed to John's apartment and cooked a big pot of spaghetti. She was pulling the garlic bread from the oven when he opened the front door.

John tossed his hat aside and put his gun on the table. "I was hoping you'd be here. Dinner smells good."

She tried to smile, but was certain it came out more like a grimace and turned her back to him, busying herself with getting plates from the cabinet. "I hope you're hungry. I think I made too much."

"That's okay. I'll eat leftovers." He came into the kitchen and wrapped his arms around her waist, putting a kiss on her neck. "Missed you, baby," he whispered before moving his kisses toward her ear.

She laughed softly, knowing where this was headed. Turning, she put her hand to his chest. "Slow down there, Officer Bowman."

His excitement faded a bit. "You okay?" He cupped her face and the concern in his eyes grew. "What's the matter, Caroline?"

"I'm pregnant." The words tumbled out before she could stop them. His eyes widened, and she nodded. She couldn't think of anything to add. Nothing else seemed to make sense.

As he silently stared, doubt started to creep in on her, but then he scooped her against him. He held her tight, hugging her as if he'd never let go. "I'm going to be a dad? I'm going to be a dad?" He pulled back, his elation looking more like panic. "Are you okay? Is everything okay?"

"I'm fine. I'm...more than fine," she said, relieved that he'd responded as she'd expected. She wasn't sure what she would have done if he hadn't wanted the baby.

"This is amazing. This is... We gotta get married."

Her face fell. Okay. That hadn't factored into her plan. "What?"

"You can't have my baby out of wedlock."

"Oh, John. This isn't 1950. Plenty of women have babies without getting married first. I've got to finish school. I don't have time to plan a wedding."

"Finish school? Caroline, you're pregnant."

"All the more reason to push through now." She tugged his hand until he followed her to the table and sat beside her. "I already talked to an advisor at school. We figured it all out. I'll go back to medical school in a few years. Being a nurse will keep me in the field. I won't lose any ground. In fact, I'll gain some. I'll have actual working experience to take to medical school. I'll be ahead of the game when I go back."

He shook his head. "No. No. You should be at home. With our kid. Like a real mom."

She gawked at him, not sure if she should laugh or smack

him for his closed-minded, sexist comment. "Like a *real* mom? Women work, John. That doesn't make them any less of a mother than a man working makes him less of a father."

"Yeah, I know that," he said, but clearly didn't believe it. His mother had never worked. "It's just... I want you home. With the baby."

"I want to be a doctor. I've always planned to be a doctor. You know that."

"But this changes everything."

"No. It doesn't. It changes how I'm going to get there, but it doesn't change the end game. I'm going to medical school, John. I'm going to be a pediatrician."

He opened his mouth, likely to argue, but didn't. "Okay. Sure. If that's what you want. But we are getting married."

"John, we're not ready for marriage."

"Hey," he said, his voice and eyes unwavering, "I'm not caving on this. Not this. If you want to work, okay. If you want to go to school, we'll figure it out. We are getting married." He knocked his knuckles against the table in his signature rhythm. "Don't move."

She sat back while he went into his bedroom. Maybe he was right. Not because the baby should be born to married parents, but because he had better insurance than she could get. She'd have to go on public assistance to cover the cost that John's insurance would if she were his wife. Insurance didn't seem like the best reason to get married, though.

John pulled her from her internal debate when he sat at the table, wearing that half-grin that always melted her heart. She gasped when he held up a gold band with a tiny diamond perched on top. The gem wasn't big, but neither was his salary.

If she had to guess, she'd say he'd saved up a long time to buy that ring.

"See that?" he asked. "I was planning to marry you anyway. Not because you're pregnant, but because I love you. More than life itself." He pushed the ring onto her finger and kissed her hand. "Fits and everything." His smile grew, causing her reservations to fade.

Okay. Okay. They'd get married. They'd get married and have a baby.

She'd figure out the rest later.

———

Carol's chest burned, reminding her that she'd been sprinting longer than her body could handle. Slowing the treadmill, she eased her heart rate down and stretched before taking a quick shower.

As she approached the RV, she saw that John was sitting in one of the lawn chairs she'd packed in the storage section. He'd set both of them out, but she had no intention of occupying the other. The sun had set, and clusters of stars littered the inky sky. Several people had small fires going in their fire pits, but John was illuminated only by the streetlight high above their parking spot. The scene seemed sad to her somehow, like the amber glow highlighted the solitude of the life he'd made for himself. Her sympathy was short-lived as she reminded herself of his shitty attitude earlier.

The crunching gravel under her feet announced her arrival.

"Hi," he said.

"Hey." She opened the bin to put her bag away.

He suddenly appeared at her side. "I didn't mean to snap at you," he said as she closed the door. "It's the headache."

"I know."

"I'm sorry."

She shrugged one shoulder and let it fall. "I shouldn't have said what I did. I'm sorry, too. I know you're in pain. I'll try to be more patient."

He gestured up at the sight he'd been admiring. "Have you ever seen a more beautiful sky? There's gotta be a million stars up there."

She tilted her head back to look at the twinkling display set against the near-black backdrop. Tobias loved sitting out like this, looking up at the night. He said seeing the universe staring back kept him humble. It had always made her feel insignificant. Even so, she couldn't deny the beauty of it. "Wait until we really get away from it all. It's amazing."

"Are you hungry?"

"Not much. You?"

"I ate a sandwich. I can make you one."

"I can do it," she said as she started for the door. "Thanks for offering, though."

He followed her into the motorhome, standing by the entrance as she got a plate from the cabinet. "You haven't asked how I'm doing."

She managed to stop her hostile laugh before it left her. Seriously? After his temper tantrum? "You didn't seem to want me to, John."

Another few heartbeats of quiet passed between them. "We shouldn't fight. Katie hated it when we fought."

She opened the fridge. "We're not fighting."

"Oh. I guess your cold shoulder gave me the wrong idea."

His voice was light, as if he were trying to tease her.

She wasn't in the mood to be teased. She slammed the door and met his stare. "I didn't ask how you are doing so I'm giving you the cold shoulder?"

The look in his eye immediately changed to barely contained anger. "The temperature dropped about twenty degrees when you got back."

She didn't care. Let him be pissed. Let him get pissed enough to storm off and leave her there. She'd jump in the driver's seat and disappear without another word to him. "What would you like me to do, John, hmm? How would you like me to be?"

"A little less bitter would be nice."

She focused on untwisting the tie around the bread. "You know, you show up in my life out of nowhere, dredging up memories better left alone—"

"You mean our daughter?"

She scoffed. "I'm not doing this."

"You're pissed because I made you remember Katie?"

She dropped the bread as she met his gaze again. "No. I'm pissed because you made me remember *you* and all the bullshit I tolerated to try to keep the peace between us."

Returning her attention to making her dinner, she ignored him until he put his hand on hers, stopping her from spreading a dollop of olive-oil mayonnaise. Shaking her head, she dropped the bread and knife. "Do you remember that night I told you I was going to divorce you? I got suspended without pay because you'd made me late for work, *yet again*. You had a bad day and instead of coming home to take care of Katie, you sat in that pub drinking. I was about to lose my job because you never seemed to be able to come home on time. I packed your bags. I was going to make you leave but you talked me out of it. You always had this way of making me believe you could change." Narrowing her eyes, she seethed, "Do you know how many times I've thought *if only*. If only I hadn't given you *one more chance*. If only I'd been stronger. If only I'd listened to my parents. If only this. If only that. If only you hadn't been such a selfish bastard."

She pushed her plate away and stormed outside, inhaling the muggy night air in a futile attempt to calm her anger. Hell. Maybe she'd be the one to vanish into the night. Let him take the RV and all these damned memories with him. She could walk into the darkness and disappear for good. That'd be okay. As long as this hell ended, that'd be perfectly okay.

She stood staring at the stars, trying to calm her racing heartbeat. She wasn't sure how long she stood there, but she'd talked herself out of a suicide mission across the emptiness of West Texas when a plate appeared in front of her face.

"You should eat," John said.

She accepted his offering. "Thanks."

"I wouldn't have given up that easy." He stuffed his hands in his pockets. "That's why when you finally did leave me, you disappeared in the middle of the night without a word. Because you knew I'd never give up that easy."

"And I'd never stop accepting your lame apologies."

"I've thought that, too. If only... There are a million if-onlys that have played through my mind. We can't change the past. That's something I've had to learn to accept. I can't change what I've done, and I'll never know what would have happened if I'd done things different. Maybe she'd still be dead. Maybe she was always meant to die. Maybe nothing I could have done would have changed that." He nodded toward her dinner. "Eat. I'm going to get some sleep. We have another long day tomorrow."

She stared at the sandwich, far too large for her appetite, then up to the stars.

He was wrong. *Everything* would be different if he'd left that night. Katie wouldn't have died. She would have lived. She would have grown up. And Carol would have still been able to hold her daughter.

———

Carol's defenses immediately spiked when John said, "This suits you." His words cut the silence that had filled the motorhome for the last hundred miles, and though his tone wasn't malevolent, she sensed his unspoken judgment. She hadn't slept well the night before. His comment about how maybe Katie was meant to die had played over and over in her mind and twisted her emotions inside out as she remembered far too many things that were better left forgotten.

"What suits me?" she asked, trying to keep her tone from sounding clipped.

"The fancy house. The fancy clothes. The overpriced motorhome. You always were too good for me. Remember how your parents blamed me for you not finishing medical school?"

"Well, I did drop out to have your baby."

His smile spread, apparently proud that her unexpected pregnancy had forced her to give up her lifelong ambitions.

"We were the 'it' couple, you know. Everyone wanted to be like us. We had it all."

She creased her brow at his assessment of the life they'd shared. "No, we didn't."

"Come on," he said, his gaze skimming over her face. "We had a nice home. A beautiful daughter."

"We also had an enormous amount of debt. You were a drunk. And all we did was fight."

He shook his head as if her points weren't valid. "There were good times, too. You don't remember them, but I do. We laughed all the time. We had good friends. Remember how we had parties every weekend?"

Amazement at how differently he saw the past rolled through her. He'd have a better chance at convincing her the Earth was flat. "*You* had parties every weekend, John. *I* cleaned up the messes that you and your friends left behind."

"You enjoyed those as much as I did."

She cast him a glance, letting the unamused look on her face dispute his observation.

"You liked our friends," he said with quiet insistence.

"They were *your* friends."

"That's not how I remember it."

Pressing her lips together, she tried to stop herself, but she couldn't let this rest. "You drank so much, I don't know how you remember anything."

Turning in his seat, he pinned her in place with a vexed stare. "We were together for almost eight years. Not all of it was bad."

He unbuckled and pushed himself up, moving back to the kitchen. She exhaled some of her frustration, debating whether it was too late to turn the RV around and go home.

The sound of the fridge door slamming made her wince. She was about to call back and tell him to take it easy on her RV when he dropped back into his seat. She chafed inwardly at how it bounced in response.

"You know," he said, cracking open a bottle of water, "I get that you hate me. I don't blame you, but fuck you for acting like we never had anything worth remembering."

"Fuck *you* for acting like you ever *did* anything worth remembering. My God, John, I spent our entire relationship mothering you. It was cute in the beginning, you know. *Look how much he needs me. He wouldn't last a day without me.* That got old pretty damn quick when I had a child to take care of. Nursing a grown man's hangover isn't nearly as adorable when you have spit-up in your hair, swollen tits, and a screaming newborn in your arms."

"It wasn't that bad."

"Where were you when Katie and I were released from the hospital?"

"I had every right to celebrate becoming a dad."

"Yeah, you did, and I had every right to leave the hospital with my husband. I waited for you for hours. I had to call your father to come get us because I was too ashamed to call *my* father. It's a damn good thing considering you were passed out on the couch when we got there."

He took a long drink from his water bottle. "I don't deny that I had some growing up to do."

"No, John. You had some *sobering* up to do. I made excuses for you like I always did. I told your dad you'd stayed up late preparing for the baby to come home. I told him we'd be fine. I told him to go home, not to worry. Then I sat in the bathroom and cried because I knew we weren't going to be fine. I knew we were going to be a disaster. I didn't know how to stop it." She swallowed hard. "I didn't know how bad it was going to get."

"I may not have been perfect," he snapped, "but neither were you. Nothing was ever enough for you. Nothing I did was right. Do you know how much that beats a man down? To know his wife is miserable and nothing he does can make it better? I remember how you used to look at me. You blamed me because you had to give up medical school. Well, newsflash, *Nurse Bowman*, you participated in making our daughter. You were there, too. You were as much to blame for getting knocked up as I was." He grunted as he shook his head. In true John fashion, he didn't know when to stop. Instead of shutting his mouth, he pressed on. "We had good times. The first Christmas after we were married. We had that ugly little tree, remember? But we worked hard to make it beautiful. We didn't have a lot of money, but I got you that necklace with little booties on it. You loved it. We had good times."

She gripped the steering wheel, irritated as hell that he was missing the point. "A few good times doesn't balance the scale of what happened to Katie."

He focused out the window at the flat topography. There was nothing for miles and miles except dry land and bright blue sky. There weren't even any clouds to try to interpret as something else. Just brown dirt and blue sky.

"You should have stayed. I would have stopped drinking. I would have been more committed. Losing Katie was a wakeup call."

"One that you didn't take." She glanced at him. "When did you say you got sober? Four years ago?"

"Nine."

"Nine years ago, John? Katie had been gone for fifteen years. It took *fifteen* years for the lesson to sink in?"

"The fifteenth anniversary of her death hit me hard. I did try to crawl into a bottle then. What'd you do, *Carol*? Go on a road trip with your new husband, living your new life, acting like we never existed?"

Actually, she'd spent that day in bed. Taking more sleeping pills than any bottle or physician would recommend. Not enough to overdose. Enough to sleep through the day. And part of the next. Tobias had forced her to see a counselor after that. She'd smiled and nodded and faked her way through the appointment, and never went back again. She didn't need Tobias *or* a doctor to tell her how to feel about Katie dying. She sure as hell didn't need the man responsible for her death to give her pointers. "I'm not comparing my grief to yours, John. I mourn every day for my daughter, and you are not going to make me feel guilty for not falling apart enough to suit *you*."

"You didn't fall apart at all," he said. "You turned to stone. Then you walked away like we meant nothing to you."

Grinding her teeth, she took a moment to constrain her response. "You don't get to be angry that I left you. You don't get to judge me for moving on and trying to find some happiness in this life. You *don't* get to tell me that I didn't hurt enough for Katie."

"You didn't even give us a chance to recover. You just left."

"Yeah. I did. You are correct. If I'd left the hundred times before when I wanted to..." Though the shoulder wasn't sufficient to park the RV, she steered off the road and threw the gearshift into park. "I lay there last night listening to you snore and thinking of all the times I debated slipping out with Katie. All the times I talked myself out of leaving you. You were her father. We were a family. We were married. Wives don't leave without trying. Mothers don't take their daughters away without a really good reason. I had a good reason, John. I had a thousand good reasons. They were never enough to make me walk away. But then you killed her," she whispered. "And I let you. I knew you weren't responsible enough to care for her. I knew you drank too much. I knew you weren't attentive enough. Still, I convinced myself that you'd never let anything happen to her."

"I was asleep."

"You were *passed out*." Her voice cracked as she emphasized the last words, as she let the accusation hang between them. "I saw the beer cans when I walked in the house, John. The counter was full of them, every one empty. She is dead because you were a drunk and I enabled you. I let you kill her."

Her eyes widened at the shock her own words inflicted. The reality of what she'd said was like a slap to the face. Katie was dead because John was an alcoholic. And because Carol had made a thousand excuses to allow him to be. She'd played as much of a role in Katie's death as John. She was as guilty.

Jesus.

She'd killed her baby. By being a doormat, by making excuses, by lying to herself about how bad things really were. The role she'd played had been passive, but she'd played it all the same.

She'd killed Katie, too.

"Caroline," he whispered, as if he could read her train of thought.

"Oh my God."

"You weren't even home," he said as if to stop the next words from leaving her lips.

"I killed her, too."

"It was an accident."

"Oh God." Her shoulders rocked as a sob pushed its way up her throat. Her chest grew tight and her gut rolled, her breakfast tried to evacuate as she struggled to unbuckle and open the door at the same time. She landed on her feet outside the RV as she lost control of her stomach.

FIVE

THICK SILENCE FILLED THE RV. John started to speak—no doubt to reassure her once again that Katie's death was an accident, and no one was to blame—but she lifted her hand.

"Don't talk to me right now," she said before swishing water around her mouth and spitting out the window. Before she even pulled the RV back onto the road, he'd climbed from his seat and disappeared into bed.

Carol didn't care how much pain John was in. They had reservations outside Grand Canyon National Park, and she wasn't going to miss checking in. She had an agenda. He had pills and a place to rest. She couldn't do any more for him than that. All she could do was drive as fast as possible to put an end to this hell. Two days down, ten to go.

She didn't hear any sounds from the back until the alarm on his watch beeped and he shuffled around to get his pills. That was good. That was perfect. She could get through this trip if he'd give her some damn space. She would have loved to drive forever without stopping, but they were getting low on gas. Pulling off an hour into

Arizona, she found a gas station and parked in front of the pumps.

"Bathroom break." She looked in the rearview mirror when he didn't respond. "John?"

She released her seatbelt and spun her chair to go to the back. Leaning over the lump on the bed, she called out to him again. "Hey. I'm getting gas. Do you need anything?"

When he didn't respond, she shook him gently. Nothing.

"Shit," she muttered as she climbed onto the bed and pressed her fingers against his neck. She closed her eyes at the feel of his carotid artery thumping against her fingertips. Confirming he was alive brought more peace of mind than she would have ever expected given their latest exchange of angry words. She exhaled, not realizing she'd been holding her breath. Until that moment, the reality that he could die in her RV hadn't sunk in. Panic rushed through her veins, making her stomach knot and her heart pick up the pace.

Pulling back the blanket, she gave him several nudges until he came to.

He blinked a few times, looking as if he didn't understand where he was. "Caroline?"

"I need to pump gas. You should get up and stretch. Use the bathroom."

He licked his lips. "Yeah. Okay."

She hesitated before leaving him. Opening the side door and feeling the dry heat envelop her face was a relief. The mood inside had been tense for too long and was becoming increasingly difficult to tolerate. Leaning against the RV after starting the pump, she relived the moment of fear that he'd passed away while she'd been cursing his very existence from the driver's seat.

Funny how easily they had fallen back into the old habits. Five minutes of being able to tolerate each other followed by hours of anger and bickering. They'd been stuck in that vicious cycle for years before she'd left. Sometimes it seemed they didn't know how to communicate without fighting.

She had a million memories to support her theory.

———

Family gatherings were rare occasions, but Katie's sixth birthday had brought both sets of grandparents calling. Caroline's dad, who avoided any family event where John was present, sat in the shade watching smoke roll from the grill.

Caroline stood by the pool while John tossed Katie over and over into the water. He never seemed to tire. He probably liked splashing in the pool more than Katie. He'd gotten a deep tan already. The pale skin Katie had inherited from Caroline was covered in about a hundred new freckles. Her sandy-brown hair was lightening from endless hours in the sunshine.

A familiar hint of mischief shone in John's eyes as he tossed Katie closer to the edge of the pool. Caroline squealed when the water splashed her. Katie resurfaced, laughing as much as her daddy.

"Not nice," Caroline insisted.

"If she didn't like that," John said to Katie, "she's going to hate this."

"Don't," Caroline warned, but he swiped his arms across the surface to send a surge of water toward her. Resting his arms on the edge, he jerked his head back, indicating that he wanted her to come closer. She hesitated, but the sweet smile on his face lured her in. "You're such a jerk, John Bowman."

"You love that about me, Caroline Bowman." He looked around the yard. "Nice, huh? Having the family together like this?"

"Yeah, it is." She kept her gaze on Katie, who was doing her best to float on her back the way John had taught her. When he distracted her with a sweet kiss, Caroline narrowed her eyes. "What do you want?"

"Can't I kiss my wife?"

"You can, but I know you. This is leading up to you asking me for something."

Looking over his shoulder, he watched Katie take a deep breath before going under. "Can you believe our little girl is six years old?"

"Six going on thirty."

"It's time. Don't you think?" he asked, returning his attention to Caroline.

"Time for what?"

"To have another one."

She jolted, surprised by his suggestion. Less than a month ago, she and John had sat at the table and had a heart-to-heart. She was ready to call it quits—for about the thousandth time—but she wanted to give him one more chance to be the husband and father she knew he could be. Not only had he agreed to cut back on his drinking, but he'd actually encouraged her to pursue a medical degree.

"We talked about this. She's going to start school full-time this year."

"I know. I can't believe it."

"We agreed when Katie started school full-time, so would I."

"Come on. That was before."

"Before what?"

"Before this... Before we were reminded what it's like to be a family. I don't want to wait another four years before having another baby. Let's do it now. You can always go back to school, Caroline, but you can't always have kids."

Damn it.

Once again, he'd only told her what she wanted to hear but never had any intention of standing by his words. Once again, he'd lied to appease her. Once again, she'd bought it.

"No."

He creased his brow, as if he'd never heard the word before. "What?"

"No, John. I'm going back to school. Like we'd planned."

He stared at her. "Why isn't what we have ever enough for you?"

Before she could retort, he swam away.

"You and Daddy fighting again?" Katie asked slightly above a whisper. The fun that had been like an aura around her all day had dimmed and sadness seemed to replace it.

Caroline hadn't realized how close Katie had gotten. Forcing a smile, she lied. "No, sweetie. No. Daddy's ready for cake. You ready for cake?"

Her face lit up and her happy aura returned. "Yay! Cake, everybody!"

Caroline made her way to the ladder and waited for Katie to climb out of the pool. She wrapped a towel around Katie's shoulders as the girl stuffed her wet, bare feet into her red boots. Caroline steered her toward her grandparents before going to find John to tell him to get over himself. Caroline's mom started pushing candles into the pink icing, but stopped long enough to cast her daughter a disapproving glance.

Caroline ignored the silent judgment. Her parents had never

approved of John. They merely tolerated him for Katie's sake. She didn't blame them for that any longer. Some days she thought she merely tolerated him for Katie's sake as well.

Caroline followed John's wet footprints inside the house, easing the door shut behind her despite her urge to slam it. "No," she said, before the door was even closed all the way. "Put it away. John, put it away."

Sneering, he cracked open a beer.

"You are not drinking at Katie's birthday party."

She marched across the living room toward him as he started to chug the drink. Smacking the can, she glared as cold beer spilled down his chest.

"Goddamn it."

"You are not drinking at Katie's party."

Spinning, he threw the half-empty can across the room. Foam exploded as the beer hit the wall. Turning, he glowered at her until the sound of sniffing broke the tension.

Caroline faced the door where Katie stood with tears in her eyes and her chin quivering. Her heart plummeted to her stomach as she rushed to her daughter. Dropping to her knees in front of Katie, she put her hands on her cheeks. "It's okay, baby. It's okay. Don't cry."

"You said you weren't fighting."

Caroline brushed her hand over Katie's hair and kissed her cheek, warm from the sun. "We're talking, kitty cat. That's all."

"You're lying, Mama."

Guilt burned through her veins. She was lying. She was always lying. About everything. Katie was far too smart to keep believing Caroline, just like Caroline was too smart to keep falling for John's lies. She couldn't fool herself, or Katie, any longer.

"Come here, baby girl." John swooped in to play hero, as he always did. Lifting Katie into his arms, he kissed her several times and hugged her close. "Sometimes Mommy and Daddy get upset, and we forget to use our inside voices. That's all."

"You threw your drink."

"Yeah, I did. I'm sorry." He pulled Caroline to her feet and into the hug with Katie, making a show of kissing her, too. "I'm sorry, Mommy. I was wrong to throw my drink."

Caroline forced a smile. "I know. It's okay. We're all okay, Katie."

Katie put one arm around each of her parents and squeezed. "Promise me. No more fighting."

"No more fighting," John whispered.

"No more fighting," Caroline agreed, though she knew, like John, she was making empty promises to appease her daughter.

———

Carol blinked away the memory as the gas pump kicked off. After putting the nozzle back, she walked into the convenience store and used the restroom. John was filling a cup of coffee when she emerged. She joined him in the corner, intent on filling her own cup when he lifted one to her.

"Got it."

"Thanks."

She gathered her drink and a few snacks and headed to the cash register. John told the cashier to add her items to his, and she didn't argue. They'd argued enough already that a few dollars for honey-roasted nuts and a drink wasn't worth the effort. When they got back to the RV, he sat in the passenger seat instead of going to the back. She buckled her seatbelt and reached for the ignition, then dropped her hand as the need to confess a long-held secret became overwhelming.

"Our first date," she said.

He looked at her, brow creased in confusion. "What?"

"One of my favorite memories, not only of you, but of my life, was our first date. You walked into the coffee shop with a handful of wildflowers. It was obvious you'd picked them from the side of the road, but you denied it."

"I was a rookie cop. I couldn't afford flowers, but what kind of chump shows up empty-handed on the first date?"

Smiling, she continued, "You drove us to Possum Creek and spread out a blanket so we could have a picnic. We talked for hours."

"You broke the dorm's curfew and had to sneak in through a window."

"No one had ever made me feel as...interesting as you did that night."

"Well, you were interesting."

"No, I wasn't." Her smile faded. "I was invisible, and I liked it that way. It was easier, you know. I didn't disappoint people or make waves that way. You listened, and you asked questions, and you actually saw me. You were the first person who ever saw me, John."

"Tobias saw you."

She swallowed and nodded. "Yeah, he did. But you were the *first*." Rolling her head to look at him, she ignored the pain hearing her husband's name brought. "We did have good times. I know we did. It's easier to hate you if I hold on to the bad ones."

He paid far more attention than necessary to flipping open the top on his coffee. "I gave you plenty of those, didn't I? I regret that. Of all the things I regret, one of the biggest is that I wasn't a better husband to you. I always put myself first and that was wrong. I should have been more supportive of your dreams. After you left, I spent a lot of time trying to figure out why I wasn't, and I think...I think I was scared you were going to wake up one day and realize you could do a million times better than me. You deserved a million times better than me. Somebody who could buy you things and take you places. Somebody like Tobias."

"I never wanted things, John. I tried to tell you that many times. I wanted you to stop drinking and start showing up when you were supposed to. That's all I wanted."

"I see that now. I didn't then. I do now, though. I wish to God I'd understood that back then."

"Me too." She started the ignition but didn't shift into gear. "I thought you were dead."

"Well, I came close a few times, but I managed to pull myself together."

"No. When I went back to wake you up. You didn't answer me. I had this flash of fear that you were dead."

The tension between them escalated again, but with a different underlying feel. Instead of years of anger feeding the stress, the knowledge that he was, in fact, going to die, sooner rather than later, hung over them.

She gave him a weak smile, hoping to break the bleak mood. "The thought of you haunting my RV is too much to bear."

"Oh, I would, too." The familiar light of mischief found

his eyes. "I'd rearrange the pantry so the cans of veggies are out of order and fold all your towels wrong."

She reached for the gearshift. "That's cruel, John. Buckle up, please. We don't need the odds of you dying on my watch any higher than they already are."

The next stretch of silence that fell between them was companionable. The smooth sound of the Moody Blues filtered from the speakers, loud enough to block out the road noise, but not deafening. Realizing that John wasn't occasionally humming or singing along, she glanced over. His head was back, his mouth open, and his eyes closed. He snorted before she had a chance to once again fear he wasn't breathing.

She chuckled to herself, thinking of the many times she'd found him like that. Her smile faded, though, as she remembered most of those times were because of the alcohol he'd consumed. Giving her head a hard shake, she dislodged the thought. She did not want to keep dwelling on offenses long past. It was time to start working on letting them go. No matter how difficult that might be.

———

Splashes from the pool at the RV park pulled Carol from the report she'd been reading on her laptop. The constant yelling set her on edge. Though she had never been one to swim, she understood the attraction. Katie had loved to swim. However, there was no lifeguard on duty and the parents weren't paying enough attention. Didn't they know how easy it was to lose a child? Didn't they know how they would never find peace again if anything ever happened to their kid?

Once again trying to tune out the sounds, she stared at her screen. She could block out office chatter, Tobias watching a game, she'd even once blocked out the noise of a Fleetwood Mac concert to answer several urgent e-mails. The one thing she couldn't block out was the sound of children playing. Every squeal of happiness felt like nails raking over her skin. She'd asked for another spot, but the park was full.

"Put that away," John said. "Let's go for a walk."

She didn't need more prompting than that. She closed her laptop and carried it into the motorhome. She joined him and they walked in silence until he heaved a sigh and shoved his hands in his pockets.

"Can I ask you something that's been bugging me?" he asked.

She felt her stomach do a flip-flop, not certain what to expect. "You can ask. I don't promise I'll answer."

"You were determined to be a pediatrician. What happened?"

She gave a polite nod to a couple walking a dog down the gravel road. John waved and wished them a good evening as Carol considered how to answer his question. They'd moved away from the screaming children, and the park was quiet. People sat at picnic tables eating, playing cards, or talking. The peace of being surrounded by nature fell over her as she inhaled the dry air deep into her lungs.

"After I left you that night," she said, "I stopped at the hospital to quit. One of the doctors asked where I was going. I told him I didn't know. He had transferred from St. Louis and still owned a house there. He said I could rent it, and offered to put in a good word for me at the hospital where he'd worked. When I got to Missouri, I had a new life waiting for me. It should have been easy to start over. My very first patient was a little girl, a year or so younger than Katie. I froze. I couldn't move. All I could do was stand there looking at her thinking about how... Thinking that I hadn't been able to save *my* little girl, what right did I have to try to save someone else's? I went straight to the head nurse and told her I had to quit and why. She moved me from pediatrics to another area in the hospital." Scanning the horizon, she tried to focus on the present, but her mind's eye was stuck in the past. "I couldn't work with kids anymore, but I wasn't great working with other patients, either. I was angry and short-tempered. Not great qualities in a nurse. I pushed through it while I went back to school, but I knew I couldn't be a pediatrician anymore. I got my degree in medical science instead. Tobias pushed me to get my doctorate. He said even if the area of study had changed, the end goal shouldn't."

"Doctor Caroline Bowman," John said with pride.

"Doctor *Carol Denman*," she corrected. "It wasn't the path that I'd always imagined, but I get to help people even if I'm not working directly with them. You might snub your nose at pharmaceutical companies, but my job is important. Without my work, millions of people wouldn't have the medications that keep them alive." She bumped him lightly with her shoulder. "Or help manage their pain."

"That is important. I shouldn't have implied otherwise. I'm glad you found your way, Caroline. I really am." He grew quiet for a minute before saying, "I don't think either one of us realized how much you covered for me. No one else had a clue how much I was drinking. Mom and Dad came over about a week after you'd left. Mom cried as she picked up dozens of beer cans and empty pizza boxes. I blamed it on you. On losing Katie. I swore I didn't drink that much until you'd left me. Mom bought it, but I think Dad knew. I think Dad realized how much you'd covered for me all those years. I think he knew the day he brought you and Katie home from the hospital because I was too drunk. Mom was in denial even after I started getting treatment."

"I enabled you," Carol admitted. "I don't know if it was easier for me or if I was ashamed of your addiction, like it somehow reflected on me, but I think I was in denial, too. Until I had to face how bad it had gotten. You were a functioning alcoholic, and I made excuses for you." She sighed loudly. "I should have made you get help. I didn't want the fight, you know. Everything was a fight with us and that was one I didn't have the strength for."

"You shouldn't have had to fight me for sobriety."

"No, I shouldn't have. Alcoholism is a disease, John. Ignoring it only made it worse." She choked on the sudden rise of a sob that she hadn't felt coming. Blinking rapidly, she managed to stop her tears from falling, but she couldn't hide the emotion that rolled through her. "We're both to blame," she whispered. "For everything."

Stepping in front of her, he put his hands on her shoulders and stared into her eyes. "Katie's death is my burden to carry. Leaving me was the right thing to do. You are right to blame me. I was the one responsible for her that day. I was the one who chose to drink too much. Not you. *Me*. Don't blame yourself. You don't want to live with that kind of guilt. Trust me." He dropped his hands from her shoulders. "I live with it every day."

"What, um...what made you stop drinking?"

He looked everywhere but at her. "One night, about five

years after you'd left, I got called to a domestic. This drunk was going on and on about how *that bitch* had packed his bags and told him he had to leave. *I'm not leaving. This is my house, damn it,*" he said, mocking the slur of the man. "Another unit got him cuffed and hauled off, and I went to take the woman's statement. I walked into the living room, and when she looked up, I saw you. I swear to God I almost said your name before I realized I was seeing things. She had tears running down her face. Her little girl was clinging to her, crying so hard she could barely talk. I flashed back to you standing in the living room, telling me I had to leave. I saw myself, drunk as always, telling you that was my house, and you weren't kicking me out. I saw Katie coming in. Crying, begging you not to make me leave." He raked his hand through his hair. "I hadn't thought about that night in years, but seeing that woman going through what you did hit me hard. I went home that night and swore that I'd get sober. I went to my first AA meeting the next day. Better late than never, right?" he asked with a lopsided grin. "I'd do okay for a while, but then something would happen. Some excuse I could use to start drinking again. It took a few times before it stuck, though."

"Sometimes it does. I'm glad you got sober, John."

"I wish..." He sniffed before meeting her gaze. "I wish I'd left that night. Left you and Katie alone until I could get my shit together. Maybe you're right. Maybe she'd still be here if I'd taken my bags and gone to Bert's."

"We can't change what happened," she whispered. "We can't bring her back."

"I know." He roughly wiped his face. "But we never should have lost her."

"Maybe *you're* right. Maybe we were always meant to. What kind of life were we giving her, John? All we did was fight and then make-believe things were okay, so we'd feel a little less guilty about upsetting her. That was no way to raise a child."

"We could have been better parents."

"Yeah. We *should* have been better parents. She deserved better."

"So did you, Caroline." John had enveloped her in his arms before she realized he was closing in on her. She stiffened, but when he hugged her tight and sobbed, she put her arms around his waist. "I'm sorry," he choked out. "I'm sorry."

She ground her teeth hard, determined not to completely fall apart in the middle of the road of an RV park. Focusing on supporting John, she waited a few moments before pulling back. "There's a restaurant up there. I'm going to die if I don't eat soon."

"You don't get to die before me. This one time I get to do something better than you."

She glanced up before chuckling. "Sorry. I shouldn't have put it quite like that."

A little boy rode by on his bike, seeming to pedal as fast as his legs and the gravel would allow. She wanted to call out, tell him to be careful, but he wasn't her child and parents these days didn't much care for others protecting their children. She had never minded when the neighbors corrected Katie. In fact, she had appreciated the help. John had been as carefree as a father as he'd been as a boyfriend and then as a husband.

The boy swerved, then corrected the bike before toppling over, and Carol exhaled with relief.

"Sometimes I think it was a blessing Tobias and I never had kids," she said without any prompting from John. "I probably never would have let them out of my sight. I'd have had a breakdown before they could grow up."

He didn't respond, and she found herself rambling to fill the silence.

"I found out I was pregnant right after Tobias and I celebrated our second anniversary. It wasn't planned. We hadn't even talked about having kids. I was terrified to be a mother again. I felt guilty, like I was somehow replacing Katie or betraying her memory. I had a million emotions, but none of them were happiness or excitement. Then I miscarried. I think I mourned as much for that baby as I did when we lost Katie. I felt as empty as I had after losing Katie, but somehow that made me realize it was okay to be a mother again. The next pregnancy was planned. Meticulously. You know how I am." She gnawed at her lip. "I miscarried again and...I fell apart. I completely fell apart. I was so depressed, Tobias was afraid to leave me alone. He flew his mother in to care for me while he was at work. She stayed for three months. When I got myself together and suggested we try again, Tobias said no. He said he wouldn't put me through that again. He said we could adopt or foster, but he wasn't willing to risk another miscarriage. We'd never fought until that night—we'd argued, of course, but we'd never really fought. God, I wanted to beat the hell out of him."

"Did you? Adopt or foster?"

She shook her head. "We buried ourselves in work and hobbies. Then we started traveling and time slipped away.

Life always goes by too quickly, doesn't it? We would have been married twenty years next month. That sounds like a long time, but looking back, it was a flash. A moment that I should have cherished more."

"I'm sorry you've had so much loss in your life. It's not right for one person to lose that many people." As they stopped outside the restaurant, he tucked his hands in his pockets. "Maybe it's best if you go home, Caroline. Go back to your life and let me...let me finish mine."

"Why?"

"Because we both know how this ends for me. It isn't right for me to put you through that. I've put you through enough hell for one lifetime."

A lump caught in her throat. "Yeah, well, I'm not here for you. I'm here for Katie." She moved around him and opened the door to the restaurant, welcoming the scent of steaks cooking inside.

SIX

CAROL JERKED her eyes open and listened intently. Staring into the dimly lit bunk area, she waited until she recognized the sound that had awoken her. Tossing her covers off, she eased down the ladder from the overhead sleeping area and moved through the RV to the bathroom. "John?"

His only answer was retching.

"I'm coming in," she warned before opening the door.

"Get out." His demand, though muffled by the trashcan he had his head stuck in, echoed through the small room.

Pressing her finger under her nose when the smells of vomit and diarrhea hit her, she took a few deep breaths through her mouth and steadied her stomach. Stepping into the room, she put her hand to his head, checking for a fever. He was sweaty, but not warm.

"I think I shit my pants," he said between hoarse wheezes.

"It happens. Did this just start?"

"I started feeling off after dinner."

"You didn't say anything."

His entire body tensed as he lurched again. She wet a washrag and, when he relaxed, held it out to him. He leaned back enough that she could scan the contents of the trashcan to verify there were no signs of blood in his vomit before leaving him alone. She flipped on the overhead light and did a quick check of the full-size bed she usually shared with Tobias. Having John climb the ladder to the overhead bed was a ridiculous notion, but she had toyed with it briefly. She didn't like the idea of another man sleeping in the bed she'd shared with her husband, but logic had won out. She couldn't possibly expect John to maneuver a ladder in his condition.

The sheets were still clean, and she said a silent thanks to the camping gods. The last thing she wanted to do in the middle of the night was strip the bed.

Carrying a cup of water to the bathroom, she held it to John's lips. "Just swish and spit."

He did.

"Are you in pain?" she asked.

"No. Just feeling sick."

"Still?"

He nodded as much as he could. "Can I drink? My throat is burning."

"Just a little. See how your stomach takes it." She helped him take a drink, then waited for his reaction. The water stayed in his stomach, and they both relaxed a bit. "Think you can get into the shower?"

"You don't want to use the shower, remember?"

"I'll make an exception."

He grinned but didn't open his eyes. "So there are perks to spontaneous bowel evacuations."

She rolled her tired, dry eyes. "Just one."

His lighthearted moment faded. Leaning back, looking pale and pathetic, he said, "I'm sorry, Caroline. I made a mess."

"It'll wash."

"No. I mean... When I told the doctor you could nurse me, I didn't think it'd be this. I thought it'd be doling out pills. Not...me shitting myself at two in the morning."

No. He wouldn't have known that. He'd been too determined to get his way to listen to what Dr. Collins had been saying. To take two seconds to hear what Carol had been saying. But she had listened. She had known. She'd done it anyway. "It's probably the new meds," she said instead of pointing out that she'd told him so. "Can you get up by yourself or do you need help?"

He looked at the shower next to him. "I got this."

"Just put your dirty clothes in the trashcan. I'll take care of it."

"You shouldn't have—"

"John, your meds have side effects. This is one of them. I knew this was a possibility when I agreed to this. Put the dirty clothes in the trash, get in the shower, and I'll take care of the rest. If you need help, yell."

Sitting there with slumped shoulders, a trashcan on his thighs, and soiled pants around his ankles, he appeared completely defeated. Her instinct was to comfort him in some way, but what could she do? In that moment, he needed to reclaim his dignity. Hugging him while he had dirty pants and a can of vomit wasn't going to do that. She left him to clean himself up and busied herself with turning on the vent over the small stovetop and opening windows to get some fresh air into the confined space.

Finally she sat and started reading up on his meds, trying to stop her mind from wandering.

———

Caroline didn't really remember the conversation about having Katie cremated. John had talked to her about it—at her, really. She couldn't seem to connect with the world. People were talking, crying, whispering, but she couldn't seem to break through the fog and connect with them. She was detached. That was okay. That was better.

Being in a state of numbness was better than the alternative...feeling.

Occasionally tears would fill her eyes and fall, but she hadn't broken down since the hospital. John, on the other hand... He seemed to do okay during the day, but at night when the house got quiet...

His crying had woken her the first night, and she'd lain in bed listening. Every wail coming from the bathroom twisted the knife of hatred in her heart. How dare he cry? How dare he mourn Katie when he was the reason she was gone? After what seemed like forever, she threw the blankets off and stormed toward the sound.

She threw the door open, determined to tear him apart, to scream until he shut the hell up. When she saw him, she stopped. The man who had always loomed larger than life was curled in a ball, sobbing loudly enough that he hadn't even heard her dramatic entrance.

She stood in the doorway watching for several seconds before stepping back and easing the door closed behind her. She hated him. God, how she hated him. Even so, she couldn't take seeing him broken. Instead of going back to bed where she could hear him cry, she went to the kitchen and sat at the table.

Katie's placemat was dirty. A shriveled flake of cereal clung to Barney's purple head. Caroline scratched at it with her fingernail. It stuck. She scratched harder. And harder. The dried flake broke free, lodging under her nail. She hissed in pain and suckled at the wound. Sweetness found her tongue, causing her to pause with a realization. That was it. That was the last bit of the last thing Katie had ever eaten. The mess hadn't been there when Caroline had left for work the night before, but it was there now. The day Katie had died. The only way it could have gotten there was falling off Katie's spoon or slipping from her mouth as she ate.

Caroline could almost picture Katie there. Sitting by herself eating as she kicked her red rain boots against the table as John slept off his six-pack. She suddenly realized that was probably the norm for her daughter. She was probably used to getting up and fixing her own breakfast. She probably ate cereal alone every morning that Caroline was at work.

Rage, the only thing that had managed to cut the fog of the pills Dr. Goodman had prescribed, filled her. She jumped to her feet, nearly knocking her chair over with the sudden movement. This time when she entered the bathroom, he knew she was there. He lifted his face. His cheeks were wet with tears, snot ran unchecked from his nose, and his eyes were bloodshot. She glared at him, hate engulfing her entire being.

"You killed her," she seethed.

"Caroline, I—"

"You fucking drunk. You killed her."

The horror on his face was clear to see. He seemed shocked that she was blaming him. He lifted his hand as she closed in on him. Caroline was not a violent person, she never had been, but then again she'd never felt such unchecked rage coursing through her veins. She wanted to hurt him like she'd never wanted to hurt anyone before in her life. She wanted to dig her hand into his chest and rip his heart out. She wanted to inflict as much pain on him as she could manage. Balling her fists, she stood over him and swung, yelling obscenities as she did.

Her punches hurt her far more than she suspected they hurt him. She only landed three before he caught her wrists and wrestled her down to him. Pinning her arms to her side, he hugged her tight. She screamed, fury tearing from her chest, calling him horrible names, blaming him for Katie's death, telling him how much she hated him.

He said he chalked it up to grief. He even reassured her that she didn't need to apologize. Apologize? She had nothing to apologize for. He, on the other hand, could never apologize enough for what he'd done.

Because Katie was being cremated, Caroline and John opted to have a small service. Family and a few close friends gathered at the funeral home. Caroline didn't hear most of what was said. She didn't speak. She simply sat in the front pew staring at the oversized photo of Katie's smiling face and the teddy bear sitting there as a representation of her daughter.

The urn filled with ashes would be ready the following week, but John didn't want to wait to have the service. He didn't see any point in waiting. He'd already decided they would take the summer trip they'd planned. They would stop at all the places

Katie had written on her list. They'd scatter her ashes, and she could be in all the places she'd dreamed of visiting.

Caroline agreed because she couldn't think of any reason to argue. What did it matter what happened to Katie now? Whether she was in the ground, in an urn, or scattered to the wind, the result was the same—she was gone. Katie was gone.

The funeral was nothing more than going through the motions, giving people a chance to say their goodbyes, giving the family closure. If only it were that simple. Maybe for some of them it had been. Not for Caroline. The seed of anger and resentment John had planted years ago broke the surface the day Katie had died. It'd grown so quickly, it had consumed Caroline in an instant.

As she sat there, listening to him sniffle while the priest talked about the loss of a child, she knew she was going to leave. She didn't know when or how, but she couldn't stay. She'd stayed too long.

And it had cost Katie her life.

———

Carol looked up when the bathroom door opened. John shuffled out, wrapped in a towel. She focused on her laptop screen again, giving him what little privacy was allotted to them in the small motorhome. A few minutes later, she assumed he'd had enough time to dress and pushed herself up to clean the bathroom, but he was sprawled stomach down and naked on the bed. "Oh, John. At least cover up," she muttered to his bare ass as she opened the bathroom door.

"I don't have the energy."

She put the trashcan into a bigger bag and carried them both outside. She wasn't going to try to clean the can. She'd replace it the next time they stopped for groceries. After tossing it in the can outside their spot, she put several plastic bags in the bathroom in case he got sick again. She checked the bathroom, seeing if there was any sign of mess she needed to clean, but found none. Another small win for the evening.

She dried out the shower to prevent mildew from growing, flushed the toilet to make sure there was enough water in the black water tank to break things down, then washed her hands and dried the sink. After tossing the towel into the mesh laundry bag, she stopped to pull the sheet over John's bare backside. "I don't need to see that."

"Temptation too much for you?"

"Yes, the temptation to kick you square in the ass is a bit much sometimes. How are you feeling?"

"Bad. Real bad."

"Stomach?"

He seemed to take a moment to assess his body before answering. "Everything. I'm tired. My stomach is off. My head is starting to throb."

"I'm going to call Doctor Collins in the morning and ask if we can cut back the dosage of your anti-epileptic meds."

He slowly rolled over, curling on his side to look at her. Even in the dim light, his face was ashen from his bout of illness. "I have no idea what you said."

"Collins put you on a new drug to try to help your seizures. The list of severe side effects includes these symptoms. Cutting back the dosage might help."

"What if cutting back causes more seizures?"

"We can try a different med." Sitting on the edge of the bed, she turned enough to see his face. "If things get too bad, we're going to find a hospital and have you admitted."

"I don't—"

He hadn't listened before, but she was hoping he'd listen now that he had a real taste of what was ahead.

"John, this is only the beginning," she said. "Do you understand that? It gets worse from here. The pain gets worse. The sickness gets worse."

"I'm prepared for that."

"And if it gets to be too much?"

He stared at her for some time before saying, "You'll help me."

"John, I—"

"Tomorrow's going to be a long day. We should get some sleep."

Turning her focus away from him, she drew a deep breath and let it out slowly. "Are you ready for this? For tomorrow?"

"I've been ready."

Looking at her hands, she twisted her wedding band. "I'm not sure I am. I've held on to her so tightly for so long. I don't know how to let her go."

"We're not letting her go. We'll never let her go. We're trying to find some peace. Despite all our mistakes, we both deserve some peace. Don't you think?"

She considered his words before nodding.

Yes. They deserved peace. Both of them. Even John. Carol wasn't nearly as convinced that spreading Katie's ashes would help them find it.

Sitting at the table, staring at the urn she'd stared at for too many years, Carol nearly gagged as she swallowed. This was it. This was the moment their path to letting Katie go started. Wringing her hands, Carol focused on the teddy bear etched on the side. "I read an article that said we should be sure to take water and paper towels."

John lifted his gaze from the urn and met hers. "What?"

"If the wind... The ash might stick to us. We need to be able to wash it off."

His face lost a shade or two. "There are articles on spreading ashes?"

"A lot, actually."

"And you read them?"

She shrugged slightly. "I like to be prepared."

"Yes, Caroline, I know." Taking a deep breath, he let it out in a rush. "Okay. This isn't going to get any easier."

"Wait." She lifted her hands to stop him before he could take the top off the urn. "Apparently, the ash won't be like the ash in a fireplace. It's more like...sand. With bits of bone." She sank back at the last part of her explanation. Tears rose in her eyes, feeling like a thousand bee stings after her sleepless night. She blinked rapidly. "I think I'll wait outside."

He swallowed, almost pleading with his eyes not to have to do this alone. She ignored him and left anyway. Closing her eyes as a breeze brushed her hair back, she breathed in. Out. In again. The sun was still low in the sky, and the air hadn't taken on the unbearable heat of an Arizona summer. Where she stood now, in a gravel parking lot lacking vegetation or any of the beauty they were about to witness, seemed fitting.

The world around her was dull. However, there, on the other side, was a world where vibrant reds, oranges, and yellows would surround her. Hues that didn't seem like nature could have made them. It was more logical that an artist, some abstract creative, had put this world together. A life-sized work of interactive art intended to make viewers appreciate how bleak their lives really were.

Standing there, she wished she had grabbed her pack to have something she could busy herself with. She wanted to make sure she had plenty of water for the two of them, John's meds, snacks, sunscreen, and all the other things a hiker might need in the Grand Canyon.

And she had to be sure there was room for a small bottle of Katie's ashes.

Can't forget that.

"I don't want to do this," she whispered to the wind. "I don't know if I can do this."

As if on cue, John opened the door behind her and stepped down. He sighed that heavy sigh of his. "It's done."

She looked at him. "How was it?"

He shrugged. Swallowed hard. Then took three big steps, bent over, and vomited.

When he was finished, she said, "If you're still feeling sick—"

"It's not the meds this time." He panted, hands still on his knees.

Closing her eyes, she nodded. "Right. Water?"

"Please."

Heading back inside, she grabbed an extra bottle from the

fridge before putting her pack over her shoulder. She paused as she glanced at the table. Leave it to John to spill sprinkles of Katie's ash on the table and leave it there. Rolling her eyes up toward the ceiling, she laughed bitterly.

"Idiot." Then she considered how hard it had to have been to put a scoop of his child's remains into a container. She hadn't even been able to stay in the RV. She'd give him this one. He had earned a pass.

Wetting a paper towel, like the article had said, she folded it over and stopped at the table. The few scattered bits of ash seemed to mock her. She couldn't stand to leave a mess, but the messes she wiped away weren't usually her daughter's remains. She opened her mouth, ready to call out to John, but he'd done his part and had proven it by losing his breakfast in the parking lot.

Swallowing hard, she wiped the table down and then held the towel suspended over the trashcan. Should she throw it away? The little specs of dirt on the white surface were part of Katie. Folding it over several times, until it was a little triangle, she tucked the paper towel in a drawer. She'd decide what to do with it later.

John squinted at her as she came out with her pack over her shoulder and locked the door. She handed him the extra bottle of water and unzipped her bag.

Mentally running down her list, she touched each item. "Where's Katie?"

He patted the thigh pocket on his cargo pants, and she opened her mouth to speak. For some reason, she felt that she should carry Katie. She had always carried Katie. John carried bags and car seats and stuffed animals, but Carol had always carried Katie. Pushing the urge from her mind, she zipped up her bag, telling herself that was the dumbest argument to start on today of all days.

She didn't have to argue. She was picking the backpack up when John put his hand on her shoulder to stop her. Without a word, he tugged the pocket on her shorts open and slipped a small container inside. He sealed the Velcro and met her gaze.

She offered him a small smile of thanks.

"Let's go before it gets too hot," he said, turning away.

They walked in silence, both lost in their own thoughts, as they headed toward the South Kaibab trailhead. Carol was so withdrawn into her own mind that she no longer cared about the colors, about nature's abstract art meant to remind her to live her best life. Her best life was in a bottle in her pocket. Her best life ended long ago. Focusing on her feet, one dusty step after the next, she put all her energy into walking—and not remembering. Not thinking. Not hearing the chatter of children around her, pointing into the distance and beckoning for their parents to see the wonder as they did.

She didn't realize they'd approached the trail until John muttered, "*Wow*," beside her. Focusing on the world around her, she saw that the horizon had changed to layers of rock kissing clear blue sky in the distance. He took her hand in his, entwined their fingers, and squeezed. Her heart seemed to stop beating before picking up a hurried rhythm with a thump.

"She'd love this," he whispered.

Carol simply nodded her agreement.

"Have you been here before?"

"Our first trip out west. Tobias was determined to stop

here. I dreaded it, but once I got here, I thought the same thing. She'd love this. I could almost hear her, you know. *Mommy, lookit. Lookit.*"

He laughed. Then sniffed.

She didn't look at him. Seeing him cry right now would break her. Instead, she started toward the dirt path that would lead them into the canyon. "It's an easy hike in but coming back will be quite a bit more challenging. Let's get going. I don't want you to tire out before we get there."

Hooking her thumbs in the straps of her pack, she walked ahead of him, again falling too deep into her thoughts to appreciate the scenery around them. She focused on her footing. On stepping to the side as mules passed. On keeping to the inside of the switchbacks to stay back from the edge. She didn't give John a second thought until she stopped at a sign that said *Ooh Aah Point.*

This was the spot. The one they'd chosen for Katie based solely on the name. She would have liked the name. She would have giggled and said it over and over, enunciating the words differently each time until she found the one that amused her most. She would have bounced along the trail, singing the name as Carol fretted over her safety and John told her to relax. She didn't have to think too hard for that scene to play out, though they'd never had a chance to make it real.

John stepped beside her. Pulling a handkerchief from his pocket, he wiped his forehead.

"Okay?" she asked.

"Yeah." He scanned the area before pointing to a ridge of rocks. "There."

She let him lead the way. The path was well-worn, but her

heart still picked up a few beats. She suspected it was more from the reason they were walking toward the edge than the potential danger. Taking her hand, he pulled her onto the top of a rock and then tugged her down to sit beside him. The constant wind whipped her ponytail until she tugged it loose and restyled her hair into a bun.

John barely moved. He sat staring, though she didn't think he was seeing the canyon any more than she had on the way down. Sitting there now, finally still, she took in the scenery. The layers of rock squished together like different colors of Play-Doh. Reds and oranges and yellows that obviously hadn't come from the same containers but had been rolled out and stacked as if they belonged together. These layers rose up to clash with the bright blue as much as they did each other.

"It really is beautiful," she said.

"Yeah, it is. Ready?"

Reaching into her pocket, she wrapped her fingers around the container and hesitated before handing Katie to him.

"We should say something, don't you think?" he asked.

She scanned the area around them. "She'd ask how it was made. Tell her how it was made."

John was silent for some time, but then he pointed to the scenery, describing how the river had carved the land and exposed the layers. He explained that the various colors were different types of rocks. He said really adventurous people camped way down at the bottom or rode rafts on the water. He said she would get to see all those things because she got to stay there forever.

Then he opened the container and slowly tapped her ashes into the breeze.

"Love you, kitty cat," he whispered into the wind as she disappeared.

Carol watched for a few moments before lowering her face and sobbing.

SEVEN

CAROL SAT IN THE RV, staring out at the Pacific Ocean, bracing herself for what came next. The thought of standing in the water as they spread more of Katie's ashes made her heart race as if urging her to drive away.

Run, run, as fast as you can, it seemed to be telling her.

"Caroline?" John called from the back before she had a chance to listen to her instincts.

She pulled the key from the ignition, unbuckled, and turned her chair to more easily see him. "Yeah?"

"Where are we?"

She could have lied, but what good would that have done? She couldn't avoid this forever. "San Francisco."

"The beach?"

"Mm-hmm."

He struggled to sit on the edge of the bed. He appeared significantly more tired today than yesterday. The hike at Grand Canyon followed by the long drive to the RV park in Bakersfield hadn't helped. She'd gotten up early to make the last of the trip to San Francisco without waking him. He'd been restless the night before. She jolted every time he made a noise, which was often. She was exhausted as well, but her body was certainly holding up better. Four days into this trip felt more like years.

She suspected he'd slept as much as he could have given the circumstances. While her RV was comfortable, it wasn't home, and it certainly wasn't the best place for a terminally ill patient to get the rest he needed. As soon as they left the beach, she would park the RV for the night. Though it was early, their next stop was over eight hours away in Eugene. She wasn't pushing either of them that hard.

They'd get to bed early and try to catch up on some sleep before continuing their trip up the West Coast.

She went to the fridge and collected the six pink roses she'd picked up before leaving Bakersfield. The article suggested having a visual to watch since ashes disappeared almost as soon as they touched the water.

Closing the refrigerator, she didn't bother looking back at him. "You get...everything else and meet me outside." She left through the side door without giving him a chance to debate. At some point she might be ready to scoop ash out of the urn and really see what was left of Katie, but this wasn't that time. She wasn't there yet. She might not ever be. That was okay.

As she stood on the concrete sidewalk, the crashing of the waves and salty air of the ocean came at her unfiltered. Even at this distance from the water's edge, cool mist hit her face, clinging to her skin and hair. She imagined most people were excited by the experience. Dread spread through her like a virus as she removed the plastic wrap from the flowers and threw it away. Like at the canyon, the wind whipped her hair around until she used a band of elastic to knot it into a bun.

Moving to the waist-high cement barrier, she leaned her forearms on the rough surface and stared out at the water. Spanning the bay in the distance to her right, the Golden Gate Bridge stood sturdy and proud. Rocks jutting out into the water appeared to dare the ocean to move them. They appeared defiant. Strong. Determined.

None of the things Carol felt at the moment. She was a bit envious of the courage they portrayed. They seemed to be goading the universe to take them on when all she wanted to do was get back in her RV and go home, back to the comfort of the little spot she'd carved out for herself in the world. Only that spot wasn't as comforting as it used to be. It was dark and lonely and a constant reminder of all she'd lost in her life.

If Tobias were here with her, he'd wrap his arms around her waist, kiss her head, and rock her in his gentle embrace. She'd sink back into his chest and let his warmth surround her. They'd stare out at the water, both content listening to the roar of the waves clashing with the shore. They did that wherever they traveled. Just stood together, soaking it all in.

He'd love this view. The constant ebb and flow of the waves. The smell of the salt in the damp, heavy air.

She couldn't stomach any of it at the moment. Not when she was standing there alone without his arms to keep her safe. Swallowing the lump in her throat, she turned as John emerged from the RV. He tucked his hand in his pocket.

Katie's ashes.

Carol faced the water again and a minute later, John leaned beside her.

"I didn't mean to snap," he said.

"I know." Not wanting to deal with the ongoing thunderstorm between them, she pushed away from the wall.

Grabbing her elbow, he stopped her from leaving. "I'm sorry."

"I'm on edge, too, John. I...I don't like the water. I don't even like taking baths, and we're about to wade into the ocean?" She faced the RV as if it could somehow rescue her. "I don't know what I was thinking. I can't do this."

"Hey," he said after a few moments. "We don't have to. See those rocks out there?" He pointed to the sign of strength she'd been envying. "We could walk right out there."

"If she were here, she'd be in the water, John. She'd run out there before we could even set up chairs." She smiled, imagining Katie rushing into the waves. "She'd want to be in the ocean."

He didn't argue her point. "I can do this one. You stay on the beach."

"I can do it. I just don't like it." Holding out her hand, she waited for him to put the small bottle into her palm, then tucked it into her pocket before walking down the stairs to the beach. She marched halfway across the dry sand before her stomach rolled. Her feet froze in place as fear overcame her determination.

"We'll only go knee-deep," John said, stopping beside her. Lifting his hand to cut off her protest, he reassured her, "There's barely anyone here. Nobody will be swimming through her ashes. She'll get washed out before that happens."

Ignoring the anxiety washing over her like a tsunami of fear, Carol slipped her shoes off and rolled the bottom few inches of her knee-length shorts up. John did the same; then he gripped her hand and took two steps.

She didn't. She stood there staring out at the water. So much water. Rushing toward her. Threatening to consume her. Pull her in. Keep her forever.

Gasping, Carol shook her head slightly.

John put himself between her and the terrifying view. He cupped her face and brushed his thumb over her cheek like he'd done a thousand times when they were younger. Whenever she needed him to convince her, to give her strength to get through something, he closed the distance between them and put his hand to her cheeks, staring at her intently until she couldn't see anything else—couldn't think of anything but him.

He still had that power. Looking into her eyes, holding her face in his hands, he soothed her somehow. "I'm right here with you. You can do this."

She didn't even realize he was slowly guiding her to the water until a wave washed over her toes. She jumped, blinking at the surprise. "It's so cold."

John stroked her cheek, pulling her attention back to him. "We're not going that far."

Giving her head one sharp shake, she met his gaze. "I don't think I can."

"I'm right here," he reassured her. "I'm not going anywhere. Look at me."

———

Caroline turned away from her parents' house to the man sitting behind the steering wheel of his beat-up '83 Toyota Corolla. "I can't do this."

Squeezing her hand, John offered a comforting smile. "Yes, you can. I'm right here. You're not doing this alone."

"They're going to kill me."

Putting his hand to her cheek, he ran his thumb over her skin, soothing her. "They might be upset, but they aren't going to kill you. No matter how angry they get, I'm still here. I'll always be right here. You know that, right? You can count on me no matter what. You're going to be my wife. We're going to be a family. Nothing your parents say or do can change that. You've always got me."

From the moment she'd taken that damned pregnancy test, she'd dreaded telling her parents. She'd wanted to do it over the phone so she wouldn't have to see the disappointment in their eyes, but John insisted they tell them face-to-face. He wanted to reassure them that he was going to take care of Caroline and the baby.

Her parents didn't think much of John. They had expected her to marry a doctor or lawyer. She was going to medical school. What they thought about her marrying a cop had become clear the first time she brought him home to meet them. They sat stiffly through dinner while John tried to woo them with his usual charms. Charms that had fallen flat with her parents.

Only minutes after John had dropped her off following that first dinner, her roommate had knocked on the bathroom door to tell her she had a phone call. The room didn't offer much privacy, so she'd huddled in the corner, listening to her mother warn her about "men like John." Her mother insisted he was too old. Caroline reminded her mother he was only five years older. She said he'd never do anything with his life. Caroline reminded her that he'd already finished the academy and was employed full-time as a police officer. She'd said he was only after one thing. Caroline insisted she was old enough to decide if and when she was ready for sex.

After twenty minutes of back-and-forth, her mother had sighed and told her she was going to get her heart broken. Then she hung up and never said a bad word about John again. That didn't stop her from frowning and casting exasperated glances whenever Caroline talked about him.

And now she was pregnant. Two semesters from finishing her undergrad. A lifetime away from finishing medical school. She'd changed majors, already taking control of her future. She'd already made a new plan for her future. That wouldn't appease her parents. That wouldn't stop her mother from crying. That wouldn't stop her father from storming out and not speaking to her for who the hell knew how long.

But she had John. Tightening her hold on his hand, she drew another breath.

John kissed her lightly. "Just remember that no matter what they say or do, they are reacting to the news. They love you, and they'll love their grandchild. It's going to be okay," he whispered when her lip trembled.

Blinking back her tears, Caroline reached for the door handle. "Let's get this over with."

He followed her to the front door, which she opened without knocking.

"We're here," she called out. She had barely walked into the living room, with John right behind her, when her mother stopped fidgeting with the TV remote. She glanced up and her eyes stopped on Caroline's face. She immediately turned an *accusing glare at John, and Caroline stiffened, certain that her mother had already figured it all out.*

John put his arm around Caroline's waist and pulled her against him as if he sensed her increased fear. "Hey, Judith. What are you watching?"

She frowned. "Nothing. I can't figure out this VCR."

John reached for the control, and her mom focused on her. Caroline almost burst into tears. She'd never been able to hide things from her parents. She twisted the ring on her finger, inadvertently drawing her mother's attention.

"What is that?" Her eyes grew wide as she stared.

Caroline was certain she actually saw the woman's heart break as she lifted her gaze and their eyes met.

"Oh my God. Are you pregnant?" she whispered.

Caroline stood immobilized. Her lungs started to burn from the spent oxygen she was holding. Her eyes stung with unshed tears.

"Oh, Jesus, Caroline." Her mother put her hand to her chest and took several steps back. "Oh my God."

"Judith," John said in his soothing tone.

She turned and narrowed her eyes at him. "You bastard! What have you done?"

Heavy footsteps announced her father's arrival. "What's going on in here?"

Judith spun toward her husband. "He got her pregnant."

Shame washed over Caroline like hot lava burning her alive. She'd expected to be upset. Nervous. Scared. She hadn't expected to feel ashamed. As an adult, she had every right to explore her sexuality, especially with the man she'd been dating for almost two years. Even so, knowing that her parents now knew she'd had sex made her feel like she'd been caught stealing something precious from her parents. Not that she'd ever been precious to them. She'd been a box on a checklist so they could continue to fit in with their peers.

Despite that, or maybe because of it, her mother had a way of punching Caroline in the gut with a look. Caroline didn't look at her father. She didn't want to see his reaction. Disappointing him was too much.

"That's great," he said quietly. "What about school?"

She couldn't answer. The knot in her stomach had moved to her throat. John answered. Something about her becoming a nurse and them getting married and being a family. Her mother dropped onto the couch and started crying. Her father stormed out, as she'd expected him to.

John didn't seem to care what they thought. He put his hand to Caroline's cheek. "It's okay," he whispered. "I'm right here. It's okay."

She leaned into him, and he hugged her close, making her feel safe. Making her forget, at least for a moment, how terrified she was.

———

"This is far enough." John pulled his hands from Carol's face.

Suddenly aware of the frigid water lapping at the edge of her shorts, she gripped his arm. He pulled his hand free, and she clung to what was left of the comfort he'd brought to her. Inhaling deeply, she fought her encroaching sense of distress as he reached into her pocket and pulled out the small container.

Clinging to his arm, she listened while John rambled off facts about the Golden Gate Bridge that he'd researched.

Things that Katie would have wanted to know. When it was built, that it was the longest suspension bridge in the world. The color was called International Orange. Over two billion cars had driven over it.

"It's amazing, Katie," he said. "You'd love it here."

Carol laid the pink roses she'd carried onto the water before them, and John sprinkled the ashes on top. They watched as the flowers rode the current, floating on the surface, moving farther and farther into the bay. She actually forgot they were standing in the water until something brushed her calf. She squealed, looked down, and then shrieked when whatever it was touched her again.

Laughing as she practically climbed up his arm, John tried to reassure her, but she'd had enough.

"Okay, that's it," she announced. "I'm done." She practically ran for shore, squealing as she went, needing to get back on solid ground and away from whatever had discovered her leg. She ignored John's laughter, not caring if she was making an ass of herself. Even so, by the time she reached the beach, she, too, was laughing at herself. Once her feet were out of the water, she faced the ocean again, shivering as the chill reached her bones. Putting her hand to her brow, she squinted, trying to see the flowers. Every other second or so, little dots would rise on the swells of the water, showing her the path Katie was taking out to sea.

After about three minutes, John joined her. They watched the water, but the roses were too far out to be seen. As he continued skimming the bay, she admired the bridge in the distance.

"You know how you said nothing was ever enough for me?" she asked.

He tore his gaze from the water, as if surprised by her voice. "I didn't mean that. I was mad."

"But you were right. I was turning into my mother, and I hated it. I swore I'd never be that way with Katie. I'd never make her feel like everything she did disappointed me."

"Your parents had high expectations because they wanted you to have a good life."

The wind caught the bitter laugh that rose from her and carried it away. "My parents wanted me to have the life they decided I should have to make the best possible impression on their friends. All they ever cared about was their social status. Even after I married Tobias, they cast those same disparaging glances whenever we visited. Tobias was brilliant and kind and successful, but he wasn't good enough. I told him it wasn't him, it was my past, but I knew the truth. Dad nearly had a coronary when I brought a Black man home to visit. Mom quietly reassured him I was rebounding and would find a nice boy to settle down with. She didn't say *White* boy, but that's what she meant. They accepted him eventually, but the wedding was interesting. Mom tipped his brother when he brought her a refill on her champagne. He was being nice, but she thought he was hired help."

John laughed, and Carol faced him, not really seeing what was funny. The memory had always embarrassed her. How could her mother have been that insensitive?

"Come on, Caroline," John said, and chuckled. "That is such a Judith thing to do. Did you correct her?"

She sighed. "No. I never did, did I? I always sank into the background hoping not to be seen."

"You're not like that anymore. You're strong now."

"Am I?"

"Yes, you are."

Scanning the bay, she analyzed the self-doubt that seemed to be festering in the dark recesses of her mind. She'd left that feeling of inadequacy behind years ago, but the last few months had seemed to give it the energy it needed to start eating away at her again. "Tobias always pushed me—"

"Don't do that."

"What?"

"Don't give Tobias credit for you becoming the person you were always meant to become. You know, if it weren't for my *interference*, as your father called it, you would have finished medical school and been an amazing pediatrician. You were always destined for greatness, Caroline, and you found it. Just not the way you thought you would. That has nothing to do with me or your parents or Tobias. It's who you've always been, who you were always going to be. I'm glad you had a great life with him, but Tobias didn't make that life for you. He made it *with* you. You've had this strength and this courage all along. You had a lot of bullshit to weed through to find it."

Looking at the bridge again, she tried to believe his words, but they felt too far from the truth to accept. "Want to know my deepest, darkest secret?"

"Yeah, I do."

She swallowed hard before confessing, "I didn't cry when my father died. Not once. Not even at the funeral." She looked at John. "What kind of daughter doesn't cry for her father?"

"The kind who had a father who made it impossible to mourn for him."

"I can't remember a time when he wasn't looking at me like I'd failed him. He always wanted a son, you know. Someone to carry on his name and take over his business. I was a disappointment the moment I was born. He never forgave me for that."

He brushed back a strand of hair that had broken free from her bun and was dancing around her face. "Speaking as a father, I have to disagree. A father's love isn't always easy to understand, but it's real and it's strong. He pushed you because he wanted what was best for you. He didn't realize how hard he was pushing. He loved you. He just wasn't very good at showing it."

"I'd like to believe that, but I don't."

He brushed his hand over her head. "And Judith? Do you think she loves you?"

"In her own way, I suppose. I talk to her once a month out of obligation, but I don't even know what to say to her half the time. I can't tell her the truth. She'd never understand."

"What truth?"

She wasn't sure she wanted to answer, but the sincerity in his question pulled the words out of her. He'd always had the power to make her talk when she didn't want to. That was one of the reasons she'd fallen as hard for him as she had. He seemed interested, *really interested*, and she'd never been able to avoid his questions.

The confession pushed forth before she could consider stopping it. "I'm so broken right now. Ever since Tobias died... No. Ever since Katie died. I've put my head down and pushed through, but when I stop and look up, I realize I'm so incredibly broken, and I don't know how to fix this."

"You fix this by letting yourself feel the pain. You have to mourn. Really mourn. For Katie, and your father, and Tobias. For the children you lost. You can't steamroll your way through grief, Caroline. If you bury it to deal with later, eventually it consumes you."

"Yeah," she said around the sob trying to push its way up from her chest. "I'm realizing that."

Putting his hands on her face, he forced her to look at him. "Katie's dead."

"Don't."

"Your father is dead."

"John." She tried to pull away, but he held her.

"Your husband is dead."

"Stop it."

"You can push the pain away all you want, but that doesn't change anything. You can bury yourself in work, but that will never fix what is broken. That won't change the fact that you were never able to have another baby."

She widened her eyes. "Shut up."

"If you want to fix what you think is broken, the first thing you have to do is acknowledge what broke you in the first place."

"Save your AA bullshit for someone else."

He grabbed her arm when she started to walk away. She turned and shoved him, cursed at him, and shoved again. He didn't let go. Anger boiled to the surface for what she thought must have been the hundredth time since he'd reappeared in her life.

She shoved a third time. Then a fourth and a fifth. He didn't release her.

"You're an asshole," she choked out. "You are such an asshole."

"I know," he said, and tugged her closer.

She wanted to escape his hold, but she didn't have enough fight left in her. He enveloped her in his arms and hugged her close.

The years that had passed and all the anger that she'd held didn't seem to matter. She found the same comfort in his hug now as she had when she had been terrified of telling her parents she was pregnant. Wrapping her arms around his waist, she buried her face in his chest as he squeezed her tight while her body shook with the strength of her sobs.

She hated how good it felt for him to hold her, but at the same time, she burrowed deeper into his arms.

He'd cut open every one of her wounds, releasing years of emotional infection that had been building inside. She didn't even know which loss she was crying over and supposed it didn't matter. She could take her pick. When she was able to control her crying, she leaned back, taking big gulping breaths.

"Better?" he asked.

"No." She tugged at the hem of his shirt. "You deserve all those snot stains."

"I'll wear them with pride. Sit." John took her hand and pulled her down next to their shoes. He draped his arm around her shoulder and they stared out at the water. "You never would have been like your mother with Katie. You were that way with me," he deadpanned. "But I deserved it. You never would have been that way with her."

"I hope not, but when I look back at how I was...bitter. I think it would have been inevitable. She would have resented me as much as I resent my parents."

"No."

"You were the fun one. I was the enforcer."

"I was irresponsible. Look where that got us."

She searched the waves, once again trying to see the pink roses that were long gone. That seemed symbolic somehow. Katie was out of her sight and no matter how much she searched, she couldn't be found. "Poor kid never had a chance with us as her parents, did she?"

"We loved her. We both loved her more than anything. She knew that. That's more than a lot of kids have. She would have turned out okay. And she would have loved you. She would have loved both of us."

"Yeah, I'm sure she would have." Silence fell between them again before Carol gently nudged him. "I want ice cream. You want ice cream?"

"That sounds good." He started to push himself up, then fell back.

Grabbing his arm, she searched his face for signs of what was wrong. "Okay?"

He tried to fake a laugh, but it didn't last. Holding his hand out, he said, "Help me up?"

She stood and bent, allowing him to drape his arms around her shoulders, and slowly lifted him. "The sand messed with your balance."

"Or I have a massive brain tumor." He found his footing enough for her to step back.

"Maybe a little of both."

"Maybe." Putting his arm over her shoulder as they walked toward the stairs, he turned his eyes to the clear sky. "She liked strawberry ice cream. Let's have strawberry for Katie."

"Strawberry it is."

They took the steps up slower than they'd climbed down. His steps were sluggish, his stride not quite as long.

His gait used to be carefree. Now he seemed weighed down by the world. By his mortality. By their loss. His walk was that of a broken man. Somehow that made her heart break a little.

She assumed the afternoon had taken more of a toll on him than either had expected. Emotions had been high, and not only for her, but seeing his measured movements concerned her. Back at the RV, he sat heavily at the table and closed his eyes.

"What's going on?" she asked.

"Starting to get one of those headaches."

Gathering his medicine bag and a cup of water, she sat across from him and checked her watch. "You know, they seem to start about this time every day. You're probably getting more tired than you realize."

He took his pills and zipped the bag without commenting.

"Maybe you should try resting earlier in the day. Might help prevent these headaches."

He put his hand to the spot where his tumor was growing. "Something tells me it won't make much difference in the end."

"Not in the end, no, but there's no need to make what time you have left worse. Go to bed, John. I'll get us to the park, and we can rest for the night."

"You wanted ice cream."

"There will be plenty of opportunities for ice cream later."

"For you." He blinked away the sudden sheen in his eyes. "I've got a lifetime of memories with you to make in the next few weeks. I should have done this sooner. I should have found you years ago."

Carol gnawed at her lip as she chewed on a truth that was hard to admit but that he deserved to hear. At this point in time, there was no point in lying, even to spare his feelings. "I don't think I would have been this kind to you years ago, John."

"Dying has its perks, I guess."

"I guess." Sinking back in the seat, she stared out the window, skimming the near-empty parking lot. "Tobias wanted me to reach out to you. He tried many times to convince me to forgive you. I just couldn't."

"I don't blame you."

"I don't know what I'm going to do with the rest of my life now that I don't get to spend it hating you." Lifting her gaze to his, she giggled.

He was a bit slower on the uptake, but he chuckled as well.

EIGHT

CAROL DIDN'T TRY to hide her disbelief. John was insane, and she let him know it by the way she gawked across the table at him. "You are *not* climbing to the summit of Mount St. Helens."

"It's only ten miles round trip."

"*Only* ten miles? You wore yourself out walking on the beach in San Francisco."

"That was two days ago. I've rested plenty since then."

"No amount of rest is going to give you the energy or the skill to hike a volcano, John." She turned her laptop and showed him the warning. "There is a boulder field. Do you really think I can carry you over boulders if you get hurt or too exhausted to continue? No. We'll take the first leg through the woods until we find the right spot."

"She'd want to be on the summit," he stated.

"You cannot make it to the summit."

Sitting back, he crossed his arms as he defiantly held her gaze, silently showing his determination.

She rubbed her forehead as she cursed. "You get fatigued

too easily. Your footing isn't as good as it needs to be. You're not capable of this kind of hike."

"I hiked at the Grand Canyon."

"On a smooth path with a steady slope. This has a *freaking* boulder field, John. There is no way around it. You can't do this."

Clearly as agitated as Carol, John slid from the booth at the table and stormed out of the RV. Turning the laptop screen back around, she finished reading about the hike. No. There was no way he could make his way to the summit. Hell, she wasn't sure she could, and she was in much better shape.

There had to be another option. When she clicked on the link to one of the various tours of the area, a quiet laugh erupted as she found the answer they needed.

Standing in the door of the RV, she watched him looking out at the volcano in the distance. From the moment she had first noticed him in the coffee shop all those years ago, she'd been taken by how he seemed larger than life. He was bigger than their problems, her doubts, the limitations her parents had put on her confidence. He'd been bigger than everything. He seemed small now. Thirty years ago, if she'd seen him facing down Mount St. Helens, she wouldn't have doubted that he could conquer the volcano without breaking a sweat.

Now, he swayed standing in its shadow. That saddened her in ways she hadn't expected. Another bit of the bitterness and hatred she'd held dear to her heart slipped away. How could she hate him when he was so small?

"Hey," she called. "Know what Katie would have loved even more than climbing to the summit?"

His only response was to turn and look at her.

"Riding in a helicopter."

After a moment, he smiled. "Seriously?"

"Apparently aerial ash-scattering is a thing. The website says the pilot will release the remains from the cockpit. We wouldn't actually be doing that part, but she'd love it."

He stood a bit taller. "Yeah. She would. Let's do it."

"I'll make the call."

"Caroline?" he called before she disappeared inside. "I don't mean to be difficult."

"I know."

He shoved his hands in his pockets. "I'm trying to focus on Katie, so I don't get caught up in my own shit, but..."

She stepped out of the RV and closed the distance between them. "You're handling this better than most, I think."

"I'm scared," he said, focusing on his feet.

"Of dying?"

He rolled his shoulders back, as if pulling on all his emotional strength. His brave façade crumbled before he even managed to get the mask in place. Slouching, he lowered his gaze again. "Of what comes between now and dying. I know you said you're only here until you get me home... You don't owe me anything. What you're doing for me now is more than I had the right to ask, but if I spend what's left of my life in a hospital they won't... I need someone who can make some tough decisions." He looked around the wilderness before meeting her gaze. "You might think I wasn't listening to the doctors, but I was. This could get bad before it's over. Real bad. I don't want to go down like that, Caroline. I need someone who will help me bow out when it's time. I need you. I know that's a hell of a thing to ask someone, especially someone you've already caused too much pain, but I don't have anyone else."

After taking a moment to digest his unspoken request, she said, "Assisted suicide is illegal in most states. I could go to prison for murder, John."

Disappointment clouded his already drawn face. "Yeah. That's a bit much to ask, isn't it?"

It was a bit much. Not just the idea of going to prison; she had enough emotional damage without taking his life, no matter how dismal the quality. She couldn't pretend she didn't understand his request. "I can't take a risk like that. That's why I have to be careful with your medications." She swallowed before continuing. "If you were to accidentally ingest..." Carol counted out a dose. "That would be fatal."

He offered her a weak smile and a slight nod.

She started for the motorhome before stopping and facing him. "John? I'd really prefer you not overdose on morphine in my RV. I don't need to add that to the long list of shit I'm never going to get over."

Giving her his signature grin, he put his hand to his heart. "You have my word."

———

Caroline bit her bottom lip as she stood in front of the full-length mirror sitting in her soon-to-be mother-in-law's bedroom. She didn't have close girlfriends. By the time she'd gotten over being a socially awkward teen, her entire life had been about John. Only now, as she stood alone in a white dress with no one around to help her get ready, did she understand how alienated she'd made herself.

She was glad John had agreed to get married at the courthouse. The embarrassment of not having anyone show up to fill her side of a church would have been more than she could have withstood. Since her parents refused to accept their marriage, all she had were grandparents and a few aunts, uncles, and cousins. They might have attended if she'd asked, but she'd decided it was better to have a judge marry them. Maybe someday they'd renew their vows and have a real wedding. One her parents would be willing to attend. But for now, all she needed was John and a judge.

Lowering her face, she tried to swallow her tears, but one escaped and landed on the back of her hand. She snuffled and wiped it away on the simple knee-length dress she'd selected for this day. Running her hand over the skirt, she tried to smile, but her lips quivered and fell.

This was her wedding day, and she was miserable.

Pressing her hand to her stomach, she reminded herself of the life growing inside her. She was going to be a mother soon. By day's end, she'd be a wife. Who cared if her parents weren't there to support her? She was a woman now. Her own person. She didn't need her parents anymore. She had John. His parents were her family now, too, and they were always nice to her.

Frannie, John's mother, had told her how proud she was that Caroline had been quick to adjust her future plans around the baby. She said it showed her that Caroline would be a good mother. The kind of mother she'd want for her grandchild.

Caroline hadn't wanted to cry in front of the woman, but she'd broken down and, without any prompting, told her how upset her own mother had been about the pregnancy. They'd barely spoken since they'd found out about the baby. Frannie had held her and promised to be there, no matter what. Thus far, she'd stuck to her word.

When she'd needed a dress for the wedding, Frannie had taken her shopping. She'd even offered to take a few of Caroline's friends. She'd thanked Frannie and said she'd prefer the two of them go alone. The afternoon had been nice. She'd helped Caroline pick out her dress and suggested they have a reception for friends and family since they were getting married at the courthouse. Again, she thanked Frannie for the idea, but said it'd be best if she and John went home and spent time together.

She had thought she'd covered well, but Frannie called John and quizzed him until he admitted that her parents weren't planning to attend the wedding. Or any reception they might have. Caroline had been embarrassed, she'd tried to avoid Frannie every time she'd come over during the following week, but the woman had been persistent and kind. Everything her own mother wasn't at the moment, so it'd been easy to start leaning on her.

Today, her wedding day, it had been Frannie who helped her prepare. It'd been Frannie who kissed her cheek and told her she made such a beautiful bride. When there was a quiet knock on the door, she knew it'd be Frannie telling her it was time to get married.

Caroline swallowed hard and practiced her smile once more before opening the door. She gasped when a bouquet, probably three times larger than the one she'd bought, met her.

"It's bad luck for me to see you," John said from behind the flowers. "But you gotta take these. They're breaking my arm."

She laughed as she took the pink roses from him. "They're beautiful, John." She looked over the flowers, touching the silky soft petals before lifting her tearstained face and catching his gaze. "You said it was bad luck."

Pushing his way into the room, he wrapped his arm around her waist and pulled her to him. "Know what's even worse than a groom seeing the bride?"

"Hmm?"

"The bride not being happy on her wedding day."

She gingerly touched one of the roses again. "It's not the wedding."

"I know. Your parents will come around, babe. You gotta give them time."

Biting her lip, she tried to hide her tears. "No, they won't. You don't know them like I do, John. They'll hold this against me forever."

He hugged her closer. "I'm sorry."

Wrapping her arms around his shoulders, she leaned into him, absorbing his support. "We have each other, right? That's all that matters."

"That is all that matters." Pulling back, he smiled at her. "I'll always be here for you. I'll always take care of you."

Some of her sadness melted away. "I know you will."

Putting his hands to her face, he brushed his thumbs over her cheeks. "You have a new family now. Me and this baby and my parents. We're your family. We're going to be here for you. Always. We'll take care of each other. From this day forward."

"Johnathan Robert Bowman," Frannie chastised from behind him. "What are you doing?"

He kissed Caroline hard on the lips before turning to his mother. "You know me, Ma. There's never been a rule I didn't set out to break."

She sighed and shook her head. "Get to the courthouse, young man. We'll be right behind you."

He kissed Caroline's head one more time and whispered, "I've got you, baby. I promise."

She watched him leave before smiling at his mother. "Whoops."

"Whoops is what got you two into this," she said lightly. "Let me look at you." Taking a moment to rearrange a few strands of Caroline's hair, she gave a loving smile. "I'm happy he has you. You're good for him. You know that? You make him a better person. I love you for that."

Tears filled Caroline's eyes again, but this time they weren't sad. This time they were the kind of tears a bride should shed on her wedding day. "He's good for me, too. He takes care of me. I promise I'll take care of him. I'll be a good wife."

Frannie hugged her tight. "I know you will. Now let's get you two married."

While it wasn't the long walk down the aisle with hordes of family filling the pews, Caroline thought their wedding was... quaint. That was a good word for it. Frannie and Mark sat on a bench and watched them exchange vows. They snapped a few photos after the ceremony ended, and then took the newlyweds out for a nice dinner.

Caroline couldn't have been more pleased with how the day ended...but it wasn't over. Instead of driving them home, John pulled into the parking lot of the pub where he and his friends hung out after work.

She stared at him, waiting for him to notice her irritation.

After several long seconds, he stopped patting his jacket, checking for his wallet, and caught her eye. "What?"

"I'm pregnant. I don't want to go to the pub."

"Just for a drink. One drink."

"You had two drinks at dinner."

His smile faded for the first time since they'd been pronounced husband and wife. "It's our wedding day. I'm allowed to celebrate."

Her heart sank at the frustration in his voice. She knew that tone. Her father used it with her quite often. She'd disappointed him. She didn't want to go to the bar. She wanted to rest and spend some time with her husband. Still, she backed down. She nodded and turned her face to the window. "Okay. Just one drink."

She should have known better. She had known better. One drink turned into two, which turned into three, as she sat at a table surrounded by off-duty beat cops sharing tales, using vulgar language, and laughing it up. John didn't seem to remember she was there until he lifted his empty glass at a passing waitress and Caroline put her hand on his arm.

"No more. I'm tired. I want to go home."

He frowned at her, but then he dug in his pocket and handed her his car keys. "Go ahead," he said. "I'll catch a ride with one of the guys."

She creased her brow. "It's our wedding night," she whispered.

He leaned closer, cupping his ear. "What?"

Swallowing, she snatched the keys from his hand and left without another word to him or his friends. She drove home, ripping the flowers from her hair as she went. She cursed him the entire ride and as she stormed up the stairs to their apartment. She threw her wedding bouquet, the dozen pink roses he'd given her, on the couch with her purse and marched to their bedroom.

Stripping out of her wedding dress, she climbed in the shower *and scrubbed away the makeup Frannie had helped her apply. She put on her nightgown—but not the lacy one she'd bought at the department store for this night—and crawled into bed. Alone. On her wedding night.*

She stared at the ceiling, listening to the silence until after one in the morning when the front door opened. John's footsteps were heavy as he stumbled through the apartment. He didn't bother getting out of his clothes or brushing his teeth. He simply collapsed in the bed and threw his arm around her, pulling her against him.

He kissed her shoulder and exhaled the scent of beer over her. "My wife. My beautiful wife."

She didn't answer. She didn't move. She lay there, smelling the alcohol drifting over her as he snored.

———

Carol slowed her pace as she crossed the lobby of the heliport. She and John had been required to sign about a hundred different releases before they were allowed to get near the helicopter, let alone have the pilot release human remains over the summit of Mount St. Helens. She'd taken the papers and the container of ashes to the receptionist and returned to where she'd left John at a round table.

His eyes grew sad as he watched her, as if he were having second thoughts about what they'd agreed to do.

"Are you okay?" she asked, closing the distance between them.

"I was thinking about the first time I saw you at that coffee shop." His lips kicked up into a lopsided grin. "I swear to God, my heart almost jumped out of my chest. You were the most beautiful girl I'd ever seen. I knew you were out of my league just looking at you."

She laughed as she sat next to him. "Wish I'd known that." She nudged him with her elbow. "That was a joke."

He acted as if he hadn't heard her. "We were good together back then. I've spent a lot of time over the years trying to figure out where we went wrong. My drinking, I know," he said before she could point out the obvious. "But we went off track before my drinking got out of hand. I think we started a downward spiral when you gave up med school."

Shaking her head, she disagreed. "We were on a downward spiral from day one, John. You spent our wedding night out drinking with your friends."

The depression in his eyes deepened. "I remember. Bert kept telling me I was an ass, and I kept telling him you didn't mind. Boy, was I wrong. Hell of a fight the next day, wasn't it?"

"We spent the first full day of marriage alternating between screaming and giving each other the cold shoulder. Should have known then. Actually, I guess I did."

He looked at his hands. "We were kids. That's all. We were too young."

"You were twenty-six," she pointed out.

"And still a kid," he insisted.

She didn't counter his opinion. She wasn't going to be baited into a fight at the heliport while they waited to spread their daughter's ashes. Drumming her fingers on the tabletop between them, she turned her focus to the framed posters on the wall.

John covered her hand with his, likely to stop her rhythmic tapping. She glanced up to apologize. Tobias had hated when she did that, too, but it was nervous habit she didn't always have control over.

However, the look in John's eyes wasn't one of irritation. He looked sad, almost as if he could cry. "I loved you," he said with such tenderness her heart ached. "More than anything. I never regretted marrying you. Not once. I regretted not being a better husband. Not being more mature. I regretted not taking better care of you. But I *never* regretted marrying you."

Holding his gaze, she tried to think of the right response. She couldn't say the same. Maybe they were working through some issues during this trip, but she'd regretted marrying him far more times than she hadn't. She wasn't going to lie and tell him otherwise, which left her sitting there not quite sure what to say.

"Mrs. Denman," someone called, demanding her attention.

She stood as a man approached the table. His walk was confident, as if he didn't have a care in the world. Carol supposed that should be a good trait in a pilot, but she would have felt better if he seemed a bit nervous. Her heart had started pounding with anxiety the moment she'd parked outside.

He introduced himself and asked to clarify the instructions on releasing Katie's ashes. Once she and John verbalized their wishes for their daughter, they followed him to the helicopter. He gave them instructions, showed them where the first-aid kit was and how to use the flotation devices, and then had them buckle in.

"I'll let you know when I'm going to release the remains," he said through the headset.

Carol swallowed hard as the helicopter whirred to life.

Within a few minutes, they were lifting off. She was nervous, but not terrified like she'd been when they were walking into the water at the beach in San Francisco. However, when she looked over at John, he was clinging to the edge of his seat with his eyes closed tight.

She pried at his fingers until he eased up and gripped her hand in his. When he turned to her wide-eyed, she offered him a comforting smile. She didn't say anything. She didn't want to alert the pilot to John's panic. Instead, she held his gaze and motioned for him to breathe in and out. He did and by the time they neared the volcano, he was occasionally glancing out the window to look at whatever view the pilot was telling them about.

Carol watched out her window as well, imagining Katie's excitement if she'd been there with them.

Lookit those trees, Mommy.

Did you hear that, Mommy?

Do you see that, Mommy?

Lookit over there, Mommy.

"I see, baby," she whispered.

"I'm going to release the ashes now," the pilot said.

Her heart flipped, knowing another bit of Katie was slipping away. Carol wanted to close her eyes, but she didn't. She stared down as they flew over the crater created by the 1980 eruption.

The hole seemed symbolic somehow. The earth had been ripped open much like she had been at the loss of her child. The jagged scar on the ground would never fade. Nothing could ever fill the void left behind. The hollow shell of what once was whole would never fully recover.

But life went on. The summit had new growth, wildlife,

adventurers. It would never be the same, but it survived. In one way that was an amazing testament to the strength of the mountain, but in another, it was a horrific reminder how very fragile the world could be.

How fragile everything she loved and held close to her heart could be. She knew better than most that life could change in an instant. What was perfect one moment could erupt into a disaster, destroying everything, without warning.

John's hold on her hand tightened and she returned the gesture, silently sharing a moment for their child. She didn't look at him. She couldn't. She was broken enough without seeing his pain.

A full minute passed before the pilot resumed his role of tour guide, giving them facts that might have bored most, but which Katie would have loved to learn.

The flight was short, a little over twenty minutes. Still, she held John's hand until the landing skids were safely on the ground again. When he released her, she had to flex her fingers several times to get the blood flowing right. They unbuckled as someone slid the door open. She was the first to put her feet on the ground, steadying herself before moving aside so John could climb down.

When he did, he swayed and laughed it off, but when he put his arm around her shoulder, trying to be casual, he leaned on her far more than he had in recent days. The man leading them back to the building reached out, clearly concerned, but she waved him off.

She supported his weight all the way back to the RV, where he dropped into a seat at the table. "You want to lie down?"

"No. Not yet."

"Water?"

"Please."

She got a cold bottle from the fridge, cracking the top for him.

His hand trembled, but he was able to take a drink, only spilling a little down his chin. He lifted his eyes to hers as he wiped it away. "I'm sorry."

Patting his hand, she dismissed his apology. "You handled that ride way better than I did the ocean."

"I mean for our wedding night. I was a shithead. I'm sorry."

"It doesn't matter now."

"It matters to me. I screwed up a lot back then." He scoffed. "That's putting it mildly, right?"

"I wasn't perfect either." Sitting across from him, she played with the lid from his bottle. "I was sad, John. My parents had all but disowned me. I was alone and scared. Even though I was as much at fault, I put most of the blame on you. I didn't give you a chance. Not really. I wasn't ready to be a mother or a wife. I don't think I was that great at either one."

"That's not true," he said. "You were great. You were always great. You put up with too much. You couldn't have been a better mother to Katie. She was lucky to have you."

Leaning back, she shook her head. "I shouldn't have been so strict. I should have... I should have been more fun. Like you. You always made her laugh. Her eyes lit up when you walked in the room, John."

"One of us had to be the grown-up. It sure as hell wasn't me. And you made her light up, too. Maybe you didn't see it, but I did. She adored you, Caroline. She really did."

She thought she'd cried herself out on the helicopter until tears filled her eyes and dripped over the lids before she could catch them. "I hope so."

"Do you think I can make it up to you? Or at least try?"

She swiped her cheeks, then ran her hands over her shorts. "Make what up to me?"

"Our wedding night."

Cocking her brow, she dared him to say what she immediately thought he was suggesting.

He laughed. "I was thinking a fancy dinner that doesn't end with me stumbling in drunk would be a nice memory to replace the shitty one."

"Oh." She relaxed her death glare. "That would be nice, wouldn't it? Let's do that."

"I'm going to rest while you get us to the RV park. Then we'll figure out dinner."

"Sounds good." She watched him gradually maneuver his way to the bed and practically collapse onto the mattress. Every day seemed to take more of a toll on him than he was willing to acknowledge. Fatigue closed in on him from the moment he woke until he gave in and napped for an hour or two. Sometimes longer. She could no longer ignore that he faded a little more each day. Unlike Katie or Tobias or their lost children, she knew what was coming with John, and the knowledge was starting to weigh down on her in ways she hadn't expected when she'd started this journey with him.

Climbing into the driver's seat, she sank down and pressed her hands to her face to muffle the sounds of choking sobs from drifting to the back of the RV.

———

Instead of waking John, once she had the RV hooked up at the park outside of Seattle, Carol opened her laptop and checked e-mails, responding to a few and leaving more to deal with later. While she was online, she found a few options for restaurants, wondering how fancy *fancy* was in John's mind. In her life, fancy was probably more than he would be comfortable with, so she downscaled her usual expectations for a *fancy* dinner out. She narrowed their options down to an Italian restaurant and a steakhouse. She'd let him make the final decision.

"Hey," she called. "We should start making plans for dinner." Moving to the back, she nudged his leg. "You awake?"

Rolling over, he moaned and ran his hand over his face. "What time is it?"

"Almost four. I need to make reservations for dinner, or we'll never get a table. Italian or a steakhouse?"

He cleared his throat. "Uh, Italian."

"Good choice." She left him to wake up as she called the restaurant and reserved a table for six thirty. She was hanging up as the bathroom door clicked closed. Her instinct was to call out to remind him they were at the RV park and he could walk to the public restroom, but she bit back her words. In the grand scheme of things, having to empty dirty water from the tank didn't really matter.

He'd done a good job of respecting her request to use the bathroom as little as possible. She wouldn't complain now. While he was in the bathroom, she opened the closet they were sharing and sorted through what she'd brought. She hadn't considered dinners out when she'd packed, but she did have a sundress that should be nice enough for where they were going.

Planning her dinner outfit came to an immediate stop at the sound of banging behind her. Tossing her dress back on the hanging bar, she closed the closet and turned around in the small space. "John?" The only sound was the continuing *thump, thump, thump.* "I'm coming in." She turned the knob and pushed, but the door only moved about three inches before bumping into something solid. When she peered through the crack, her heart sank.

Only his feet were visible. His muscles were stiff and trembling, kicking the wall, as his body seized uncontrollably in the confined space.

Thump. Thump. Thump.

Putting both palms against the door, she pushed again. It was no use. Even if she were strong enough to shove his weight aside, there wasn't enough room for him to sit on the floor and the door to fully open. Sinking to her knees, Carol stuck her arm through the crack and put her hand to his leg.

"It's okay," she said as soothingly as she could. "You're okay." Knowing he was on the other side of the door suffering broke through what remained of her years of anger and the cool, calm façade she'd developed as a nurse long ago. She rested her head against the door as her heart crumbled and tears filled her eyes. "I'm right here, John. I'm right here."

Forever seemed to pass before his spasms eased and he gripped her hand. Wiping her cheeks, she sniffed and took a deep breath. "Can you move away from the door, so I can come in? John? Move back a little. I can't get to you."

He managed to curl into a ball and she was able to open the door enough to see him. His eyes were dazed, seemingly unable to focus. Drool soaked his chin and shirt. He opened his mouth, but only a moaning sound came out.

"It's okay," she whispered. She still couldn't get to him, but at least she could monitor him with more than a hand on his leg. "That was a bad one, huh?" His response was another inaudible moan. "Just breathe. It'll pass. Give your body a few minutes to recover."

She sat, comforting him through the door until she could see his eyes begin to clear as his brain started functioning properly again. His posture straightened somewhat, and his breathing evened out. After a few minutes, he dragged his hand over his chin and blinked a few times before meeting her gaze.

She offered him a weak smile that he didn't return. "Can you get up?"

With a sense of uselessness, she watched from the door, unable to help until he struggled to his feet and she could open the door all the way. Putting her hands to his face, as he'd done to her in the past, she stroked her fingers over his cheeks, waiting for him to look at her. Their eyes locked, but he clearly wasn't fully connected to his body yet. Snagging the hand towel, she wiped his chin dry and eased his shirt over his head. He helped as much as he could, which wasn't much at all. Then she guided him from the bathroom toward the bed.

Instead of scooting back on the bed, he fell with his legs dangling off the edge. She sat next to him and put her fingers to his wrist, checking his pulse. Not that she could do anything, no matter what the count was, but it made her feel as if she were doing something assertive in the moment rather than simply waiting for him to recover. Checking her watch, she noticed how much time had passed and started to stand. John grabbed her wrist, weakly clinging to her.

"Don't leave me," he mumbled.

"I need to cancel our reservation."

"Don't leave me."

She stared at her phone sitting on the table, a few feet away. It would take seconds to grab it and return to his side, but walking away from him felt heartless.

Screw proper etiquette. The restaurant would figure out soon enough they weren't coming. Resting her hand on his chest, she saw a three-inch scar down the front of his left shoulder. That hadn't been there twenty-four years ago.

Running her finger along the discolored skin, she asked, "What happened?"

"Druggie with a knife."

"Ouch."

He moaned his agreement. "I think I can move now." He struggled, but was able to scoot back on the bed and put his head on the pillow.

"Water?" she asked.

"No." He held his hand out.

She hesitated in taking it. When she did, he pulled her toward him. Instead of resisting, like her initial instinct told her to, she crawled up onto the bed next to him. Propping her head on the palm of one hand, she let him hold the other.

"Don't leave me," he said again.

"I'm right here."

He lightly squeezed her hand and almost instantly drifted off. Dropping her head down beside his, she watched him sleep. Brushing her hand over his, she stopped when she felt his wedding band. Tracing it lightly, she sighed. The ring she'd put on his finger was a drastic contrast to the one she wore—the one Tobias had put there.

Her ring was gold, too, but the band shone like it was brand new. On their tenth wedding anniversary, Tobias had upgraded the diamond to two carats. He'd said on their twentieth, he'd bump it up to three. She'd laughed and told him he might want to save his money for retirement.

Their twentieth was coming up in a matter of weeks. She'd never know if he meant it. If he really intended to add an even bigger diamond to her ring. She would have told him not to. She would have told him to spend the money on a trip. Someplace they hadn't been before. Someplace where they could make memories that were just for them.

Rolling onto her back, she stared at the ceiling, thinking of the many memories they'd made in the very bed where her ex-husband now slept next to her. How the hell had her life come back to this? Back to nursing John? Back to seeing him through yet another rough night? How had she ended up reliving the very life she'd run away from years ago?

She'd laugh if it weren't so damn sad.

Next to her, John heaved a sigh and murmured her name. She put her hand to his chest to soothe him, as she'd done a thousand times during their marriage. He put his hand to hers, closed his fingers around hers, and eased back into his slumber. As he'd done a thousand times.

And like all those times before, the sense of desperation and loneliness that filled her as he slept was enough to consume her and bring tears to her eyes.

NINE

AS ON MANY other nights since starting the trip, Carol hadn't gotten nearly enough rest. On the rare occasions when she did drift off, she'd dreamed of starry nights and staring at the mountains with Tobias by her side. She'd woken with a warm body pressed against her back and a heavy arm holding her down. She would have been content to stay there all day, but her mind started to clear, and she remembered Tobias was dead. The warm body behind her was John's.

A strange pang hit her, a mixture of guilt and anger and resentment.

She pushed John's arm off her and sat on the edge of the bed, taking a minute to finish waking up before heading for the closet. After grabbing the bag that held her shower supplies and a fresh set of clothes, she marched to the park's public shower area. She attempted to wash away the shame she felt at having slept next to John in Tobias's bed, but the feeling was under her skin.

There was no reason to be ashamed. Her night next to

John had hardly been romantic and Tobias was dead. She really doubted he gave a damn who slept next to his wife.

But *she* did, and it shouldn't have been John.

Standing under the shower head, she let the lukewarm water run over her. The camps tended to have a limit on how long the water ran. When it automatically stopped, she pushed the button again. After the third time, she actually washed.

John was sitting on the edge of the bed when she returned to the RV. "Morning," he said with a sleep-slurred voice.

"How are you?" She hadn't meant her words to be curt, but even she'd heard the sharpness of her tone. With her eyes closed, she inhaled a cleansing breath as she dropped her bag in the closet. Easing the door closed, she tried again. "Feeling better?"

If he'd noticed her previous edge, he didn't let it show. "Just exhausted. Hungry." He gave her his sad eyes, the ones that used to move her. "I'm sorry about dinner."

"It's okay. We'll try again another night."

"I still owe you ice cream."

"There's time for that, too."

"I hope so," he said, standing.

She didn't rush him, though she wanted to. She wanted to get the RV unhooked and on the road, but his movements were even more calculated than they'd been the day before. He staggered as he stood, holding his arms out and pressing his palms against the paneled walls. After two small and unsteady steps, she realized he'd never make it to the RV shower house. She should have known this was inevitable.

Maybe she had and had embraced denial, as she tended to do.

"Shower here," she told him.

He lifted a questioning gaze to her. She had been adamant that he not make more work for her by using up the fresh water and filling the gray-water tank. The time for that foolish notion had passed. He didn't have the strength to cross the park and shower on his own. She'd be cruel to make him try.

A simple tilt of her chin served as her acknowledgment. "I'll make us some breakfast. Yell if you need me."

He didn't thank her, but his relief was palpable. He shuffled around as she dug eggs and cheese out of the small fridge. Though she focused on scrambling eggs and making coffee, she listened to the sounds coming from the bathroom. He was considerate enough to take his shower military style —water on to soak, water off to wash, water on to rinse. When he emerged in sweatpants and a T-shirt, he dropped at the table, looking even more exhausted than he had when he'd woken.

She slid a plate in front of him and filled one for herself. "You should try to sleep today."

"So should you."

"Sleeping while operating a motor vehicle is frowned upon by most."

He ignored her joke and focused on stabbing at his eggs. "You were restless last night. You're restless every night, actually. You never used to toss and turn that much."

"Hmm. Is that why you had me pinned down when I woke up?"

"Probably."

Sitting across from him, she wrapped her hand around her coffee mug. "That was a pretty serious seizure yesterday."

He took a bite instead of responding.

"I'll let Dr. Collins know, so he can—"

"Change my prescription and remind you that I should be in a hospital?"

She wanted to lash out but stuffed her mouth to stifle the urge. That was progress, she thought. A week ago, he would have snapped and she would have snapped back and one of them would have stormed off. Instead, he heaved a sigh and backed down, and she kept eating.

"He can't do anything for me," John said in a calmer tone.

"Lowering the dosage on your anti-epileptic meds helped your other symptoms, but it may be too low now. There's a balance; we have to find it."

"I'm not a guinea pig."

"Didn't say you were." She grinned. "Guinea pigs are cuter. Probably smell better, too."

He met her gaze before snickering. "You look like hell this morning."

"Did you look in the mirror?"

"Yeah. I did, actually. Can we take it easy today?"

She went for the stack of papers she'd printed at home and studied the trip she'd plotted for today. "I made reservations in Missoula, but..." After a moment of looking at the map, she tapped a spot. "Let's get to Spokane. That's about six hours without stops. We can stretch it out. Think you can make that?"

He scowled at the suggestion.

Carol didn't want to make this trip longer than necessary, but she had to agree she needed the rest as much as he did. A week on the road, pushing day after day, was wearing her out, too. "I'll see if we can stay here one more night. I need to do laundry anyway."

At that, his softer posture returned. "Sounds good."

They finished breakfast in companionable silence and once she finished her eggs, she walked to the office to pay for another night. When she returned, John was stripping his bed and stuffing the sheets into the laundry bag. As he did that, she gathered the sheets from her bed.

"I got it," she said when he started to lift the bag. "You can stay here."

"I want to help," he insisted. She gave him the smaller one that held detergent pods and the charger for her phone, which had sat on the table overnight.

John headed out of the RV first, moving with deliberate ease. She didn't mind since she was hefting the heavier laundry bag by his side. Luckily the laundromat wasn't far from where they'd parked. She claimed two of the old and battered mustard-yellow washing machines, managing to get all their laundry started at the same time.

Sinking into one of the cushioned chairs next to him, she stretched her legs out and crossed them at the ankle, silently admitting she was glad she wouldn't be spending the day driving.

"Thank you," John said after a few moments of watching their clothes spin in circles as bubbles started to lather. "For taking care of me last night."

"You're welcome."

"Old habits, huh?"

She considered sharing that she'd had those same thoughts, but she was getting tired of rubbing his alcoholism

172

in his face. They'd turned the tide on the past. Letting it go was for the best. "This is different."

"Not really. You still had to put me to bed like a child." Sitting forward, he rested his elbows on his knees. "I never could take care of myself, could I?"

"Well, I'm guessing you learned sometime in the last twenty years or you wouldn't have made it this long."

"Mom took care of me after you left. I'd date someone for a while, and she'd try but... They never could live up to you, you know?"

"Oh, John. We were such a disaster. You really should have let us go and moved on with your life. You could have found someone."

"I didn't want to." He sat back but didn't look at her. The spinning of the teal sheets seemed to have him mesmerized. "If they got close, I walked away. I refused to imagine my life without you in it."

Carol let his words sink in. "That's sad. That's really sad. You could have had a better life. You could have had more children. You shouldn't have wasted all these years clinging to the past."

This time he looked at her. "I didn't waste it. I spent that time becoming the man that I should have been for my wife and daughter. I spent it becoming someone who deserved you. That wasn't a waste. It might be too late for us to ever try again, but it's not too late for me to be the man I should have been."

———

Caroline ignored the discomfort in her back as she shifted in her seat. The speaker at her graduation was droning on and on about the bright future of medicine, not seeming to care that the graduates were sitting in hard seats with even harder backs. Not the most comfortable option for any of them, but most especially the one due to give birth in a matter of days.

"Are you okay?" the woman next to her asked.

She recognized her from a few classes but hadn't ever really talked to her. She had to look at the program in her hand to check her name. Listed right after Caroline Bowman was Marie Braun.

"Mm-hmm."

"Are you sure?"

"Yeah, I'm fine." She shifted again and gave a forced smile as Marie creased her brow with obvious concern.

After what seemed like hours, the speaker announced the class of 1989. That was their cue to stand. Caroline struggled a bit, but Marie took her arm and helped her to her feet. As she did, something shifted low in her abdomen followed by a trickle of warmth down her leg. Horrified at first, she thought her bladder had given way, but she couldn't control the flow.

"Oh no," she whispered, lifting her gaze to Marie. "I think my water broke."

They both looked down. She guessed Marie was relieved to see she wasn't standing in a puddle of amniotic fluid.

"You're in labor," Marie stated as if confirming what she'd already guessed. "Um. We should get you to the hospital."

"No," she begged. "Please. I want to walk. Please. My husband and his parents came to see me graduate."

"Okay. Okay. Um." Marie exhaled, then grinned. "Hey. This is my first real emergency."

She laughed, but it quickly turned into a wince. "Oh. Those are contractions, aren't they?" Caroline asked.

Marie held Caroline's arm and whispered soothing words as, graduate by graduate, contraction by contraction, they made their way to the stage. When Caroline's name was called, Marie helped her up the stairs but let her walk the stage alone.

"Are you okay?" the head of the nursing department asked as she shook his hand and accepted her degree.

"I'm in labor."

"Of course you are." He chortled. "How far apart are your contractions?"

"Three minutes or so."

He gestured to one of the other administrators on the stage, who joined them. "She's in labor. Take her to the exit."

The woman took her by the arm and helped her the rest of the way across the stage as the director said into the microphone, "Can Caroline's family meet her by the side exit? She's about to have a baby."

Gasps and applause erupted as they headed for the nearest door. The woman she'd seen in the halls of the nursing department was coaching her through another contraction when John ran up, fear in his eyes.

"Okay," he said. "Okay. I got this. We got this. We can do this."

"Calm down. She's fine. You've got plenty of time to get to the hospital."

"Okay," he said, trying to sound calmer. "Okay. We got this."

"John," Caroline said between gritted teeth. "Go get the car."

"The car?" John's head went up and down like a bobble-head doll. "Right. Right. I'll go get the car. Don't move."

He ran out the door as the pain in her back eased and she could stand normally again.

"Oh, honey," Frannie cooed, slipping her arm around her shoulders. "Just try to relax. Your body knows what to do."

Caroline focused on the techniques she'd learned as Frannie and Mark walked her out to the waiting car. John slipped into the backseat beside her while his mother sat in the passenger seat and Mark drove. John held her hand, kissed her head, and coached her through each contraction. The fear didn't hit her until the frenzied pace died down and she was settled in a hospital bed. His parents were in the waiting room, the nurse left to get the doctor, and it was just her, John, and a baby on the way.

In that moment, panic crushed down on her like a mountain. Clutching his hand, she squeezed as tight as she could.

"Okay," he said. "Just breathe."

She shook her head. No. This wasn't a contraction. This was the worst sense of fear she'd ever known. "I can't do this," she whispered. "I can't be a mother. I don't know how."

The terror on his face eased into that smile he seemed to save for her. Smoothing her hair back, he did his best to calm her. "Are you crazy? You're going to be the best mama anybody's ever had. Just look at how you take care of me. Look how good you are to me. You're going to be an amazing mother. You're going to be the best. The absolute best."

She panted as another contraction tightened her entire body. "Oh, God. It hurts."

Cradling her to him as much as he could, John coached and soothed and kissed her head until the pain eased. Her pain and fear didn't go away, but having him there made it all much more bearable. Nobody could comfort her like John. Nobody made her feel as brave as he did. He seemed to always know the right things to say; he said everything she needed to hear right when she needed to hear it.

As she gave that final push, as their baby came into the world, the amazement on his face made it all worth it. There he stood, her husband, holding a tiny little bundle as tears fell from his eyes. He looked at Caroline as if she'd given him the world. In that moment, it was all worth it.

She collapsed back on the pile of pillows. If she were honest, her relief wasn't from giving birth or hearing her daughter cry for the first time. She'd been scared, deep down in a place she had ignored, that John wouldn't be there. That he wouldn't be the father he promised or the husband she needed. But there, in his eyes, in that moment he was everything she needed him to be.

She should have known it wouldn't last.

She had hoped he'd spend both nights with her in the hospital, but on the second night of her stay, Frannie suggested he go home to rest and make sure everything was in order. Caroline was hesitant to let him leave, not because she needed his help—she had her mother-in-law and great nurses—but because she knew where he'd go. He wouldn't get things in order. He wouldn't even go home. He'd go straight to the pub.

When he didn't answer her phone call to say good night, she swallowed her doubt, telling herself to trust him. Then he didn't answer her call to say good morning. Or her call to let him know she and Katie were being released and his mother had gone home to rest. She'd needed him to pick her up. He didn't answer when she was released and was handed a newborn but had nowhere to go. And he didn't answer when she called twice after that.

Two hours after being released, Caroline still sat in a wheelchair with her daughter waiting for her husband. A nurse, *with so much pity in her eyes Caroline nearly cried, suggested she call someone else. Caroline nodded and dialed Frannie and Mark's number. Thankfully, Frannie had thought ahead and bought a car seat for their car. She figured she'd be spending a lot of time with her new granddaughter and didn't want the hassle of switching car seats all the time. Mark drove Caroline and the baby home, but they didn't say much.*

She didn't want him to know how hurt and angry she was. When they got to the apartment and found John asleep on the couch, she excused John's bad behavior. Like she always did. She convinced Mark that everything was fine. That she was fine, and John was fine, and Katie was fine, and everything was fine. She sent him on his way and stared at her husband, sitting there in the same clothes he'd worn the day before, looking dazed and confused and...hungover.

She didn't have the energy to fight. She put Katie in her crib, locked herself in the bathroom, and tried to convince herself this wasn't the horrible omen she knew it was.

———

Carol leaned back as the waiter took her near empty plate and offered dessert. She passed on his suggestion of raspberry cheesecake. She'd stuffed herself on lobster and crab ravioli while John occasionally glanced at her plate with a hint of disgust in his eyes. He was never one for seafood. He stuck with his tried-and-true medium-rare steak, baked potato, and green beans. Being with him again really was like stepping back in time. He hadn't changed all that much in the last twenty-plus years.

Leaning on the table, he gave her that boyish lopsided grin. "What are you thinking?"

"That you are pretty much the exact same person you were when we met."

"No." His smile faded. "I'm nothing like him."

"I didn't mean it as a jab. I mean, you still look the same, you still eat the same, you still use some of the same phrases. Sometimes it feels like nothing's changed."

"If we hadn't split up, we'd be closing in on thirty-three years together."

Bulging her eyes, she did the math, confirming his statement. "*Wow*. That makes me feel old."

His grin returned. "You're as beautiful now as you were then."

"Aww. You're as handsome. And charming. And... emotionally manipulative."

"Ouch."

They laughed as she raised her eyebrows, confirming her assessment.

"We should have someone take a picture before we leave," he said. "We don't have a single photo from our trip."

"We'll ask someone on our way out." She was sipping her wine when the waiter handed the bill to John. She set her glass down and reached across the table. "I've got it."

John pulled the check closer, looking offended. "I asked you to dinner. My treat."

She opened her mouth to argue. The restaurant wasn't in his budget, but he liked to remind her whenever he paid for something that he might as well spend his money while he could.

"Thank you," she said instead.

He stuffed cash in the black check presenter and put his hands to the table for balance as he stood. His movements had been more deliberate all day. She stood as well, waiting for him to round the table. When he did, he clutched her arm.

"Okay?" she asked before taking a step.

"Yeah. A little lightheaded. It'll pass." He closed his eyes as if to give his head a few seconds to stop spinning. "I'm good."

Sliding her hand in his, she guided him around the tables to the exit. As she'd suggested, they stopped at the maître d' stand and asked the young woman to take their photo before leaving. John hugged her close, until he was pressing his cheek to her head. To the outside world, they probably looked like just another couple having a nice dinner.

Like always, the truth was much darker and more depressing than they let on to those around them.

Stepping out into the temperate Seattle evening, she was surprised at the contentment that filled her. The weather was a bit cooler than she was used to, but she loved the lack of humidity in the air. Houston was like a sauna in June. Sometimes she found the hot air too hard to breathe. Pulling her hand from John's, she started to open her purse. "I'll call for a car."

"Not yet. Let's take a walk."

"Are you up for it?"

"Sure. Are you?"

She nodded. "Yeah."

They made it half a block before he pointed to an ice cream parlor, reminding her he still owed her dessert for the day at the beach when he hadn't been up for the treat.

Though she wasn't really up for it now, she let him steer her that way.

John ordered a scoop of strawberry, one of chocolate, and nuts on top. He turned to her, silently asking what she wanted.

"Just get two spoons," she instructed instead of ordering something for herself.

They continued their walk, sharing the treat and taking in the scenes of downtown Seattle.

"I like it here," she said after a while.

"Yeah?"

She stared up at the buildings surrounding them. "The weather and the atmosphere. This is nice. Serene."

"You should move here."

"I've got a few more years before I can retire."

Tossing the now empty container in the trash, John said, "Don't wait, Caroline. Trust me. You don't want to wait to start living again. If you like it here, you should move. Give it a try. The worst that can happen is you change your mind and leave."

"You make it sound easy."

"It is." Stepping in front of her, blocking her way, he held her gaze. "What do you have in Houston that is worth putting off doing what you want?"

"Well, for starters, I have a job and a house."

"Is that enough?"

Lifting a brow, she smirked. "Aren't you the one who always told me a good job and a nice house should be enough?"

Her teasing didn't budge the sternness in his eyes. "Yes. And you were the one who said there was nothing wrong with wanting more. You were right. Like always. What are you going to do when this trip is over? When you go home, what are you going to do with your life? Sit in your office and read reports all day?"

"My work is important."

"I didn't say it wasn't. But does it make you happy?"

She opened her mouth, but the answer stuck in her throat. She would have said yes a month ago. A week ago. She wouldn't have hesitated. Now she couldn't bring herself to say the word.

"You told me earlier today that I should have let you go. I should have lived my life," John said. "You were right. I should have. I didn't want to, but I should have. You may not want to let Tobias go and move forward, but you should. He'd want you to. Wouldn't he? He'd want you to be happy. I didn't even know him, but I believe that."

"Yes, he'd want that."

"So do I. I want you to live the rest of your life *living*. Not hanging on to the past or trying to reach some expectation your parents pounded into your head from the day you were born. You should eat the ice cream. Move to a new city. Start a new adventure."

She laughed tenderly. "Easy for you to say. You aren't sticking around to see me fail."

"Who cares if you fail? Failing means you tried, right?"

"I don't want to talk about this, John. This is depressing."

She started around him, but he stepped in her way.

"You know what's depressing? Standing at the finish line and realizing there's no going back. There're no do-overs. When it's done, it's done. I had everything. I had the world in my hands, and I pissed it away. You have no idea how much I wish I could go back." Cupping her head, he put his forehead to hers the way he used to. "Jesus Christ, I wish I could go back. I wish I could take everything back and do it right. I'd still have you. We'd still have Katie. I'd have been the husband you deserved. The father I should have been. I'd be better. I swear."

"I know," she said, because she believed him. Spending time with him now, she believed he would have tried harder if he knew then what he knew now. "That doesn't mean anything would have changed, John."

"Maybe not, but at least I could look back and know I had tried my damnedest." He pulled her even closer, wrapping his arms around her. "You don't want to feel like this when you get to the end. You don't want to look back and regret every goddamned day of your life." Leaning back, he searched her eyes. "Promise me. Promise me you won't go home and live the same day over and over when I'm gone."

She heaved a sigh. "Okay. I promise."

"You're saying that to appease me, aren't you?" Rolling his eyes, he dropped his hands from her. "You never were very good at keeping promises, anyway."

"Oh my God. You really think you have room to talk about broken promises? *Really*?"

His laughter rang out as he put his arm around her shoulder and they started down the street again.

TEN

CAROL TIGHTENED her grip on the steering wheel when John pushed himself up again. He'd been restless all day, leaving her nerves on edge. She continually glanced in the mirror, watching him pace. He'd open the fridge, scan the contents, slam it and walk to the bed. Then he'd sit at the table, stare out the window, and get up and pace again.

"What's going on, John?" she asked.

Dropping into the passenger seat, John narrowed his eyes as he glowered at her, making his agitation clear. "You're a liar."

Glancing at him, she pressed her lips together, choosing not to remind him of his years of practice in that department. "Oh, yeah?"

"I'm a cop, Caroline." His voice turned hard and filled with accusation. "I know how to read people."

"Is that so?"

"Who is he?"

She stared at him longer than was probably safe considering she was driving a motorhome along the highway.

Traffic grew heavier with every mile closer to Spokane they traveled. Swallowing, she focused on driving. "You're getting confused. You need to go rest."

Shaking his head, he slammed his hand into the dashboard.

"Hey!" Seeing an exit ahead, she moved to the right lane. By the time she pulled into a gas station and parked, he was pacing again. Turning off the ignition, she left the keys dangling as she unbuckled and turned her chair.

He took the four steps needed to cross the small area, turned, and took more steps, muttering the entire time. Agitation was a side effect of his tumor—he'd snapped at her more than once for no reason—but this was the first time she'd seen his temper this flared up. She wasn't sure what to do. Probably let him go, let the episode play out, but then he turned to her and her heart lurched in her chest. He looked completely broken inside.

"I love you," he said as tears filled his eyes. "Why can't you understand how much I love you?"

"Get in bed, John."

Shaking his head, he begged with the look in his eyes. "Who is he? Just tell me who he is before you leave. You owe me that much."

"Get in bed. You need to rest."

"Fuck you." He started for the side door.

Jumping up, she blocked his way. "No! You're not leaving."

Psychotic episodes and bouts of dementia were inevitable. Dr. Collins had warned her about this possibility when he'd pulled her into his office to try to talk her out of this trip. He'd warned that John could become violent and if he did, he'd have to be put on antipsychotic meds and possibly hospitalized. For her safety. That was what Dr. Collins had said. She'd have to have John admitted for *her* safety. She didn't fear John, even as he stood there scowling at her. They had years of practice manipulating each other. They had a lifetime of pressing each other's buttons. She didn't need antipsychotic meds to control him.

"Don't leave me, John," she whispered, putting her hands to his cheeks. "Please. Don't leave me."

The edge of his anger visibly slipped away as she brushed her thumbs over his cheeks. Dropping back to his seat at the table, he rested his elbows on the top and pressed the balls of his palms into his eyes. "My head hurts."

"I know. You need to rest."

Lowering his hands, he met her eyes, looking at her like she'd somehow crushed his soul. "Are you cheating on me, Caroline?"

She shook her head. "No."

"Are you going to leave me?"

"No."

Grabbing her hands, he squeezed them tight. "I need you. You know that, right? I can't get through this life without you."

"I know."

"I don't make things easy for you. I don't mean to be difficult. You gave up so much to marry me. I know that. I know. I'll make it up to you. I promise. Things will get better. Just don't leave me, okay?"

"I'm not leaving."

He toyed with her wedding ring before bringing her hand to his lips and kissing her knuckles. "I love you."

"I know."

"My head hurts."

She offered him a small smile. "You've had a long day. You should get in bed. Get some sleep."

His eyes caught on hers for a few heartbeats before he finally nodded. Easing from the table, he moved to the bed. She sat, making sure he stayed there, before grabbing her phone. She started to call Dr. Collins, but hesitated.

If John heard her whispering into the phone right now, he might fall back into his delusion. The call could wait. She'd leave a message for the doctor after they stopped for the night. Sinking into the driver's seat, she started the engine and got back on the highway. The sooner this trip ended, the better.

For both of them.

———

Caroline swallowed hard. This was her last chance. She had no doubt Eve, the head nurse, meant it this time. No more warnings. No more forgiveness. The next time Caroline was even one minute late, she was fired.

Everyone in the pediatric unit knew the score. They all knew John was a worthless drunk and Caroline tolerated him for reasons no one could understand, though they'd never said it bluntly. She tried to hide it, but the gossipers had caught wind as to why she was always late. Now everyone knew. She couldn't let Katie stay home alone, and it was too far to drive her to her grandparents' house. And her husband was always out drinking.

"Get a sitter," Eve said, no longer trying to be sympathetic to Caroline's problems.

She nodded. "I've been looking—"

"Stop looking. Find one or find another job."

"Okay."

Eve's eyes softened, but only a touch. "It's not fair to the nurses who have to cover for you."

"I know. I won't be late again." Lowering her head as she walked away, she hoped to hide her quivering lip.

She turned into the first vacant room, closed the door behind her, and slipped into the bathroom. Leaning against the sink, she let go of the tears she'd been fighting since the confrontation with her boss started. Mostly because she knew this was the end of her career. She would be late again. It was only a matter of time, because John had had a fit the last time she'd hired a sitter. He didn't want a stranger looking after Katie. He promised he'd be home on time.

He always promised. He never delivered.

"Hey," a voice said from the bathroom door. Simon Miller, the pediatric pulmonologist who always seemed to be on duty, stepped into the small space and pulled her to him. He didn't say anything as she melted into his embrace. He didn't promise everything was going to be okay. Doctors didn't make false promises like her husband.

He simply held her until she could control her sobbing and then let her step back.

Caroline kept her face down, muttering an apology as she snagged several rough tissues from the box on the sink. She wiped her eyes and nose and snuffled back as much mucus as she could. "I should quit."

"Is that what you want?"

"No. I don't want to get fired, either. Eve's right, it's not fair to everyone else. I just... I don't know what to do anymore. I don't know what to do, but I can't keep letting John drag me down."

She ran her hand over her hair and let out an audible breath. Lifting her face, she was expecting some kind of confirmation from him, but the look in his eyes was anything but understanding of her situation. The intensity in his stare was something she'd seen time and time again since he'd come to the hospital eight months prior.

Whenever she caught him watching her, which was frequently, the world seemed to stop spinning. She had to give them both credit. They'd resisted the pull for months, but standing there, feeling downtrodden, something in her broke. She couldn't do this anymore. She couldn't keep lying to herself that her marriage was more than a façade held together by her determination to not break up Katie's home.

The last little bit of loyalty she had to her husband shattered in that moment. Not only because of the trouble he'd caused her time and time again, but because Simon Miller's desire for her was plainly written on his face. She needed that. She needed to be wanted. She practically threw herself at him. He was right there, meeting her in the middle to catch her.

Their mouths crashed together, and all her troubles disappeared.

Caroline never would have considered herself the kind to commit adultery—she'd always prided herself on her ethics—but John had worn her down to the point that she simply didn't care anymore. She couldn't care. The latest lecture she'd received from her boss was the last blow her soul could take. She was broken.

John had broken her. She needed something—just one thing—that felt right in her life. Having a handsome and successful man desire her was a pretty good start.

Pulling away from the kiss, she licked her lips. She wanted

189

that man more than she could ever remember wanting John. That said a lot considering how enraptured she'd been with him when they'd started dating.

Simon brushed his hand over her hair. "You have no idea how long I've wanted to do that."

"Me too."

Awkward silence fell between them. She was married. They worked together. Too many things were wrong with what was happening. Still, he put his hands on her hips, drawing her against him, and she forgot all the reasons she shouldn't let him. Wrapping her arms around his neck, she kissed him again, slowly this time, savoring the feel of his mouth working against hers.

He smelled like a doctor—like rubbing alcohol and soap— and his breath was fresh and his mouth sweet. Nothing like John. Nothing like the bitter taste of beer he left on her tongue that made her want to gag.

She rarely let John kiss her anymore, but when she did, she pulled away from him as quickly as she could. She wanted to never stop kissing Simon. She wanted to taste him forever, but that wasn't possible.

"We should talk about this," he whispered. "Someplace private so no one can eavesdrop."

Guilt punched her gut. "If I meet you someplace private, I'm going to do more than kiss you."

He cupped her face, lifted her chin, and looked into her eyes. "I hope so." Frowning when the pager on his hip went off, he read the screen as she bit her lip. "Gotta go. I'll write down my address for you later."

Her stomach dropped as a mixture of fear and excitement hit

her like a lightning bolt. She should tell him no, but the word didn't even come close to forming on her tongue.

He turned toward the door, but then stopped and looked at her. "I want to make one thing very clear, Caroline."

There it was. The catch. The small print. The inevitable disappointment.

The intensity returned to Simon's eyes as he stared at her. "You're amazing. You're beautiful. Your job is important. You are important. You deserve someone in your life who makes you feel that way every single day."

Her smile returned as he left her standing there, letting his affirmations soak in. An hour later, she was scribbling in a chart when Simon stopped at her side. To anyone else, it might seem he was reading over her shoulder, but as he pointed to something on the chart, he dropped a slip of paper, said, "I'll understand if you don't show," and walked way.

She didn't react then, but before she put the chart away, she tucked his address into her pocket. Walking straight to the restroom, she locked herself in a stall and pulled the paper from her pocket to read his address over and over until she had it memorized. When the apartment number and street address were cemented to her brain, she flushed the paper and any evidence that he'd ever given it to her.

She was torn the rest of the night, not sure what she should do. When her shift ended and she climbed behind the steering wheel of her car, she sat for at least ten minutes, wrestling with her emotions.

She loved John. Not like she had five years ago, but she loved him. He was the father of her child. He wasn't all bad. But his drinking. God, his drinking was taking over their lives. Anytime she tried to point that out, she got excuses and guilt trips and fights. She couldn't do it anymore. She couldn't fight with him one more time about the beer, the hangovers, the cancelled plans, her consistent tardiness to work.

She couldn't fight him one more time. She was damned tired.

Being with Simon, even at the hospital, was a reprieve from that. The stress of her life evaporated when she was at work, but most especially when she got to work with Simon. He was a fantastic doctor, compassionate and understanding with his patients. He put the kids at ease and calmed frightened parents.

She'd been with him when he lost a patient, not long after he started at the hospital. He'd damn near broken down. Not all doctors did that, not all doctors let themselves feel the loss of patients. Simon had felt the loss deeply, and that had moved her. She felt connected to him in a way she'd never felt connected to John. That connection was pulling her in. That connection seemed to be the only good thing in her life some days—besides Katie, of course. Katie would always be the light in her life.

But Simon... Simon was a beacon in her storm, offering her warmth and comfort. Something she desperately needed.

The internal battled ended, and she started the car and steered it toward an apartment complex a few blocks from the hospital.

———

Caroline was walking down the hospital corridor when someone rushed behind her, gently gripping her hips and steering her toward the stairwell. She instantly smiled and complied with the unspoken directive. Simon reached around her, opened the door, and nudged her through. She turned and caught his mouth with hers before the door had even closed. He hugged her close as she parted her lips, letting him deepen the kiss.

He backed her to the wall as his lips broke from hers. "Hi."

"You're going to get us caught." She intended for her warning to sound dire, but she was winded from his kiss, making her voice sound as husky as it did when he was making love to her.

"I don't care." He leaned in, tilting his head as he moved toward her neck.

She put her hand to his chest to stop him. "Easy for you to say. It's the nurse who always gets fired, Dr. Miller."

"What would they do if we were both doctors?"

"What?"

He held up a key ring, dangling it between them.

Her smile faded to confusion. She watched light dance off the flat edges before looking back at him. "I already have a key to your apartment."

"Yes, and I'm going to need that back. This is a key to our new place."

She didn't point out that he'd given her partial ownership of his new living space. "I didn't know you were moving."

"I didn't want to say anything until it was a done deal. I bought a house. For us, Caroline. For you and me and Katie."

Her heart dropped. "What?"

"I'm tired of talking about the future we could have. I want it. I want everything we've dreamed about. You should be a doctor, like you've always wanted. Katie should have a stable home. I'm moving in this weekend. You and Katie can move in whenever you're ready." He put the key in her palm and wrapped her fingers around it. Bringing her hand to his mouth, he kissed her knuckles. "The address is on the key ring. Stop on your way home to take a look around. You're going to love it."

He disappeared, and she stood staring at the key as if she hadn't a clue what to do with it. Countless mornings, after their shifts ended, they'd sit in a coffee shop or head for his apartment and talk about what the future held. Countless mornings, they made plans that seemed like faraway dreams that she'd never see come true.

Now she had a key to their house. Their future. And she was terrified.

She did as he suggested and took a detour on her way home. The neighborhood was peaceful with meticulously cared-for lawns. The houses weren't huge but were significantly larger than the one she and John had purchased—and were on the verge of losing thanks to their never-ending battle of the budget. She'd left Married...With Children territory and gone straight into an episode of Growing Pains. That felt damn good. That felt right.

This was a neighborhood she could see Katie growing up in. Pulling into the driveway next to a SOLD sign, she laughed. The white-and-gray brick ranch had a two-car garage that was far too nice for her scratch-and-dent silver-and-black '78 Challenger. Big red bows adorned two rocking chairs that beckoned her to sit as soon as she stepped foot on the porch. She had no doubt Simon had put them there for her.

How many times had they sat on his balcony looking directly into the building across the street as she told him how someday she'd have a nice front porch with a rocking chair where she could watch Katie ride her bike?

Using the key Simon had handed her, Caroline unlocked the front door and stepped into the tiled entryway. Clean, plush carpet surrounded the space where she stopped and slipped her shoes off so she didn't dirty the carpet. The living room spread into a dining area that was adjacent to a countertop separating the rest of the room from the kitchen.

She would be able to cook dinner and see Katie no matter where she was in the living area. Off to one side were two bedrooms separated by a bathroom. On the other side of the house sat a large master suite with sliding glass doors out to a patio and a bathroom that was about the size of Caroline's current bedroom.

The house was perfect. Absolutely perfect. Simon couldn't have found a house more fitting for the image Caroline had always had.

Returning to the kitchen, she ran her hand over the white tiled countertop, stopping when she found a stack of papers. Simon had scribbled a note in his terrible handwriting, but she'd become accustomed to reading doctors' chicken scratch.

Classes start soon! Better get on it, Dr. Caroline.

Beneath his note was an application to Wright State University.

She swallowed hard. This was it. This was the life she was meant to have. The life she'd given up the moment she'd found out she was pregnant. She always knew she'd get back on track and find her way to medical school somehow, but she'd never calculated Simon into the equation.

Accepting what Simon was offering meant leaving John. Leaving John meant tearing Katie's world apart. Though Caroline had always known she and John wouldn't last forever, she'd somehow convinced herself she could stay long enough for Katie to grow up.

Only recently, she'd started to realize she couldn't. If she stayed, she was going to lose her job. She was never going to go to medical school. She'd always be stuck in a financial rut. She'd always be fighting John to survive.

No, she couldn't stay. Not any longer. She was ready. She was ready to give herself and Katie the future they should have. She should do it now, while Katie was still young enough to recover from her parents' divorce. While Caroline was still young enough to go to school and start a career and maybe, if Simon wanted, have a few more children that she and John would never be able to afford to have.

Yeah. Oh, yeah, she was ready. Taking a pen out of her pocket, she scribbled on the note that she couldn't wait to start their life together.

She took the long way home. Playing over in her mind how she was going to tell John. What she was going to tell John. Not that she really needed an excuse to leave him. He had given her plenty of those. She hated giving up. She'd never been good at knowing when to let go. Honestly, she should have walked out on John when he'd abandoned her on their wedding night. Or when he'd failed to show up the day after Katie was born. Or a thousand times after that. She'd never had the courage, but knowing Simon was going to be there to help her land on her feet made all the difference in the world.

She wouldn't have to ask her parents for help. She wouldn't have to listen to the "we told you so" lecture they were dying to give her. She could pretend she didn't see their disapproving looks, as long as she didn't have to ask them for help. She wouldn't. Simon would take care of her.

After settling the fear in her stomach, she drove home. She walked in, ready for the fight, ready to tell him she was done with their sham of a marriage. She stepped inside and her *decision was cemented when she was met by the sound of retching from the back of the house.*

"Goddamn it." She'd seen this play out far too many times. He'd stayed up drinking all night, had probably put Katie to bed and had friends over for a poker game that he had no business hosting while his daughter was sleeping in the next room.

Caroline stuck her head into Katie's room, but the bed was empty. John retched again, drawing Caroline's attention. Moving to the bathroom, she found him with his head in the toilet while Katie stood next to him in her nightgown and the bright red boots that had replaced her security blanket, running her little hand over his back as tears ran down her cheeks.

"It's okay, Daddy. It's okay."

"Hey," Caroline called, disrupting Katie's mantra.

Katie looked up and the relief in her eyes was like a wave crashing on the shore. "Daddy's sick, Mama."

Rage flashed through Caroline. That son of a bitch had sunk so low his five-year-old was nursing him through his hangover. Then John rolled his head to her, and Caroline realized he wasn't sick from liquor. A stomach bug had been going around and apparently had struck the Bowman household while Caroline was at work...or dreaming of a new life without her husband. Putting her hand to his head, she checked his temperature. He was hot as hell.

She pulled Katie from the bathroom and squatted down to look at her face to face. "Thank you for taking care of him."

She sniffled. "I gave him water and a wet washrag like you do when I get sick."

"Good job, big girl. How are you feeling? Feeling bad in the tummy?"

"No."

"*Throat hurt?*"

"*Uh-uh.*"

"*How's your head?*"

"*Okay.*"

"*Good. I want you to do me a big favor and go take a shower. Wash your hands and face real good, the way I taught you, okay?*"

Katie nodded and rushed off toward her bathroom. Moving back to where John was leaning against the tub, Caroline frowned, but he looked up at her as if she were an angel.

He reached for her and she closed the distance between them, ready to help him to his feet, but he wrapped his arm around her leg and leaned his sweaty forehead to her thigh. "Jesus, I'm sick. I thought you'd never get home."

She ruffled his hair. "It's okay. I'm here now. You're going to be all right." She'd take care of him. She'd done that a hundred times before, but usually the smell of bile and beer filled the room instead of the sick stench that was in the air now.

She helped him stand, got him to bed, and went in search of a thermometer. She slipped it into his mouth and ran her hand over his head. He closed his eyes and visibly calmed at the feel of her touch. He always seemed to be soothed by her touch, as if knowing she was with him was all he needed in the world.

Caroline sighed. She couldn't very well tell him she was leaving him when he was this sick. That'd be mean. What was she supposed to do, pack her bag in between his bouts of vomiting?

No. It'd keep. She'd get him healthy, and then she'd leave him. She actually heard Simon's voice ringing in her mind as she put her fingers to John's wrist to check his pulse.

"You always have an excuse to stay," he'd told her over and

over. He was right. She always had a reason to stay. This was different. John was sick. She couldn't walk out on him when he was ill.

Taking the beeping thermometer from John's mouth, she frowned at the number on the screen. This wasn't an excuse. This was real. She'd leave him when he got better. Offering him a weak smile when he whispered her name, she put her hand to his chest to soothe him as she always did.

———

Less than four months later, Caroline stared at Katie's urn. She hadn't slept in weeks. Every time she closed her eyes, she saw Katie's limp body lying in a hospital bed.

John had gone to bed though. He wanted to be well rested for the trip he intended to take. Katie's list was still on the fridge. Caroline hadn't had the heart to take it down after her daughter's death. Sometimes John read it over and over for what seemed to be hours on end. When she finally asked why, he insisted they were going. They were taking that trip. They were going to leave little bits of Katie behind at every stop.

"She wanted to go to all these places, and we're taking her," he said. "I promised her we would."

John and his goddamned promises.

Caroline hadn't argued, mostly because she didn't have an ounce of fight left in her. When the box had arrived, John had opened it. She couldn't see through her tears as he carefully unwrapped the urn. She only knew it was silver with a pink teddy bear engraved in one side and Katie's name and dates of birth and death on the other.

KATHRYN ELIZABETH BOWMAN
BORN JUNE 5, 1989
DIED JUNE 22, 1995

Caroline had sat and sobbed. John had run his fingertips back and forth across Katie's name.

"We should pack now," he said, breaking the silence. "We'll leave in the morning. I have it all mapped out."

She didn't respond. She couldn't. He set Katie's ashes on the table and went to their bedroom. Half an hour later, he came out with two suitcases.

"I packed your bag. Get some sleep, Caroline."

She sat, playing the morning of Katie's death on repeat until she knew what she had to do. She couldn't let John leave Katie alone in all those places. She couldn't leave her daughter scattered in the wind. She'd failed Katie when she was alive—she wouldn't fail her now.

Grabbing the urn and her purse, she took the suitcase John had packed for her and a few of Katie's favorite things. She stared at Katie's favorite red boots. Katie had worn those every day. She'd loved those boots. Caroline started to reach for them, but stopped and grabbed Katie's teddy bear instead. Then she left. Without a word to him. Without a plan. With nowhere to go. She just took Katie and left.

Which was what she should have done years ago.

———

The campground in Missoula was probably one of the nicest they'd stopped at. Carol left John sleeping in the RV and went to the community building to take her stress out on the treadmill. She hadn't run nearly as much in the last ten days as she should have. She was tired and beat down, not only from taking care of John but from spending so much time behind the steering wheel.

She and Tobias had always shared driving duty, allowing the other to stretch and rest. Being the sole captain of this ship was taking a toll on her. The never-ending stroll down memory lane wasn't helping either. Her emotions were drained. She felt as if she were teetering on the edge of a breakdown from being forced to relive all her past mistakes. Mistakes that had cost her far too much.

She hadn't thought of Simon in years, but as her feet pounded on the belt that went round and round as she ran, she could practically hear his voice in her mind. How many times had that man begged her to leave John? How many times had he said she didn't have to worry about finances? How many times had he promised to take good care of her and Katie? He'd given her the perfect out, and she'd turned her back on it.

Why?

Why hadn't she packed her and Katie's bags and walked out of that shithole house she and John had lived in and right into the beautiful home Simon had offered?

Because she'd loved John. Despite his drinking. Despite his immaturity. Despite all his many faults, she'd loved him more than he ever deserved. He had a way of looking at her that made her feel like she was the most amazing thing in the world. He had a way of making Katie smile that made Carol's heart swell with so much love she thought it might explode.

When the Bowmans had good times, they were so good Carol could forget the all-too-frequent bad times.

And while Simon had been a wonderful man, and his intense gaze stirred a longing deep inside of her, he'd never once made her feel like she was everything to him. John could do that with nothing more than a glance. The lust she had for Simon, the longing she had for the life he offered her, wasn't strong enough to tear her from whatever hold John had over her.

What a goddamned fool she'd been.

That was exactly what Simon had told her when she'd explained she couldn't leave John.

"You're going to regret this, Caroline," Simon had told her.

Boy, had she. When she'd gone to the hospital to tell them she was quitting, that she couldn't stay in Dayton now that Katie was gone, he'd pulled her into a room. She expected him to tell her that if she'd left when he wanted her to, Katie would still be alive. God knew she'd told herself that a hundred times over the last few weeks.

But he hadn't. Simon was better than that. He was kinder than that. He'd taken her hands and kissed her forehead and asked what he could do for her. She'd fallen against his chest and cried. She had no idea how long he'd held her, but when he eventually eased his hold on her, she told him she was running away. She didn't have a plan beyond getting on the highway and driving.

He told her that his house in St. Louis was still for sale. He offered to call the real estate agent and request they take it off the market and give Caroline the keys. He even offered to call the hospital where he had worked and see if there were any open positions.

He'd taken care of her, like he'd promised he would. He'd given her the fresh start he'd told her he was going to give her while they were lovers. Unfortunately, she'd waited too long to accept his offer; her fresh start was with nothing but memories and ashes.

When she arrived in St. Louis, she had a home and a job and a new life.

In the end, she'd repaid him by mailing him his key and a thank-you note when she and Tobias moved in together. She might have deserved more than John, but Simon definitely deserved more than her. He'd given her the means to get back on her feet. All she'd ever done for him was a few months of passionate sex and empty dreams of a future she never had the courage to pursue.

Hopping off the treadmill, she used a towel to wipe the sweat from her forehead and caught her strained reflection in the mirror. She never did deserve Simon. Or Tobias. Hell, maybe she'd been wrong all along. Maybe she *did* deserve John.

She hadn't exactly been as compassionate to him as she could have been. Then or now. No matter their past, no matter how jaded she felt, the father of her child was slipping away right in front of her. He needed her now as much as he had then, and she'd spent so much time over the last ten days sitting in judgment of him for mistakes that were decades old. As if she were innocent.

She stretched and showered before making her way back to the motorhome. Back to John.

He smiled from the swing that had been built into the lot provided by the park. She was reminded of their first stop in Texas, when he'd admired the stars while she resented his very existence.

Dropping her bag, she sat next to him. "I'm sorry."

"For what?"

"For everything. For making our marriage more difficult than it had to be. For leaving without telling you. For blaming you for every moment of misery I've ever had in my life. I'm sorry. For everything."

Putting his arm around her, he curled his fingers into her damp hair and pulled her head closer. He kissed her temple. "I'm sorry too, kiddo." They sat quietly for a few minutes before he spoke again. "I don't know what that was about earlier. I'm not sure where that episode came from. Guess I'm getting worse, huh?"

She nodded.

"It's true, though, isn't it? You were planning to leave me for someone else."

She debated how to answer. "No. I did have an affair. It was brief, but intense. He was a doctor. He bought a house for us. He told me I could quit work and go back to school full-time and be there for Katie. He said he'd support us and take care of us. He offered everything I had ever wanted on a big ol' silver platter. But I loved you, John. No matter how miserable we made each other, I loved you so much and every time I found a reason to leave you, I found a bigger reason to stay." She focused on the ring on her hand—the one Tobias had put there. "I don't think I was running from you when I left. I think I was running from myself. From my own guilt and shame. I think all this hatred I've aimed at you all these years is a reflection of how I feel about myself. Things didn't have to be the way they were."

"I was a high-functioning alcoholic, Caroline. You couldn't have changed that."

"No. However, I could have helped you get treatment. I

could have fought for us. I didn't have to be as angry and selfish as I was."

He put his hand on hers, stopping her from fiddling with her ring. "We were kids."

"How long are you going to tell yourself that?"

"Probably just for the next few weeks or so."

She lifted her eyes to his, instantly horrified, but then he flashed her a grin and she chuckled. "You're awful."

"I know. I don't want to live the rest of my life rehashing our mistakes."

"Isn't that why you sought me out? You wanted to put this to rest, right?"

"For my own peace of mind, not to hurt you more than I have already."

"I hurt you, too," she admitted. "I've felt guilty about that for too long. I don't want to feel like this anymore, John. I'm tired of feeling like my heart and soul are being torn apart. I need it to stop."

"We both made mistakes. We were young and inexperienced at life. We aren't those people anymore. We wouldn't make those mistakes again. We grew. We learned. That's what life is about. Let go of the guilt and the blame and accept that you're better now."

Staring up at the sky, she considered the mistakes she'd made. "As soon as our divorce was final, I did everything in my power to erase you from my memory. Tobias and I were together for over a year before I even told him about you and Katie. He understood. He said he couldn't imagine how difficult it must have been to go through what I had. I told him how horrible you were, how much Katie and I had suffered at your hands. Never once did I tell him that I'd been so cold to you that I gave myself frostbite sometimes. I never told him I'd had an affair. I never told him how hard you tried to make me happy." She swallowed when her voice cracked. "I made you out to be a monster to justify my actions. You weren't a monster. You were a drunk. You were irresponsible. But you loved us, and you never meant to hurt Katie." She squeezed his hand. "Even though it was an accident, I had to blame you because I felt guilty about everything else."

He hugged her closer. "Let it go. None of that matters now."

"Doesn't it?"

"No, it really doesn't. What matters is the here and now. I'm dying, Caroline. We're out of time. The only thing that matters is what we do before I'm gone. We have to make peace now so we can say goodbye to our daughter. The past is the past. This, right now, this is what matters. This is what Katie would have wanted. I forgive you," he said. "For whatever mistakes you made. I forgive you. It would mean a lot if you could forgive me."

She swallowed. "I...I'm working on it."

The silence between them was heavy for a moment, but then he chuckled. "Fair enough."

ELEVEN

"EASY," Carol warned as John stumbled down the RV steps. Grabbing his shoulder, she did her best to stabilize him as he took the last, longer step to the ground. Slipping under his arm, she supported him as they walked to the rock wall that separated tourists from the never-ending drop that overlooked one of the many views Yellowstone had to offer. He pulled Carol closer as they stared out at the valley. Though it wasn't John's first or second choice, the spot was perfect.

Initially, he had wanted to release Katie's ashes at the Grand Prismatic Spring, but Carol convinced him he'd never make the walk. Though the trail was a somewhat level and well-kept boardwalk, the distance was more than he could handle. His second choice was Old Faithful. He said they could let her go as the geyser was gushing. Carol had shaken her head before he even finished making the suggestion. He still would have had to walk from the parking lot, through the museum, and out to the geyser. She didn't think he could make it, and she couldn't carry him that far.

He was disappointed, but hadn't put up too much of a fight, which she thought said more about his waning condition than his obvious fatigue and thinning face. Instead, she'd started driving and pulled off at a random spot. As with any stop in Yellowstone, the sights before them were breathtaking.

A waterfall in the distance had cut through a mountain, making the earth dip down to a valley below. Evergreens shot up, reaching for the sky on either side of the river. The distant water rushing over rocks had a quiet but distinct sound. The moment was one of the most peaceful that she'd had since starting their trip.

"Look at that." His voice filled with the awe that only witnessing a miracle of nature could bring. "Isn't that amazing?"

"It is."

"This is perfect. She'd love this."

Taking his arm from around her, John pulled the little container from his pocket and worked to remove the lid, giving Katie some of the facts he'd researched about Yellowstone. Serenity washed over Carol as the ash scattered on the breeze and disappeared. This was the first time she'd watched the ashes leave that she hadn't felt some sense of failure as a mother. This was the first time the ashes didn't carry some of her guilt along with them.

She was at peace here. She was calm. She wasn't thinking in the back of her mind how she wouldn't be standing there if John hadn't been such a worthless drunk. She wasn't blaming him. She was simply here, in the moment, coming to terms with the loss of her daughter.

She jolted when a flock of birds left the trees below. She watched them rise up to the sky, flapping desperately as they took flight.

"There she is," John whispered. "She's right there. With the birds."

Carol felt it, too. Something was different this time. Something in her heart and her mind and her soul felt lighter as they let Katie go. She sensed her daughter there, smiling down on them. The birds seemed to be a sign that Katie acknowledged the harmony between them. The flock was her way of thanking her parents for letting go of the anger and blame they'd been clinging to.

They stood in silence, watching the birds rise to the sky.

———

Caroline spread a blanket out next to one of the fishing ponds at Possum Creek Metropark. The park was where she and John had spent their first date. No matter how bad things got between them, an afternoon spent by the pond seemed to soothe their wounds. The nostalgia of the scene reminded her why she'd fallen in love with John in the first place. Being here made her feel like they were a family.

She leaned back on her elbows, watching John walk Katie to the edge of the water. Finally, Caroline thought, those red boots were being put to use as they were intended—keeping Katie's feet dry as the water lapped against them. They kneeled down, observing something. Katie's curiosity never ended. That had been a blessing Caroline hadn't expected when she'd had her. John had no interest in the world around him or learning about how things worked. At least not until Katie got old enough to ask about everything.

"How do clocks work, Daddy?"

"Why do dogs bark, Mama?"

"Daddy, what kind of clouds are those?"

She wanted to know everything. She wanted to absorb and understand everything. That had ignited a need in John to know and understand, too. He'd spent an hour the night before studying the different kinds of fish in the pond so he would be able to tell Katie all about them no matter what kind she caught.

He didn't like not being able to tell her about things. More so, he didn't like that Caroline usually knew the answer without researching it. The perks of being a lifelong nerd.

Stretching out, Caroline let the sun soak into her skin as John taught Katie how to bait a hook. Her daughter giggled, squealed, giggled again, and Caroline couldn't help but smile. John had offered to buy a pole for her, but she wanted to watch. She preferred to stand back and observe life. She liked to let these moments scorch her mind where she could keep them forever. Harmony was getting harder to find in the Bowman household, but this day, this moment, was one she simply wanted to let in.

When they finished fishing and were ready for the picnic lunch, John helped Katie wash her hands while Caroline unpacked the cooler.

"Where's my beer?" John asked, peering in while Caroline unwrapped a sandwich.

"No beer today, John. Not today." She glanced up to see a spark of anger light his eye, but he looked at Katie as he grabbed a bottle of water instead.

Caroline felt his rage. She sensed his anger, but she ignored it. She bit into her lunch and listened to Katie ramble about fishing and how she thought Daddy was the best fisher in the whole world. As the afternoon wrapped up, all three of them stretched on the blanket to watch the clouds rolling in.

Katie thought all of them looked like teddy bears. Caroline didn't see what her daughter did, but she agreed. She was happy to let Katie perceive the world however she wanted.

When it was time to call it a day, a strange sense of sadness washed over Caroline. Somehow, she felt that they'd never have a day like this again. As John and Katie talked about bugs, Caroline followed behind, once again observing every moment between father and daughter. Their bond was strong. Stronger than Caroline could have ever dreamed of having with her father.

Katie loved her daddy, and John loved his little girl.

Though Caroline had struggled with her decision to end her affair with Simon, she knew in that moment she'd made the right one. Katie needed John in her life. And he needed her.

"You okay?" John asked as he started the ignition.

Caroline peeked back at Katie, who was too busy looking at the rocks she'd collected to be paying attention to her parents. With a full heart, she took John's hand. "Yeah. You?"

"I'm good. I'm real good." His smile faded a little as sincerity touched his eyes. "We're going to be better now. I promise. We're going to have more days like today."

Again, she sensed that they wouldn't, but she didn't voice her concern. "I hope so."

She'd been right. They'd never visited the pond again. They'd never spent another day fishing and looking at clouds. They'd never been a family again like they had that day.

Katie was gone before they ever had a chance.

———

"We have to talk about something," Carol said as she slid John's dinner onto the table.

"Uh-oh. That doesn't sound good."

She didn't fix a plate for herself. Instead she sat across from him, twisting the ring on her finger. "It's time to head home, John."

He stopped lifting his fork halfway to his mouth. "We have more stops to make."

"This is getting to be too much for me," she explained as gently as she could. "You're starting to struggle with mobility. You're too heavy for me to lift. If you fall—"

"I know."

Astonished at how easily he'd given in, she sat back in her seat. Giving in without a fight wasn't like him at all. Of course, if the dark circles shading his eyes were any indication, he was too exhausted to resist. His spirits had been lighter after spreading Katie's ashes in Yellowstone, but that hadn't lasted long. His illness was starting to take a visible toll on him. Every day he seemed weaker, more easily fatigued. Neither of them could deny his declining health if they'd wanted to.

Easing his fork down, John sat back as well. "I don't want to burden you more than I have, but we have more stops. I already looked into options. We can stop in Cody and get me a wheelchair."

She lifted her brows.

"Yes, I know," he said with flat sarcasm. "I've been a pain in the ass for so long, you weren't expecting me to be reasonable in the last weeks of my life."

"Something like that."

"If we get a wheelchair, I can get around. If I can get around, we can finish the trip. We gotta finish the trip, Caroline. There are more places Katie wanted to see."

Caroline read the last three stops on the list that was now stuck to the RV fridge with a magnetized photo of Carol and Tobias at a St. Louis Cardinals game. "We're getting close, aren't we?"

"Next stop, Devil's Tower."

"Okay, let's agree right now we aren't even attempting to go up the trails there."

He started to laugh, but the sound cut short as he panted a few breaths. "I think you underestimate your own strength. Surely you can push me."

"Oh, I'll push you, all right. Right off a cliff."

They grinned at each other, and he reached for his fork. She didn't miss that he struggled a few times before wrapping his hand around the handle like a young child would do. His fine motor skills were fading.

The fact that he'd started wearing sweatpants and T-shirts every day should have been a clue that he could no longer work with buttons, but she hadn't thought much of it. She was in more of a yoga pants and T-shirt mode herself. Extensive travel tended to do that to a person's wardrobe. Jeans weren't exactly comfortable when she was sitting in the driver's seat for several hours at a time.

But now that she was really paying attention, the signs were clear. His health had started a steady downhill slide. The emotion of her observation took hold and broke the heart that was starting to mend.

"Caroline?"

She had to blink several times to clear her head and focus on him. "Hmm?"

"You okay?"

She had to clear her throat before speaking. "Yeah."

His shoulders sagged a bit, as if some of his energy had suddenly been drained. "Don't lie. We're beyond lying to each other. What's wrong?"

"Your motor skills are going. That's...not good, John."

He turned his attention to his hold on the fork. "No. I guess not."

"I can't do anything for you other than make what time is left as good as I can."

He stared at his hand for another few seconds before looking at her. "Well. Seeing as every meal I eat could literally be my last, maybe we could have a little less grilled fish and steamed veggies and little more fried chicken and stuffed-crust pizza?"

She considered his suggestion for a moment before shaking her head. "Dead men may not have to count calories, but living women in their fifties certainly do."

She smiled as he rolled his head back and laughed.

———

Carol gave the woman at the medical supply store a sympathetic look. The cozy store sat off the main street that went through the town. She'd been hoping they could get back on the road quickly. Unfortunately, John's surliness was putting an end to that dream. He was all but pouting and throwing a fit. Sure, the woman was likely used to grumpy clientele, but Carol still felt bad that John continually dismissed her instructions.

"My wife is a nurse. She can help me." He'd said that three times.

Not wanting to irritate him more than he already was, Carol didn't correct him on their marital status or her vocation. Arguing moot points seemed counterproductive at the moment. However, when he swatted at the woman who kneeled beside him to show him how the wheelchair brake worked, Carol stepped in.

Putting her hand on his shoulder, she waited for him to look up at her. "It's her job to show you how to do this."

"You can help me. You're a nurse."

"I can and I will, but let her do her job."

He stared at her for a few seconds before easing back and returning his attention to the woman beside him. She went through her routine of showing him the various parts and how to use them. He was as patient as Carol suspected he could be, which wasn't much. Eventually, he rolled his face up at her and scowled. "You could have shown me that."

"Just stay here," she said, following the woman to the counter. "I'm sorry. His illness makes him irritable."

"I'm used to it. Which hospital do you work at?" she asked, making small talk as she rang up Carol's purchases.

"Um... We're from Texas." That was easier than delving into the long story of how she'd ended up at a medical supply store with her ex-husband in Cody, Wyoming.

"Oh. Traveling, then?"

"Yeah. He's, um...he wanted to see some things."

Sympathy filled the attendant's eyes and she used a softer, less clipped tone. "I'm glad you got a chance to."

Carol slid John's credit card and ID across the counter as she peeked back to check on him. He sat in the wheelchair, staring out the window at the mountains in the distance. The day had been long; his exhaustion showed in his short temper.

When the sale was final, Carol joined him, taking a second to try to pinpoint what had him enthralled. "What are you looking at?"

"I was wrong. You shouldn't move to Seattle."

She had adapted to the sudden changes in topic. Even so, this one threw her. "No?"

"You shouldn't move anywhere. You should sell everything and never stop moving." A tear fell down his cheek. "There's so much out there I'll never see. So much Katie never saw. You have to see it for us, Caroline. You're the only one left."

Carol bent down to get a better look at his face. "Nobody ever sees everything. The world is a big place full of mystery. That's what makes it amazing. Nobody ever sees everything, John."

"Can we walk for a while before getting back on the road?" His lips quirked. "You can walk. I'll roll."

"Sounds fair." She handed him his card and ID, then opened the door and waited while he found his groove with the wheels and was able to maneuver himself out of the store. "Want me to push?"

"No." He was winded but seemed determined enough to not accept his weakness yet.

They crossed the street toward the center of town and

window-shopped, admiring various locally made keepsakes. Carol gasped as they stopped at a display of turquoise jewelry spread on fake busts, wrists, and fingers covered in black felt. She stared at one bracelet in particular, mesmerized by the row of coral beads set in antique sterling silver with tribal patterns stamped on the edges of the cuff. The simplicity was captivating.

"A little help here, Caroline."

She tore her attention from the window to find John trying to open the door and back up in his wheelchair at the same time. She didn't get a chance to argue, to tell him not to go into the store. Someone rushed to the door and held it open for him. He thanked the man and rolled inside.

She offered a less enthusiastic thank-you and followed behind him. "Did you see the price tag?"

"Says the lady who drives a Mercedes motorhome for fun."

Her objection was interrupted by an overzealous employee who seemingly appeared from out of nowhere.

John let the young woman know how she could help before Carol could dismiss her. "My wife would like to try on the bracelet in the window. The red one."

The girl walked away, and Carol scowled at him. "Stop telling people I'm your wife."

"Ex-wife raises questions."

"Friend doesn't."

He waggled his brows. "Wife's friend?"

She didn't know why she was surprised at his wicked humor, but she couldn't stop herself from laughing. "God, you are awful."

"Ma'am," the saleswoman said, drawing Carol and John back to the jewelry.

Carol hesitated before accepting the bracelet, slipping the cuff around her wrist. The bright red stones shone like fire against the stamped silver. The piece was simple but elegant. She loved it. Absolutely loved it. She didn't have to say so; her cheeks hurt from smiling.

John reached in his pocket and handed his debit card to the woman.

"John," Carol chastised.

"Consider it a wedding present."

"Oh, are you newlyweds?" the woman asked.

"Not exactly," John offered. "I'm sucking up for years of misdeeds."

Carol shook her head when the woman flicked uncertain eyes toward her. She seemed more than happy to dismiss John's awkward joke as she rang up the purchase and removed the tag from the bracelet.

"That wasn't necessary," Carol informed him as they left the store.

"Which part?"

"Any of it, but mostly spending five hundred dollars on a bracelet for your *ex*-wife."

He didn't seem fazed. "I can spend my money on you now or you can fight the collectors for it when I'm dead."

"I don't want your money, John."

"Well, that's too bad, because my will names one beneficiary: Caroline Elizabeth Denman."

She stopped walking. "What?"

"Who else was I going to name?"

Looking around the main street, she didn't see the shops or the people strolling by. Her mind was processing the implication of his words. "Bert. A charity. Anyone else but me. Why would you do that?"

"Because you're my wife." His happy mood faded in an instant. "I don't care what you say. You're my wife and when I die, everything I own should go to you."

Her mouth went dry. "I don't want it."

"Well. Tough."

"John, I don't—"

He pinned her down with his stare, effectively ending the argument. When a few moments of tense silence passed between them, he pointed to a storefront down the block. "Let's have a coffee before getting back in the RV."

They didn't speak as they headed down the street and waited in line to place their orders. When they got their drinks, Carol carried them while John navigated himself to the patio. She moved a chair from a table in the shade to make room for his wheelchair. Sitting across from him, she was content to take in the scenery as they sipped their hot drinks, but she felt John staring at her.

Heaving a sigh, she turned her attention to him. "What?"

"I knew you were going to leave me."

She felt her stomach drop, instantly fearing another episode like the one they'd had when he accused her of cheating on him. She didn't want that scene to play out in public.

"As soon as we lost Katie, I knew I'd lost you, too. I knew you were only staying for her. I wasn't surprised when I woke up in the morning and you were gone. I saw it coming."

The pain of the past knotted in her stomach. She focused on her cup. "Our marriage was over long before Katie died."

"I know. I sat on the couch looking at the spot where I'd last seen Katie's ashes and tried to figure out where you'd go, but I came up empty. I knew you'd never go home to your parents, but I couldn't remember the names of any of your friends." His already sad eyes seemed to darken even more. "That was when I started to think that maybe I hadn't been the victim in our marriage after all. Maybe you had a point when you called me selfish. How could I not even know who to call to check on you?"

"You were selfish, John, but I didn't disclose a lot about my life outside of our house to you. I liked to keep you out of that part of my life. My work was my safe place away from you, and I didn't want you involved. I was selfish, too. Just in a different way."

"I spiraled. My drinking got so bad I had to take an extended leave from the force and almost lost the house. Mom and Dad had to step in and get me back on track." He looked at her. "I'm not saying this to make you feel guilty. You were right to leave. I'm glad you found the life you wanted to have with Tobias. All I ever wanted was for you to be happy."

"Then why are you telling me this?"

"Because I want you to know that I was broken. I was broken when you found me, and I was broken when you left me. It was never your job to put me back together, but for some reason, you're the only person who ever tried. Maybe it isn't saying much, but the only time I ever felt whole was with you. It's not your fault you couldn't save me. I fought you every step of the way. You stuck around a lot longer than I thought you would. Thank you for that."

"You know, John, you weren't the only one that was broken. My parents had beaten my ego down to the point that I barely had the confidence to string two sentences together when we met. You gave me the courage to crawl out of the shadows. I'd never felt like a real person until I met you. You convinced me I was worthy of being." She rested her hand on his. "Thank you for that."

"We could have had everything we wanted. Man, did we screw up."

"We're not looking back anymore, remember? We're moving forward."

"I don't know how much time I have left. I have to say all these things I should have so you know."

"I do know, John." She squeezed his arm. "I know. I appreciate you thinking of me when making your will, but you should have talked to me about it first. I'm assuming when you say you left everything to me, you're including the house in that?"

"Yeah."

Closing her eyes, she tried to stop the image of the run-down ranch from filling her mind. "I don't ever want to see that house again. I don't ever want to think about that house again. I don't know how you stayed there without going insane. She died there."

"It was all I had left of our family. I couldn't have left if I'd wanted to. When we get to Dayton, *if* I get to Dayton, I'll change it. Okay?"

Frowning, she sank back into her chair. "No. The last thing you need is the stress of that. Who's the executor?"

"Bert."

"I'll talk to him. We'll figure it out."

John's lips sank as he stared at his coffee. "I keep making things worse for you, don't I?"

She covered his hand. "Oh, John. Nothing's ever been easy between us. Why would that change now?"

He brought her hand to his lips and kissed the back. "I'm tired. Let's head back."

TWELVE

TURNING HER FACE TO JOHN, Carol blinked. He'd said something, but she hadn't heard him. She'd been lost in thought as she stared at the pine trees surrounding the visitor center outside Devil's Tower. They seemed taller than most trees, like they were in competition with the jutting rock. They didn't sway with the breeze that made her hair tickle her cheek or cooled the sweat on her neck. They seemed too sturdy for that, too focused on outshining the Tower behind them. "I'm sorry," she said. "Say that again."

"I said you're a million miles away."

"Yes, I was."

"What are you thinking?"

She took a drink of her coffee to delay, not really wanting to ask, but knowing she had to. Setting the bitter drink down, she met his gaze. "Have you planned a funeral?"

"I'm retired PD. The department will handle it."

"Should I let Bert know if..."

"If I die before we get to Dayton, tell the coroner to call

the department. They'll take care of everything. You don't have to."

She nodded. "Where...where are you going to be buried?"

"I'm not. I'm getting cremated. Like Katie." He focused on his hands. "Actually, I'm glad you brought this up. Now that we're better, do you think you could..." He gave her his crooked little smile. "It sounds creepy as hell, but maybe you could ask them to put our ashes together. Mine and what's left of Katie's."

"It's not creepy," she said. "Morbid, but not creepy."

He watched a group of tourists hiking toward the trail. "Don't leave me sitting on a shelf for twenty-four years, though, okay?"

"I won't. I'll hang on to you for a while and then...flush you down the toilet like you deserve."

She smiled at the sound of his laugh.

"Good luck explaining that to the plumber."

Her lips fell as she returned the topic to his demise. "What do you want me to do with you, John?"

"This. Do this, Caroline. Go places. See things. Take a little bit of us with you when you do."

"John, I—"

He grabbed her hand, silently demanding that she look at him. When she did, he said, "Don't hide yourself away in that office for the rest of your life. Please. That's not living. We'll be gone. Tobias is gone. *You* are not. Don't live like you've already died. Live for us. For all of us."

Swallowing the bundle of raw emotion in her chest, she choked out, "You make it sound easy. I'm the one that will be left behind. I'm always the one left behind."

"Because you're the strong one. You always were."

She didn't want to be strong. She wanted to curl in a ball and let all the storms of her life pass. Considering how rapidly John's health was decreasing, she might get the opportunity sooner rather than later. Pushing herself up, she tossed her cup in the bin and wiped her hands down the front of her shorts. "Come on. Let's do this and get to Mount Rushmore before you tire out."

John clutched her hand and stopped her movements to admire the bracelet on her wrist. "I never would have been able to buy you things like Tobias did."

"When I married Tobias, he couldn't buy me things. We were up to our eyeballs in student loans for years. He worked hard to turn that around. You worked hard, too, John. You had the career you always wanted." Caressing his hand, she reassured him, "Success isn't about income any more than affection is about gifts."

Happiness shone in his eyes. He looked more at ease today than he had since they'd started this crazy journey. "It's a pretty bracelet."

"It is. Thank you."

"Do you have Katie?"

She patted her pocket before stepping behind him and releasing the brakes on his wheelchair. He sat unspeaking, taking in the scenery as she pushed him along the flat part of the path. They didn't make it far before she stopped to survey their surroundings. Pine trees shaded the area, but the base of Devil's Tower loomed to the west. The view wasn't as spectacular as it would be farther up the trail, but they'd gone far enough.

Pushing him to the side of the trail to allow others to pass easily, she set the brakes and squatted beside him. Holding out the container, she smiled up at him, waiting for him to start his history lesson. When he finished talking about igneous rock and Native American legends, he gripped the container. After a few moments of watching him struggle to turn the top, Carol took the bottle. He didn't argue as she twisted the top off and handed it back to him.

Moving out of the way, letting him sprinkle Katie's ashes on the pine-needle-covered ground, she held her breath. No flock of birds took flight this time. It was a silly notion, one she hadn't realized she was clinging to. Still, she was a little disappointed that they didn't experience the same display they'd watched in Yellowstone. Turning her attention to John, though, she found him searching the sky as well. Ruffling his hair, she leaned down and gave him a half hug.

"Let's go," she said. "We've got a couple hours' drive to get to Rushmore."

At the RV, she helped him up the stairs and to the bench at the table. He was finding that seat easier to get in and out of than the passenger seat. Funny how a week ago, she would have loved for him to stay at the table and let her drive in peace. Now that he didn't have much choice, she missed having him next to her. Sure, his humming was annoying, and he was always touching the AC and radio controls, but he was company. More company than she'd had since Tobias had died.

She climbed into the driver's seat and buckled up. The drive to Mount Rushmore was unnervingly serene. Every time she glanced in the mirror to check on John, he was staring out the window, his face devoid of any expression. He was involved in some serious contemplation, and she dreaded finding out what it was about.

After paying the fee to get into the park, she steered the RV as close as she could get to the monument. She really should have requested a handicap parking pass from Dr. Collins. The thought hadn't occurred to her in the stress of preparing for the trip. It was a testament to how shaken she'd been at having John in her life again. She'd never been one to forget the small details.

John frazzled her as much now as he had back then. He'd always had a way of knocking her off balance. No one else had ever been able to do that. Not even Tobias. No, Tobias centered her, helped her focus. John? John was like a tornado to her heart, mind, and soul. He shook her up. Sometimes that was a good thing, an amazing thing, but usually the insanity he brought ended with her falling flat on her face.

Sadly, she was beginning to accept this time was no different. He'd come in like a whirlwind, making a mess of things, and then he'd disappear as quickly. As always, the mess would remain for Carol to clean up. This time cleaning up after him wouldn't be as easy as tossing away beer cans and empty food containers.

Clearing her throat, she turned her seat. "We're here."

He tore his gaze from the window and gave her a slight nod.

She moved back to the table and took the seat across from him instead of grabbing his chair. "Want to talk about it?"

"It's just... It's sinking in, you know."

"Yeah. For me, too."

A tear rolled down his cheek. "I'm dying, Caroline."

"I know." Laying her hands on the table, palms up, she offered him as much comfort as she could.

He clung to her with so much desperation in his eyes, it

stole her breath away. "I'm glad she's not here. I wouldn't want her to see me slipping away."

Carol bit the inside of her lip and swallowed hard to stop herself from sobbing. "You were her hero, John. Bigger than life. This wouldn't have changed that in her mind."

"It does in mine," he whispered. "I don't think..." He looked at their entwined hands. "I don't think I can fill the container anymore. You're going to have to do it."

Her heart dropped to her stomach. It was only fair, really. He'd filled the container with ash at every other stop. She'd known she would have to take over at some point. Swallowing hard, she got up and put her mind on autopilot, gathering the ashes and a few paper towels. Sitting back at the table, she inhaled a deep, cleansing breath and let it out slowly.

"It's not that bad," he said. "Just use your fingertips to grab the spoon."

"Spoon?" She creased her brow.

He shrugged.

She took the top off the urn and peered in, then frowned at him. "John. You used my silverware to scoop Katie's ashes. We eat off those."

His cheek twitched. "Maybe not this one anymore."

She didn't want to laugh, but a chuckle left her. "You are such a handful." Bracing herself, she reached in for the spoon.

"Slow and steady," he advised.

She met his gaze, holding his stare, before finding the courage to lift the spoon from the urn.

Don't think about it. Don't think about it. Don't think about it.

And there. She was done. Ashes in the container. Top on the container. Top on the urn. Done.

"Okay. That happened," she muttered.

"Good job. Are you ready?"

She answered by pushing herself up and taking his chair outside, readying it for him. He met her at the stairs and eased down. He could walk, but his steps were labored and slow, even more so than the day before. For the first time, Carol was beginning to worry he wouldn't make it back to Ohio.

She didn't tell him that. They had one more stop on the list after Mount Rushmore. One that she actually wasn't dreading.

The Gateway Arch in St. Louis.

She hadn't been back since they'd had a small family gathering to lay Tobias's headstone. His mother had wanted him buried in the family plot, and Carol had no reason to disagree. That was six months ago. She missed her family.

They didn't know she was coming, though. She was going to have to make that call soon, and what a call it would be. Mary, her mother-in-law, would be supportive of what Carol was doing; she didn't doubt that. She was still going to have to explain herself.

"You're smiling," John said.

She released the brake and looked up at him. "I need to call Tobias's mother to let her know we'll be in St. Louis in a few days."

"Am I going to meet her?"

"Yeah, I'm sure you will."

"Do they hate me?"

"No. Nobody hates you."

"You hated me."

She shrugged. "Well, I was married to you."

Though he was growing weaker by the day, he still managed to laugh as she pushed him toward the monument entrance. She was happy for that. Too many times, people spent the last days of their lives sulking. While John had plenty to be bitter about, she was glad he was finding moments of light in the darkness.

They took their time moving along the Avenue of Flags to the Grand View Terrace. This visit was bittersweet to Carol; she didn't want to rush their time here. John seemed to have the same sense. Of all the places Katie had wanted to visit, this was the one that seemed most important to her. She'd stared at the pictures of this monument many times, mesmerized by how the faces had been carved in stone. She said she thought they must be bigger than anything else in the whole world. Carol hadn't pointed out that wasn't possible. She'd soaked in Katie's wonderment and still carried it in her heart.

When they made it to view the mountain face, her breath rushed from her chest. "There it is. Mount *Hushmore*."

"She never could get that right." He held his hand out until Carol took it. When she did, he clasped her fingers tight. "This was it. This was the big one. The one she couldn't wait to see."

Damn it. Carol didn't want to cry. She'd spent so much time the last few weeks crying, but she had to blink away her tears anyway. "I think...I think she would have grown up to be a photographer. She would have traveled the world. We would have seen her pictures in magazines, and she would have called us to check in from places we'd never heard of. I'd have a shelf full of knickknacks from all her travels."

John sniffed and wiped at his face with his free hand. "That would have been something, huh?"

"Yeah, it would have been."

"I think she would have been a nurse. Like her mom. Remember how she'd put bandages on all her toys and tell them how they were going to be okay."

Carol ground her teeth together in an attempt to control her emotions. "She was a great nurse."

She moved her eyes over every inch of the view before her, committing it to memory. She'd been there before, but this was different. This was special. This was for Katie, and she didn't want to forget a thing. Before long, though, a crowd gathered and Carol pulled John's chair from the railing.

As she had at Devil's Tower, she pushed him down one of the trails far enough away from the visitor's center that sprinkling Katie's ashes wouldn't interfere with anyone's happy vacation.

"There." John pointed to a spot off the trail where the sun was shining through the trees. "In the sun. Put her in the sun."

She parked his chair and squatted beside him as he rambled off the information he'd memorized for the moment —from Doane Robinson's conception of Mount Rushmore to the time it took nearly four hundred workers to finish the sculpture with dynamite and a drilling technique called honeycombing. When he was done, Carol took a few steps off the trail to tap the contents of the container into the sunlight.

"You made it, kitty cat," she whispered. "Mount *Hushmore*."

Putting the bottle in her pocket, she joined John back on the path.

He sat staring at the spot for a long time before looking up to Carol. "The Arch is the last stop. One more to go."

The finality of reaching the bottom of the list suddenly seemed too much to bear. When the list was done, the only place to go was Dayton. The only thing left to accomplish was helping John pass as peacefully as possible. "You ready to get back on the road?"

Sighing, he returned his attention to the particles dancing in the sunlight. "Yeah. Yeah, let's do this and go home."

———

Home. Carol couldn't believe she and Tobias had moved into their first home together. Standing in the empty living room of the second-floor apartment, staring out the large window, she smiled as he slipped his arms around her waist and rested his cheek against her temple.

"What are you thinking?" he asked.

"How lucky I am to have snared you in my trap."

He rocked her for a moment before holding out his hand. "Are you sure I'm the one who got trapped?"

She inhaled at the shock of seeing a diamond ring sitting in his palm. Lightly touching the band, she assured that she wasn't imagining the moment. She wasn't. The ring was real. The apartment was real. Tobias was real. Despite everything she'd been through, she was standing in the arms of a man she loved more than life, looking at the future she'd always wanted.

Her heart skipped a few beats, though. Because this moment, as wonderful as it was, had a shadow looming over it. Turning, she simply stared and the excitement in his eyes faded.

"I know we've only been together a year—"

"No," she cut him off. "It's not that. Tobias," she started, and then stopped. "There's something I have to tell you."

A hint of suspicion found his eyes. "Girl, if you're about to tell me you're already married—"

"Divorced. It was final before we started dating."

His excitement returned. "Okay. That's all right. We all make mistakes, Carol."

"We had a daughter."

That gave him pause.

"Her name...was Katie." Carol's voice cracked. She hadn't said her baby's name out loud in so long. She blinked rapidly, but a tear still seared down her cheek. "She was six years old. I left him because...it's his fault she died. He was a drunk. Still is, I'm sure." She had to swallow hard. "I worked the night shift and one morning, when I got home..." A sob ripped from deep in her chest as she flashed back to what she'd seen. How she'd found her daughter.

"Okay," he soothed. Pulling her to him, he cradled her against his chest and dug his fingers into her hair. "Okay." He exhaled slowly. "You don't have to tell me this right now."

Though they didn't have a single chair in the apartment yet, Tobias scooped her up like she weighed nothing and dropped down. Sitting with his legs crossed, he snuggled her into his lap and held her until she stopped crying enough to breathe.

When she leaned back, her eyes burned and her nose felt like it'd been filled with wet sand. "I wanted to tell you sooner. I couldn't. I can't...I can't talk about it."

"It's okay. It's okay. I understand."

"She was just a baby," she choked out.

He pulled her back into his embrace and kissed her head. Stroking her back, he soothed her, told her how sorry he was, and assured her he loved her even more than before.

———

Carol and Tobias had a huge wedding, mostly because his mother wouldn't have it any other way. Mary was crazy about her son and was incredibly proud of the man he'd become. She accepted Carol into his life and his family without a moment of hesitation.

When they were planning the wedding, Mary had made it a point to suggest ideas to include Katie. One pink rose had been added to Carol's bouquet and the others were wrapped with one pink ribbon. The night before the wedding, at the rehearsal dinner, Mary gave her a necklace with a little pink heart pendant to symbolize the girl who was missing from the wedding party.

Letting Tobias and his family in on her pain had been the first step to healing. Katie was never forgotten in their family. Every prayer included her name. Every Christmas a donation was made to honor her memory. Someone in her new family always remembered her even though they'd never known her. The sense of unity they'd brought to Carol's life was like nothing she'd ever felt.

She had always tried to hide things from her parents, from John, and even from Frannie and Mark. She was always lying and making excuses so they didn't know how bad things were. She never had to do that with the Denmans. They had loved her and the daughter she lost long before meeting them.

As she walked down the aisle to where Tobias stood waiting

for her, she knew in her heart that Katie was there and was happy for all the little touches that brought her into this new family.

Marrying Tobias truly was second only to the day Katie had been born. Carol couldn't have asked for a more perfect day. She was so caught up in her own happiness, she was even able to forget that her parents sat rigid, looking completely miserable as their daughter married yet another man they didn't approve of.

At least they took the time to show up to this wedding. Then again, Carol realized during the reception, she would have been happier if they hadn't. Not only had her mother treated her new brother-in-law like a waiter, but her father had refused to partake in the traditional father-daughter dance, reminding her that he didn't dance...even for special occasions.

Someone must have forgotten to tell the DJ that, because he announced it was time and Carol actually felt her father start fuming. She told him it was a mistake, but he glowered at her like she'd done it on purpose. No matter, though. Mary grabbed her hand and pulled her to her feet and out to the dance floor. Everyone laughed—everyone except her parents. Halfway through the song, Carol was passed off to her husband.

He kissed her head, hugged her tight, and gently rocked her. "I love you. You know that, right?"

"I love you, too."

"Good. Can we agree that we never have to visit your parents? Like ever?"

"I wasn't planning on it. Ever."

He was too tall for her to rest her forehead to his, but she could put it to his lips, and he always kissed her when she did.

"I'm sorry for them," she said.

"Don't apologize."

"No, I mean, I feel sorry for them. Can you imagine being that cold all the time?"

"Are they always this cold?"

Peering back at them, she nodded. "Always."

"Well, it's a damn good thing you found me, then."

"You have no idea." Leaning into him, she nearly melted, as she tended to do.

"Save it for the honeymoon," someone called.

Carol didn't want to, but she couldn't help glancing at her mother. The reaction—pure horror—was priceless. She giggled and burrowed back into the safety of Tobias's embrace, knowing that he really didn't have any idea how lucky she was. She knew, and she wouldn't blow her second chance. She was older and wiser now. She knew what being a wife meant, how amazing it could be to be the second half of something. She was ready now. She was ready for this new life.

His family truly had become hers. She would cherish them, and her husband, forever.

———

Carol stepped out of the RV and under the bright stars. They were leaving from Rapid City in the morning and headed to more populated areas. An overnight stay in Sioux City, Iowa, would be the last before they made it to St. Louis.

This was the last bit of real quiet Carol expected to have on this journey. John was sleeping soundly, finally. He'd been struggling quite a bit with twitching in his legs, which made it hard for him to rest. After she'd given him a higher dose of one of his meds, he'd eventually drifted off.

The end was near. If the tumor didn't take him soon, she

figured he'd take her suggestion of swallowing pills. His depression was deepening. The long stretches of silence were filled with obvious contemplation on his part. He'd been staring down death for some time, and seemed to be coming to terms with it.

He'd barely spoken during the day. When he did, he'd say something like, "remember when," or "promise me that," followed by something that never failed to surprise her.

"Remember when Katie made pancakes for Mother's Day?"

"Promise me that you'll have cake on my birthday, too."

Little things that he seemed fixated on throughout the day would pop from his mouth and she'd nod in agreement before he started thinking of something else.

She was glad he was sleeping. She needed a break from him as much as she did from driving. Pulling out her phone, she checked the signal. God bless technology. Finding her mother-in-law's name in her contacts, she connected the call.

"Child, where have you been?" was the hello she received. "I've been worried sick about you. You aren't answering your phone."

"Sorry, Mary. I've been out of range for most of the last week. I'm in Rapid City, South Dakota, at the moment, but I'm headed your way in the morning. Are you up for a quick visit?"

"Quick? I haven't seen you for months."

"I know." She eased onto the seat of the provided picnic table. "I'm sorry about that. I was burying my head in work."

Mary's voice softened. "I know. I know how you are. You work too hard. Always have."

"Listen, I'm not alone. Katie's dad is with me. He found me in Houston."

"*Okay*," she said.

"He's dying, Mary. His last wish was to spread Katie's ashes like we had planned all those years ago. That's where I've been. Letting her go." She blinked, surprised at the way her voice cracked. She didn't think the reality could still hit her so hard after living it for the last twelve days.

"Oh, baby," she said, the sympathy in her voice causing Carol's tears to fall. "Haven't you been through enough this year?"

She sniffed, wiped her cheek, then dried her hand on her shorts. "I've been through more than enough, but he's sick. He's incredibly sick. I needed this, too, though. I needed to face this. You were right. Tobias was right. I never processed my grief."

"But right now, Carol? You just lost your husband."

"I know." She swallowed hard. "Oh, boy do I know. John doesn't have time, though. He really doesn't. He has a terminal brain tumor, and he's starting to lose control of his body. It won't be long now."

"That man put you through enough, baby. Your precious little girl..."

She exhaled heavily. "You know, seeing him again after all this time and looking back made it clear that he wasn't the only one to blame. I wasn't the best wife to him. I could have been a better mother to Katie."

"I don't believe that."

"Well, I do. I made mistakes, too, and I've got to let them go. She had a list of all the places she wanted to visit. We've been going through it. The last stop is the Arch. We'll be there in two days, and we are two serious hot messes, Mary. Are you up for it?"

"I'm here for you. Always and forever. You know that."

"Good. Because I don't know how much longer I can hold myself together without a little help."

THIRTEEN

PEACE WASHED over Carol's soul as she pulled into Mary's driveway. Not only was she home, but there was a welcoming committee waiting for her. She'd recognized the cars parked along the street. They belonged to Tobias's brother, his wife, and their uncle, Jerry. This scene had played out before when she and Tobias had stopped on their trips.

Elijah, Tobias's baby brother, jumped over the railing on the porch to guide Carol into the yard and under the trees where they always parked the RV. He waved her back, back, back, then put his hand up to stop her. She barely had the ignition turned off before he was opening the door. She unbuckled and hopped down into his arms. Like Tobias, Elijah was at least six inches taller than Carol, so her feet didn't hit the ground until he eased her down.

He muttered something about it being good to see her before pulling back and looking at John in the passenger seat. "Where'd you find that white guy?"

"Be good," she warned with a playful swat to his arm.

He laughed before moving around the RV. Carol heard

him introducing himself to John about the time Mary wrapped her arms around her shoulders. Tears came too easily to Carol these days, and sinking into the comforting embrace brought another round. She pulled back and wiped her face, mumbling an apology.

"This is my thing now," she said, rubbing her hands together. "It's all I do."

"Because you're putting yourself through hell," Mary chastised.

Carol couldn't deny that assessment, but she did ignore it. She smiled widely when three girls came running from the house calling to her. Elijah's daughters had been the light of her and Tobias's eyes and they were growing up too fast. The oldest had recently turned thirteen but when she came bouncing toward Carol, she looked as much a little girl as her youngest sister did at eight. Tobias had spoiled those girls like mad. She hugged each one before the trio disappeared around the side of the RV. As per tradition, the first thing they wanted to do was rush inside and play.

She turned as Elijah, with his arm around John's waist, walked around the RV. "There's a wheelchair inside."

"We got this," Elijah said. "Right, Johnny?"

"Make sure you tip him, Caroline," John said, sounding like his usual mischievous self.

She sighed and rolled her eyes toward the overcast sky. "I really wish I hadn't told you that story."

"Carol's mother is crazy, man," Elijah said, still grinning at John's comment.

John agreed. "You don't know the half of it. She cried every time she saw me for the first three years of our marriage."

"That isn't true," Carol stated. "It was only two years."

They all laughed as John and Elijah slowly moved toward the house.

"I made up both guest rooms," Mary said as they followed behind. "I don't want to hear any argument out of you. You're staying here tonight and getting some real rest. I know you don't sleep well in that camper."

"He can't make it upstairs."

"Elijah is staying tonight to help out. He can get him wherever he needs to go."

"How does Lara feel about that?"

Mary gripped Carol's hand, slowing their stride. "About having the house to herself? She's probably wondering why he doesn't stay here more often."

She watched Elijah helping John up the stairs one at a time. "So you told him the score with me and John?"

"You mean that you've lost your ever-loving mind? We already knew that." She gestured toward the chairs on the porch. "Sit."

Carol hesitated at the door where John and Elijah had disappeared.

"Sit. He'll be fine."

Easing into a rocker, Carol soaked in the sense of belonging she felt being back with her family. However, she couldn't ignore the feeling of emptiness lingering in the back of her mind. Tobias was missing. He'd always be missing. However, this house, this porch, these people...this was home, and Carol *really* needed to be home right now. "I know it sounds crazy, but I had to make this trip with him."

"I know you did. You've needed to for a long time. That's

not what I'm worried about. It's the timing, Carol. It's only been eight months since Tobias."

"I know." She swallowed hard at the reminder. "When John showed up at my office, I couldn't get rid of him fast enough. I wanted him gone. The next morning I got a call from the hospital. He'd had a seizure at the hotel and had been admitted. The doctor told me he might not even survive the trip. I really felt like Katie was telling me it was time. Now or never, you know? She sent him to me to face the past and I was not getting another chance. The last two weeks have been hard, but we've made progress. We said what we needed to say, no matter how harsh we were to each other sometimes, and we're letting go of years of resentment. I needed that as much as he did."

Mary patted Carol's hand. "I worry about you."

"I love you for it, too."

"You look exhausted."

"I am *beyond* exhausted. I am...tapped out." A car slowly cruised by as the driver looked at the RV on the lawn. "I want to go to the cemetery in the morning. Would you mind if I leave John here?"

"Of course not."

"I won't be gone long."

"You'll be gone as long as you need. I'm a retired nurse. This guy can't toss anything at me I haven't dealt with before. Besides, Elijah is here to help. You need a break. I could hear it in your voice the other night, and I can see it on your face now. Let us ease your burden while you're here."

Squeezing Mary's hand, Carol nodded. "Thank you." She creased her brow when the girls emerged from the RV with arms full of laundry. "What are they doing?"

"What they were told. You don't need to be taking care of that thing right now. Let the girls clean up and do your laundry. They're old enough."

She smiled as they stumbled up the stairs. "Thanks, girls."

A round of "You're welcome, Aunt Carol" rang out as they trudged inside. The door closed and a moment later Carol lifted her nose to the air, inhaling the scent lingering on the light breeze. "Do I smell ribs?"

"Damn straight you do. I couldn't let you visit without having Tobias's favorite dinner. You ready to eat?"

"I'm starving. Let me check on John first." After pushing herself up, she kissed her mother-in-law's head and walked inside. She found John standing in the living room, taking in the collage of photos that kept growing. Stepping beside him, she skimmed the images, letting the overlapping voices in the dining room fade to white noise.

"I've never seen you look that happy." John touched a candid photo, taken while she and Tobias were laughing at a joke Elijah had told. A Christmas tree filled the background, creating a magical scene. "Look at that smile."

"Those were good times." She hadn't meant her voice to sound sad.

"You found a good life here. I'm glad." He pointed to another picture. "That's our girl."

Carol touched the frame that surrounded her daughter's smiling face. "Mary wanted her on the family wall, too. She considers Katie to be her firstborn grandchild even though she never met her."

"That's nice. I'm glad they think of her."

"Me too. Are you ready to eat?"

Patting his stomach, he said, "I am after smelling those ribs. Elijah said Mary's ribs are award-winning."

Widening her eyes, she tried to warn him against saying anything more. "Go ahead and ask if you want to hear the two-hour history of her family recipe and how she beat Myrtle Cummings—"

"That woman's ribs are dry as sand," Mary said, coming in behind them. "And taste as bad, too. Sit down and I'll fix you a plate, John. This recipe came from my great-granddaddy."

"Oh boy." Carol chuckled as she took John's arm to help him walk to the dining room table.

———

Who knew the smell of food could break someone's heart? But that was exactly what happened when Carol walked down the stairs toward the church basement, where the preacher had directed the funeral attendees. She'd held herself together fairly well as she'd laid her husband to rest, but the moment the scent of Mary's ribs hit her, Carol lost the minute amount of strength she'd retained, and her knees grew weak.

Every trip back to St. Louis—every single one—Tobias spent the last hundred miles telling her how much he was looking forward to his mama's ribs. And every single time, Mary had a batch waiting for them.

"Man," he'd say, "I can almost smell them."

Elijah caught Carol before she stumbled down the steps and helped her the rest of the way down. A man stood, turning the chair he'd been sitting in her way. Between the two of them, they eased her down before she could faint.

"I can't breathe," she panted out. "I can't breathe."

"What happened?" Mary demanded, rushing toward the scene Carol had unwittingly caused.

Carol wanted to reassure her that she was okay, but the words wouldn't form. The weight of her grief had suddenly fallen on her chest, crushing her. She squeezed her eyes shut, ground her teeth, and tried to focus on getting air into her lungs. The moment she inhaled, though, the scent hit her and whatever had remained of her composure crumbled.

"Come here, baby." Mary wrapped her arms around Carol. "This has been a long time coming. You can't keep the pain inside. It always finds a way out."

Clinging to her mother-in-law, she let loose the sob she'd been choking back for days. When Katie had died, she'd accepted the doctor's prescription to numb the pain. By the time she swallowed the last pill, she was able to fake the numbness she'd felt for weeks. When Tobias had died, she'd gone into autopilot, focusing on each and every little task to get through. There were no more little tasks. The funeral was over. He was in a box in the ground. The women of the church were in charge of the luncheon. They had stacks of disposable plates on hand. The napkins had been purchased in bulk long before a truck had robbed the world of Tobias's light.

There were pitchers of lemonade and sweet tea ready to go. Mourners had filled the tables with food. There were no little details for Carol to obsess over here. Those details had been ironed out during the hundreds of funerals that had happened before her husband's. The planning of Tobias's funeral luncheon went off without a single snag because it was just like the ones that had come before it.

There was nothing for Carol to distract herself with here.

There was only the pain and the scent of Mary's ribs to remind her that Tobias wasn't there to eat them.

Carol didn't know how long she sat there with her face buried in Mary's stomach, hanging on to her and crying, but when she could catch her breath, she was exhausted. Mary tilted Carol's face back and wiped her eyes and nose as if she were a child before putting a kiss to her head.

"Take her home," Mary told Elijah. "Put her to bed."

"No," Carol croaked. "I should be here."

"This is all for show," Mary said. "Anybody says a word about you not being here, I'll tell them where to go. You've been through enough today."

"Mama, you shouldn't be here alone," Elijah said.

"I'm not alone. I'm never alone. I've got Tobias with me everywhere I go." She put her hand to her heart and smiled at Carol. "You know that feeling all too well. Now go home. Get some sleep. You've been through enough for today," she said again, and nodded as if to confirm her assessment.

"I'll take her," Lara said. "I think the girls should get some rest, too."

Carol looked beyond Mary and saw her three nieces huddled together, watching the scene play out. "I'm okay," she mouthed to them, and offered them a smile.

"You stay with Mary," Lara said to her husband, and kissed him lightly.

Elijah helped Carol stand. She hugged Mary tight, whispered that she loved her, then let Lara take her out to Elijah's car. The girls settled in the back, quiet as mice.

Carol turned to look at them. "I'm sorry, girls."

"It's okay," they said, in almost robotic unison.

She wanted to reassure them, but she couldn't find the words *or the energy to lie. She sat silently as Lara drove the few miles to Mary's house. Once they arrived, Carol said, "You don't have to stay with me. You should be there with Mary and Elijah."*

"You shouldn't be on your own."

"Actually, I think I'd like to be on my own."

"Mary would slap me silly if I left you alone right now."

Wiping her eyes, she sighed. "Tell her I beat you up." She cleared her throat when her voice cracked.

"Like that could happen." Rolling her head back against the headrest, Lara frowned. "I should be here. I want to take care of you. Tobias would want me to take care of you. He wouldn't want you to be alone."

"But I want to be alone, Lara. Please. Take the girls home and let them get some sleep. I promise, I'll be okay. I need to do this alone for a while."

She exhaled before nodding. "Okay. Okay. But if Mary kicks my ass, I'm kicking yours."

"Deal."

Carol used Mary's spare key to let herself in. The house was quiet. Too quiet. She walked into the living room and stopped at the wall of photos that chronicled the evolution of the Denman family. The framed images continued to accumulate. In a few years, there wouldn't be any wall space left.

She started on the left side, when Tobias and Elijah were babies. Mary's husband had walked out when Elijah was a toddler. Tobias had almost always been the man of the house. His sense of responsibility had shown even when he was pre-teen. He'd taken care of his brother from the tender age of four and had never stopped. They were closer than any two siblings Carol had ever met. They were a team and were fierce about protecting their mother.

That strong sense of family and loyalty was what had drawn Carol to Tobias. When he'd stood up for her in their chem class, he might as well have shot Cupid's arrow through her heart. She'd been smitten from that moment on. Her admiration had never wavered. Not once in twenty years.

He had started working as a paperboy as soon as he was able to bring in money to help ease his mother's burden. Carol smiled at the photo of him beaming as he held up his first paycheck. He might have been a child in that photo, but she had seen that smile on his face when he had graduated college. He was so proud of his accomplishment.

As the pictures progressed, the boys grew, as did their triumphs—Tobias in his football uniform, holding the MVP trophy, and Elijah standing on the baseball field. Both boys at their high school graduations. Then on to college. The photo that made the tears in her eyes fall was of their wedding day. A photo of Katie hung next to one of Carol and Tobias on their honeymoon in the Ozarks, which was all they could afford at the time. Elijah's graduation and wedding came a few years, and photos, later, soon followed by picture after picture of his daughters.

The photo that drew Carol back, though, was the one taken a couple of Christmases before. She sat next to Tobias, leaning into him as they both laughed at Elijah. Lara had caught the moment that perfectly reflected their lives as a family. Happiness. That was the only word she could think of to describe what it was like to be in this house with her family.

Happiness.

Happiness that had been easily ripped away from her. She hadn't felt pain like this since Katie had died. No. She'd never felt pain like this because she'd never let herself really feel Katie's loss.

She'd numbed the pain with drugs and then buried her head and her heart and her hurt. All that was coming for her now. She could feel the monster closing in on her.

Grief was pulling her down, threatening to overtake her, and all of a sudden, the last twenty-plus years of swallowing the pain weren't working. She no longer had Tobias there to be her rock. He wasn't there for her to look to as a reminder that she could move on, that she could live another day...one more minute.

He was gone. All that was left was searing-hot pain, ripping her apart.

Pressing her hands to her mouth, she tried to stifle the scream building in her chest, but just like when the doctor had told her Katie was dead, the sorrow ripped free, burning her throat as it did. Just like when Katie had died, the agony brought her to her knees.

Only this time when she fell, there was no one there to catch her.

Like so many nights in the last two weeks, Carol jolted from her sleep, then lay frozen as she listened.

Thump. Thump. Thump.

"Shit." She tossed the covers aside. Jerking the bedroom door open, she rushed across the hall into the room that had two twin beds for the girls when they stayed with Mary. Elijah leaned over John's seizing body, looking panicked.

Dropping to her knees, Carol put her hand to John's chest. "John. I'm right here. I'm right here. You're okay."

"This is bad," Elijah said. "I'm going to get Mama."

"Let her sleep," Carol said. "There's nothing she can do."

Mary shuffled into the room, pulling her long white terrycloth robe closed. "Like I could sleep through this noise. Did he fall off the bed or did you pull him down?"

"I pulled him down."

"Good boy."

John's seizure seemed to last forever before he started to relax under Carol's hand. The soothing words she offered did little to help, but she couldn't stop them from pouring out. Eventually he quit shaking and twitching and stared up at the ceiling, blinking lazily. She held his hand and rubbed her other over his chest, his arm, occasionally brushing over his hair as his mind slowly started connecting with his body again.

When he looked at her and she could tell he really saw her, she smiled. "There he is."

He mumbled, but she didn't even bother trying to make out what he said.

"We're going to get you up, John." She nodded to her brother-in-law.

Elijah bent over John and lifted him as if he were filled with crumpled paper before easing him to sit on the bed. John swayed, and Elijah kept his hands on his shoulders but stepped to the side while Carol looked into John's eyes.

He muttered again as a towel appeared over Carol's shoulder. She thanked Mary without looking at her and wiped John's face clean, drying the drool off his chin and the tears from his cheeks. He took a few long, deep breaths before reaching up.

His fingers trembled as if his hand weighed a thousand pounds as he touched Carol's hair and frowned. "You look better as a brunette."

"And he's back." She stood upright and put her hands on her hips.

"Praise the Lord," Mary said flatly, clearly not impressed with John's post-seizure observation.

"I'd like to blame his illness, but he's always that uncouth."

Mary shook her head at John before running her hand over Carol's arm. "Let us take care of this. You get yourself back to bed."

"I can't—"

"Carol Elizabeth Denman, that was *not* a request."

Elijah physically winced at Mary's maternal tone. "*Ooh*, Mama used your middle name. You better run, sis."

Carol lifted her hands. "I'll never sleep now. I'm going to fix some tea. Anybody want anything?"

"Bourbon," John slurred.

Carol simply lifted a brow at him before leaving him in the care of her in-laws. She did hear Mary chastise him, though. A gentle but firm warning that he had better start being nicer to Carol or she'd kick his ass. Carol didn't stop to hear John's response, but imagined he told them her name was Caroline. *Car-o-line*. Not Carol.

She'd just put the kettle on the stove and turned the flame to high when Mary came into the kitchen. Mary leaned against the doorjamb with a dramatic sigh and shook her head slowly.

"Something on your mind, Mary?" Carol asked. She didn't have to ask, really. Mary would have told her all about her concerns even if Carol hadn't asked.

"This is too much."

She focused on getting two mugs from the cabinet,

intentionally avoiding picking Tobias's favorite Cardinals mug. "It hasn't been easy."

"Carol—"

"Mary." Turning, she faced the woman. "He's dying. Katie's father is dying. Despite all the problems in our past, he *is* her father, and he has no one else in this world."

"And whose fault is that?"

"His. Believe me, he knows it." She returned her attention to adding honey and tea bags to the mugs. "You and Tobias have been pushing me for years to make peace with him."

"Not like this." Crossing the kitchen, she stopped next to her. "You're torturing yourself."

"No."

"*Yes*. You think I didn't hear it in your voice? You think I can't see it in your eyes? You're putting yourself through hell. And for what? A man who let your baby girl—"

"*Don't*." She closed her eyes, knowing she'd unintentionally snapped. "I'm sorry. I don't mean to bark, but... Yes, this has been tough and, yes, I am exhausted. But you were right. Tobias was right. Even John was right. It's time to face Katie's death." Carrying the mugs to the stove, she waited for the telltale whistle from the kettle.

Mary joined her. "There is a difference between grieving and punishing yourself. That man should be in a hospital."

"He knows that. He doesn't want—"

"To hell with what he wants. I'm talking about you. You've seen enough death in your life. You shouldn't have to be there for his. It isn't right that he's asking you to do this. It hasn't even been a year since you lost your husband, Carol."

"I don't want to fight about this. Please." She scoffed. "If I wanted a fight, we would have visited *my* mother."

Mary brushed her hand over Carol's hair. "We're not fighting, baby. I'm worried about you. With damn good reason."

The kettle whistled, giving Carol a reason to ignore Mary's comment. She filled the cups and carried them to the table. Sinking into a chair, she dipped the tea bag a few times before dropping the tab to let the leaves steep. "It's my fault, too," she whispered. Swallowing hard, she lifted her gaze to Mary. "Katie's death. It's my fault, too."

Mary narrowed her eyes and pressed her lips together. "Don't you let that man screw with your mind."

"I knew he was a drunk. I pretended he could control it. That he could somehow be responsible when he needed to be."

"Is this what he's been telling you?"

"Mary, I left my six-year-old daughter alone with an alcoholic, knowing that he couldn't stay sober long enough for me to get home to her. I knew that he started drinking the moment he put her to bed. Every night. I knew this, and I still left her with him." She blinked, stopping her tears before they could fall. "All this hatred and anger I've been clinging to, it's not only at John."

Mary shook her head hard. For the last twenty-one years, whenever John came up—which wasn't often—Carol had been more than happy to tell her mother-in-law how horrible the man had been.

Carol's lips quivered. "I should have left him. I *could* have left him. I chose to stay. I chose to trust him with my daughter. That was my choice. My mistake. One that cost Katie her life."

Mary gripped Carol's hands. "You are no more to blame

for that girl's death than you are for Tobias's. Do you hear me?"

"But it's the truth. Mary..."

"Stop this nonsense," Mary nearly yelled. "Right now." Pointing her finger to the ceiling, indicating the second floor, she clenched her jaw tight. "Is this what he's doing to you? Making you believe you could have saved Katie? Twisting your guilt? Because I will kick that boy's ass. I don't care if he's got both feet in the grave."

Carol didn't mean to giggle, but the sound slipped out before she could stop it. "I love you. God, how I love you. But he doesn't blame me. He accepts the role he played. I realized this on my own. We were both to blame. He was irresponsible in his drinking, and I was irresponsible in letting him keep her. Everything between us was a fight toward the end, and I didn't want the fight. I didn't want the inconvenience of forcing him into rehab, so I screamed and yelled about everything else and ignored that he had a real problem. My denial killed Katie as much as his alcoholism."

Mary sat back, clenching her jaw and shaking her head. "Don't you carry this guilt for the next twenty-four years of your life. You've held on to this pain long enough."

"I'm realizing that, too. I hate to say this, but I don't think I could have reached this point if I hadn't lost Tobias. Losing him—" She cleared her throat when her voice broke. "He always stopped me from hitting bottom with Katie, but I bottomed out emotionally when I lost him. I shut down."

"I know you did."

"If John hadn't shown up, I would have spent the rest of my life on autopilot—work a lot, eat a little, sleep even less. Rinse and repeat. Facing this has been like falling into a pit of broken glass, but all this is necessary. I have to process the grief I've bottled up. Painful as it is." She dipped her tea bag again. "He still owns the house where she died. He never moved."

"Don't you go back there," Mary warned with a stern whisper. "Don't you do that to yourself."

"I told him I wouldn't. Damned if that place isn't calling out to me, though." She focused on squeezing the excess tea from the bag and setting it aside on a napkin. "I never told you but, I...I went to where Tobias was hit."

"Carol," she whispered in a tone of disbelief.

"I stood there staring at the marks the police had put on the pavement. A line where the impact happened. One where the truck stopped. Another where he landed. I could see it playing out in my mind. I got so angry, Mary. All this rage boiled up and erupted. I got the tire iron out of my car and started beating it against the asphalt, screaming like a madwoman."

Mary gasped and lifted her hand to her lips. "You didn't."

"The cops showed up and pulled their guns on me."

"A rich white girl like you?"

Carol laughed quietly. "Yeah. Imagine that." Her amusement faded. She still had a hard time believing that what she was about to share was the truth. It was. "They held me in the psych ward for evaluation for forty-eight hours."

Mary's face sagged as she finally seemed to understand the seriousness of her confession. "You never told me this."

"I didn't want you to worry. The counselor convinced the judge to drop the charges if I did three months of grief counseling. It didn't help." Her voice cracked again, and she covered her face.

As she had at Tobias's funeral, Mary wrapped her arms around her and hugged her close as she sobbed.

Finally Carol leaned back. "I'm okay."

"You haven't been okay since he died, baby."

"I'm working through it."

"You're working through it? Is that what all this is? What you're doing is opening every single wound you've ever had and hoping you don't bleed to death. Self-inflicted torture."

"Not quite that drastic."

"Mm-hmm." Easing back in her chair, Mary pursed her lips together and lifted her brows. "You're going to go to that house, aren't you?"

Carol considered the question that had been whispering in the back of her mind for nearly two weeks. "I don't want to. I think I *have* to. I don't know how else to let the rest of this anger go."

"I'll go with you."

"No."

"You need help taking care of John anyway."

Taking Mary's hands, Carol squeezed them tight. "Thank you. I mean it. Thank you, but no. She was my daughter. *Our* daughter. We've got to do this as her parents."

Mary sank back. The frown on her face spoke volumes about how unhappy she was at Carol's decision, but she didn't continue to argue. "You come back here on your way home. I need to see with my own eyes that you're okay."

"I will."

"Tobias would not approve of this."

"Actually, I think he would have. If it was the catalyst to healing, I think he would have."

———

Carol hadn't been to Tobias's grave since the day she and his family watched his headstone carefully set in place six months prior. Still, she knew exactly where to walk. She felt as if he were pulling her to him until she stopped in front of the monument with *Denman* stamped in large letters across the stone. Under their last name, *Tobias James* had been carved in smaller letters on the left, *Carol Elizabeth* on the right. Below Tobias's name were the dates of his birth and death. Beneath the intertwined wedding bands that separated their names was their wedding date, July 2, 1999.

She had never considered her name before, but looking at Carol instead of Caroline struck her. She'd always felt that Caroline died with Katie. Now it seemed that, to some extent, Carol had died with Tobias.

John might have insisted she was strong, but she knew better. She'd grown up hiding from her parents, avoiding any kind of spotlight to keep their harsh judgments from her ears. Then she grew into the Caroline John wanted. The mommy Katie needed. When that was lost, she morphed into Carol— the serious, ambitious wife to serious, ambitious Tobias.

Here she was, a fifty-one-year-old woman whose only identity was as a childless mother and husbandless wife.

Easing to her knees, she placed a bouquet of white and blue delphiniums and purple salvias against the headstone and traced his name with her fingertips. The flowers were the same as he'd grown in their garden that had brought him so much pride.

"Hey, you," she whispered. "It's been a crazy year, huh?"

Sitting the rest of the way down, she crossed her legs and

inhaled until she couldn't hold any more air. Her exhale sounded loud to her ears, and she glanced around to make sure she hadn't disturbed anyone. Sounds always seemed amplified in cemeteries. She was glad they hadn't put Katie in one. She would have hated the quiet. Katie was never quiet.

Even as an infant she'd babble to herself constantly. She never could tolerate silence. John had been right about leaving her on a shelf for twenty-four years. That hadn't been right. That wouldn't have been what Katie would have wanted. She should have been front and center in the living space. Her urn should have been on display for all to see the way Katie had always drawn people to her.

She had a natural charisma she'd gotten from John. She was a people person. Not the introvert Carol had always been. No. Katie never should have been left sitting on a shelf. Carol was changing that; she was honoring Katie the right way now. That was all she could do. She guessed by finally facing her grief like he'd wanted her to, she was honoring Tobias, too.

Running her fingers over his name again, Carol replayed the year in her mind. Losing him, breaking down, turning her grief inward and burying herself in her work. And John. She never would have thought he'd show up in her life after all these years.

They certainly had come a long way in the last two weeks. Further than she would have ever thought possible.

"I guess you know about all that. You probably had a hand in it, didn't you? Jerk." She smiled. "You got tired of telling me to reach out to him, so you brought him to me. Not nice, Tobias. Not nice at all."

She swallowed and exhaled harshly to keep from crying. "We've been taking Katie around the country, leaving her in all those places she wanted to see, and I thought... She would have loved you, Tobias. She would have absolutely adored you, and I know you loved her even though you never met her. She'd want to be here with you, too." Reaching into her pocket, Carol pulled out the little container holding Katie's ashes and held it tight. "You should have her here with you."

After sprinkling Katie's remains in the grass at the base of the headstone, she put the flowers over them to prevent them from blowing away. "I love you guys." She kissed her fingertips, then put them to his name before pushing herself up and walking away.

When she got back to the house, John was eating brunch with Mary and Elijah. Despite Mary's clear resentment of his intrusion into Carol's grief process, she was being as kind to him as she would be to anyone sitting at her table.

He looked up, grinning through the smear of barbeque sauce on his face. "I'm trying to convince her to adopt me. My mom never cooked this good."

"Oh, I don't know," Carol said. "Frannie's apple pie was pretty memorable."

John's smile widened. "It was the best."

"Sit down. Let me fix you a plate," Mary ordered.

Carol looked at her watch. "It's barely ten in the morning. I'm not up for ribs."

Elijah stopped chewing. "Good thing Tobias never heard you say that."

"He would have divorced me."

Mary kissed the top of Carol's head. "That boy loved you more than anything. But, yes, he probably would have." They laughed as Mary slid a plate of fresh-cut fruit and a cup of coffee in front of Carol. "I know my girl."

"Thanks."

"John says you're getting back on the road today?" The concern on Elijah's face was there for Carol to see.

"Yeah. Next stop Dayton." She didn't even try to sound upbeat as she said it. Dread had been crushing in around her heart for days. With the trip to Ohio imminent, she feared her heart would shatter under the pressure.

"I can go with you," he offered.

She lifted her face to him, holding his stare. Mary had put him up to that. He wouldn't have offered otherwise. Not that Elijah wouldn't be there without hesitation if Carol ever needed him, but he had a job and was already taking the morning off to be sitting there.

"You've done enough already," she assured him.

"I have vacation."

"That I'm sure you'd rather spend with your family."

"*You're* my family," he said unwaveringly.

"I know that. I meant Lara and the girls." Reaching across the table, Carol waited until he took her hand. She squeezed his tight. "I'm fine. I've got this."

"I want you to stop on your way home," Mary said from behind her. "That's not an option, young lady. I want you to stay for a few days. None of this passing-through business. You understand?"

Carol nodded. "Got it."

Elijah gently tugged her hand, demanding her attention. "I can be there in six hours. One phone call, and I'll drop everything."

"I will call if I need you."

He released her hand. "Tobias would be pissed if he knew you were doing this alone."

She chuckled. "He'd be pissed that you're eating his share of ribs."

Lighter chatter filled the rest of the meal. Carol and John gave a brief rundown of all the places they'd seen in the last two weeks, talking as if it'd been a vacation rather than a memorial trip for their daughter. After the dishes were cleaned up and all Carol's and John's belongings were tucked into the RV, Elijah helped John toward the door, one measured step at a time.

"You staying with him until the end?" Mary asked.

Putting a top on the travel mug she'd filled with coffee, Carol shrugged. "I don't know. I don't know what's going to happen when we get to Dayton. Part of me wants to kick him out at the city limit and run as fast as I can, another part of me wants to finish this thing the right way."

"What's the right way?"

Facing Mary, she said, "Honestly? I have no idea. I guess I'll know when I get there. Thank you for letting us stay. I know it wasn't easy with John's health being what it is."

"That was nothing. *You*"—she put her hand to Carol's cheek—"are everything, and I'll be here to do whatever you need me to do to help you."

Carol hugged her tight. "Thank you. I needed to hear that."

"Don't you let this thing pull you under. Elijah and I will be there in a heartbeat if you need us."

"I know." Exhaling, she looked out at the RV. "We're stopping at the Arch and then getting on the road. We should be in Dayton by dinnertime."

"Let me know you're okay."

"I will. I love you."

"I love you, Carol. I'll see you soon."

Carol's next stop was a big hug from her brother-in-law. He lifted her up and held her like he did his girls. They always squealed and protested, but Carol let the feel of his embrace fill her. She would never admit to anyone how much she needed a soul-squishing hug, but she did. Since Tobias wasn't there to give her one, she'd accept Elijah's and let it heal her a bit.

"Love you, sis," he said with one more squeeze.

"Love you." When her feet were on the grass, she looked up and smiled. "Kiss the girls for me."

"Will do. You get through this and come home and let us take care of you, okay?"

"Yup. Mary already gave me my marching orders."

He held her gaze. The determination in his eyes was reminiscent of Tobias. "I meant what I said. I'll drop everything and come running if you need me."

"I know."

"Get outta here before the crowd beats you to the Arch."

She accepted his kiss on the cheek, then climbed into the driver's seat. "All right. One more stop. Are you ready?" she asked her passenger.

John looked out at the sunny sky. "Ready as I'll ever be." He seemed content to sit in silence as she drove the familiar route. She was content with his silence as well. Her emotions had been rubbed raw over the last two weeks. The quiet didn't last, though.

"I like them," he said. "Your family."

"I like them, too."

"Mary didn't cry every time I entered the room like Judith did."

Carol giggled at his observation. Glancing at him, she was glad to see him smiling as well. His face had gotten thinner; his clothes hung noticeably looser than they had when they'd started the journey. She hadn't wanted to accept what that meant, but her heart grew heavy with the knowledge that he was rapidly losing his battle.

"Don't look at me like that," he said.

"Like what?"

"Like I'm dying."

"Didn't realize I was."

"The seizure last night..." He looked out the window at the Arch in the distance. "I'm ready, Caroline."

"Ready for..." She trailed off as understanding took hold.

"This is the last stop. The last thing I can do for Katie. I've done everything I promised her I'd do. I quit drinking. I made peace with you. I forgave myself. And we're about to finish her list. There's nothing else for me to do here. I'm ready."

She pulled her lips between her teeth and bit hard to try to stave off her tears. "That's good, John. It's good to be ready."

They didn't speak again until she'd parked and was helping him into his chair. He shielded his eyes until she slid his sunglasses onto his face.

"Better?"

"The light hurts a little."

"It's bright today."

"That's good," he said as she started pushing him toward the Arch. "She liked the sunshine."

"She liked the rain, too. Remember how she'd wear those red rain boots and jump in every puddle she could find."

"Splish-splash, Mama's gonna make me take a bath," he sang, remembering Katie's chant.

Carol's heart seized for a moment. "I haven't thought about that in a long time."

"She was such a mix of us, wasn't she?" His voice wobbled, filled with emotion. "An angel like you and a mischievous devil like me."

"She was a handful sometimes," Carol admitted. "Just like Daddy."

He swiped at his face as she pushed him to the edge of the grass and set his brakes. Looking up at the Arch, he sat staring for some time as Carol squatted next to him.

"That's it, kitty cat. The last place on your list. Isn't it great?" Holding his hand out, he waited for Carol to take it. "Mommy and I miss you very much. We're so happy we made this trip together." Looking at the woman beside him, he smiled as much as he seemed to be able to manage. "You should tell her about this one, Mommy. This is your home. You should tell her about it."

Carol wiped at her face and swallowed to steady her voice before telling Katie what the Arch symbolized and how tall it was and how it had been built. When she finished, she opened the container. Instead of sprinkling the ashes, she put the container in John's weak fingers. With her hand on his, she helped him empty Katie's remains into the grass.

A sob ripped from his throat, causing one to leave Carol's as well. Turning to him, she leaned up enough to pull him into a hug. His arms, weak as they were, went around her, holding her as they supported each other now, as they should have done twenty-four years prior.

It was a few years late, but they were finally mourning their daughter as they should have done—together.

FOURTEEN

THE DRIVE FROM ST. Louis to Dayton took longer than Carol expected. Between construction and increased traffic, the time was closer to seven when she saw buildings looming in the distance. Every highway sign telling her how much farther she had to go before reaching Dayton made her stomach clench a little tighter. As evidence of the city started to pop up around them, she glanced at John. He had refused to go to bed but had fallen asleep in the passenger seat somewhere east of Indianapolis and hadn't stirred since. However, he seemed to sense they were getting close and started to stir.

"Hey," he said a few minutes later. He blinked before looking around. "Are we home?"

Staring at the road ahead, she tightened her hold on the steering wheel. "I...I can't take you there. I'm going to find a hotel."

He took a moment to process her words. "Okay."

"I'm sorry. I just... I can't. Not right now."

"It's okay." He looked out the window again. The tension

in the RV hadn't been this thick since their first days of traveling together. The peace that had somehow settled between them had turned into something else. The stress wasn't necessarily between them but was definitely there, like a riptide hiding below the calm surface, waiting to pull them in.

Her awareness of her surroundings heightened. The streets were the same, some of the buildings had barely changed, but the city had evolved into something more modern. The sense of doom was the same, though. The strangling hold she'd always felt in the city returned, shaking her down to her core.

She hated this place. For many reasons.

Carol shook her head hard, dislodging the ghosts from her mind.

"Are you okay?" John asked.

"Yeah." Her voice cracked, exposing the lie in her brief answer.

"If you clutch the steering wheel any tighter, you're gonna break it."

She forced her fingers to relax. "I swear to God, I can still feel my father here. Looking down his nose at me like he always did. You know the only time I ever came back here was for his funeral. When Mom called to let me know she'd decided to sell the house and move to Florida, I was relieved. I'd dreaded having to settle her estate and sell that place. I'm glad I don't have to worry about that now."

John looked at the bottle of water in his hand for a few moments before saying, "I was there."

"You were where?" she asked, creasing her brow.

"Your father's funeral."

The bottom seemed to drop out of her stomach. "What? You're just now telling me this?"

He shrugged and turned toward the windshield. "When I saw your dad's obituary, I knew you'd be at the funeral. I had my chance to confront you for leaving like you had. I had this whole speech in my head, ready to tell you what a shitty person you were. When I walked in, that all faded away. My first thought was that you were even more beautiful than when you left, but then I noticed how you looked so...numb. I knew that look. That was the same look you had after Katie died. You were pushing to get through the service so you didn't break." He smiled sadly. "I couldn't... It would have been cruel of me to pick a fight when you were grieving your father. I sat back and watched you."

"That's creepy, John."

He chuckled. "Yeah, I know. I'd always known you were too good for me, but seeing you standing picture-perfect next to your mother proved it. Your hair was perfect, your suit was perfect, you smiled and nodded on cue. That's what was really creepy. You looked like a Stepford daughter."

She glanced at him. "I don't doubt that. Even though he was in a coffin, I was terrified of misstepping and embarrassing him."

"Tobias wasn't there."

Her brief amusement faded. "No. If you read the obituary, you know my mother left out the fact that I was married. *Survived by his devoted wife Judith and their daughter Caroline.* Most people include their children's spouses. But nope. Not a single mention. Not even a note that my last name was Denman. Just *Caroline.* I didn't take offense—that was expected—but I did take the hint. Dad didn't want Tobias at his funeral any more than he wanted us to visit at Christmas. Not that I would have. I was perfectly happy to spend holidays with Tobias's family."

"Was Tobias angry?"

"No. I think he was relieved when I told him it was probably best if I went on my own. My mom was better at hiding her disapproval, but you know how Dad was. Nothing brought him greater joy than letting me know how disappointed he was in me."

"Did he do that heavy sigh thing whenever Tobias walked in the room?"

Carol hit the steering wheel with the palm of her hand. "*Yes*. Every time."

"He did that to me, too. Never failed. Sometimes I'd leave the room and walk back in to hear his reaction."

Carol laughed. "God, he was such a jerk." She glanced over, and her smile softened. "Thank you for not approaching me. Being back here was hard enough. That would have been too much."

"I know. I saw it on your face." He stared at her for several seconds. "You said you didn't mourn for your father. I would disagree. You were shaken by his death."

"I said I didn't cry. I was shaken, mostly because he's always seemed indomitable. I never considered that he could die someday. That seemed impossible. He went without a fight. Mom said he was there one minute and gone the next. I would have expected him to fight."

He looked out the window again. "Sometimes there's no fight to be had. I could have tried surgery or chemo, but the doctors said the odds weren't with me. Why spend the rest of my life in a hospital or sick from treatment? That seemed pointless."

"It might have worked."

He shook his head. "I don't think so. Besides, this was worth it. This trip with you and Katie. This was all I ever wanted. Well." He scoffed. "I would have preferred she not be in an urn when we made it to all her places. This was worth not being in a hospital. I'd rather be here with you."

She glanced at him. She had to admit she wasn't nearly as offended by his presence as she had been two weeks ago. "I'm glad. I guess." She smiled, and he snickered in response.

He exhaled, forcing the air through tight lips, accentuating the sound. "Things are winding down. Don't you think?"

She considered his words for a moment before deciding he meant his health. "Yeah, I think so."

"Are you leaving? Now that I'm home."

She forced her gaze to stay on the road as she inhaled. "I don't know. I can stay. If you want."

"I do. But I don't want to...you know."

"I know. I'm not ready to face that house yet."

"You've had a pretty rough year already."

"Yeah. I can handle it, John. Just...not yet."

He gave one firm nod. "Of course you can. You're the strongest person I ever met."

She laughed softly. "Hardly."

"You are. Don't ever doubt that, okay? Don't ever think you weren't enough. Because you were."

Blinking her tears away, she swallowed her emotions. "I gotta drive here, John. This trip won't end well if I can't see through my tears. Maybe we can hold this chat for a few minutes, huh?"

"Sure. It'll keep."

She took an exit a few miles from the neighborhood where the little ranch house she'd used to live in nestled. Pulling into the first decent chain hotel she found, she parked. "I'll be back."

His only response was a slight nod of his head. Taking her purse, she entered the lobby and smiled at the receptionist as she asked for a handicap-accessible room with two queens. Relief settled in her heart to hear there was a room available. She hadn't realized how much she'd feared not being able to find a place to sleep and having no choice but to take John home.

"Got a room, huh?" John asked when she climbed in through the side door instead of getting into the driver's seat.

"Don't sound so disappointed."

"I am disappointed. Maybe you could take me home."

She unbuckled his seatbelt and turned his chair. When he was facing her, she shook her head. "Call Bert if you want to go home. I'm sure he'll come get you. I am *not* ready. I've already said that." She took a quick assessment, making sure his feet were square under him. "Ready?" They maneuvered gradually until John was out of the RV and seated in the chair.

His lips twitched with a weak grin. "You should call Dr. Collins and tell him I made it home. No doubt he lost a bet on that one."

Carol ignored his bad joke. A few minutes later, she dropped one overnight bag with clothes and toiletries for both of them in his lap and started pushing him toward the entrance. "I'm starving. Let's figure out something for delivery. My treat."

"Pizza," John said without hesitation. "I don't know how you never eat pizza. I've gone two weeks without pepperoni, and I feel like I'm dying." He rolled his head back to look up at her. "Get it? I said—"

"I heard what you said, John. Yet another death joke. Funny. Do you have a preference on where I order?"

"Nope, as long as you get stuffed crust and extra pepperoni."

She stopped at room 114 and used the keycard to unlock the door. Stepping in, she waited for him to maneuver his way inside, which took so long she almost gave in and helped, but she resisted the urge. For both their sakes, she really needed him to be independent as long as possible. Finally he was in far enough that she could let the door close.

"I'm going to order dinner and then freshen up. Do you need the bathroom first?"

"Naw," he said, scanning the room. "I'm good. Nice digs, Dr. Denman. This must have cost a pretty penny."

Carol ignored his assessment as she grabbed the hotel-provided local guide off the desk and picked a pizza place. After placing the order, she went to the restroom and used cool water to splash some of the weariness away. When she stood up and patted her skin dry, obvious signs of exhaustion remained.

No wonder Mary and Elijah had been worried. She really did look like hell. She felt like hell, too. She hadn't been treating her body right the last few weeks. She needed to take a run to clear her head and get her muscles moving. Then maybe she could get some real sleep and get rid of the bags and dark circles that had taken up residence under her eyes.

Until then, any attempt at making herself appear any less miserable was futile. Folding the towel, she set it aside and left the room. John was sitting in his chair, staring out the window. The only thing visible in their view was the parking lot, but he didn't seem to be seeing that.

"You okay?" she asked.

He took a moment, as if considering his answer, before nodding. "Tomorrow, okay? Take me home tomorrow."

Carol swallowed. "Tomorrow is..."

"The day she died."

Twenty-four years. "I don't think... John, I don't want..."

Turning in the wheelchair, he met her gaze. "You can't hide from her forever."

"I'm not hiding."

"You've been hiding from everything your entire life," he said quietly before facing the window again.

She opened her mouth to push back. He was the one who had insisted she was strong—the strongest person he'd ever met. But then she closed it and simply glared at him instead. They could go back and forth for hours if she didn't end the fight. She knew that from plenty of experience. "I'm going to go grab my gym bag so I can run after dinner."

"You shouldn't exercise on a full stomach," he called as she marched toward the door.

Turning, she managed to bite back the words that wanted to rip from her mouth. Instead, she counted to three and said, "Thanks for the advice. I'll consider it." She would have jerked the door shut, but the damn thing had a hydraulic brace at the top to stop the door from closing too fast. Damn it.

She stormed to the RV and grabbed the bag from the compartment and slammed that door. That one slammed fine. Dropping the strap over her shoulder, she stared at the hotel entrance, not really interested in going back to her room. She wasn't going to fight with him anymore. The man was dying right before her eyes, she couldn't keep fighting with him, but damned if he didn't push every single button.

She eased down in a chair in the lobby and tried to tell herself that being home couldn't be any easier for John than it was for her. Their journey had ended. He'd said goodbye to his daughter. The only thing he had left to look forward to was dying.

That wasn't easy. That couldn't be easy. He didn't have much time left. She needed to be patient and help him through it. And obviously that meant finding the courage to take him home.

She needed patience and courage. Unfortunately, both were a lot easier to find in theory than in her current reality.

The doors slid open and a pizza-delivery man walked in.

"Is that for one fourteen?"

"Yes, ma'am."

She stood and signed the credit card receipt the man held out to her before accepting the dinner. Carrying it and her gym bag, she went back to the room. John hadn't moved. "Pizza's here."

"I want to go home."

She eased the box on the table in the corner of the room. "Tomorrow."

"Why? Why are we waiting?"

"Because I'm not ready. If you want to go home," she said as calmly as she could manage, "call Bert."

He was quiet for a moment, as if debating the option. "Tomorrow. Promise me."

She sighed. "I'm not promising anything, John." Turning, she stared at the back of his head. "That house is tied to a lot of really bad memories for me. You've had twenty-four years to learn how to be there without Katie. I'm not ready. I need you to understand that."

He looked over his shoulder at her. "You shouldn't have left."

"Are we back to this? Really?"

Looking down, he stopped himself from saying whatever was on his tongue. She thought that was for the best, but that didn't stop her from pushing the issue.

"I left, John. I walked out. I can't change that. I *wouldn't* change that. Maybe you never let go of us, but I did, and I don't think we need to rehash all the reasons why. We've done this. We've settled this. I did what you wanted. I drove you to all those places and we said our goodbyes. I deserve time to gather myself before I have to face the place where my daughter died." She didn't mean to raise her voice, but she was damn near yelling by the time she finished.

"I just..." He faced the window again. "I'm ready to go home, Caroline."

"Tomorrow. Come eat before it gets cold."

She focused on opening the box and prying apart the disposable plates that had come with it. She'd set the table by the time he pushed himself from the wheelchair to join her.

"Admit it," John said flatly. She was expecting him to

continue the fight, but he grinned and said, "That smells a hell of a lot better than asparagus."

"I never cooked asparagus on this trip. Not once." She put a slice on his plate, then lifted a smaller one out for herself. She took a moment to smell the pizza. "Yeah, I can admit that smells damn good."

"Yes, it does." He shoved nearly half a slice into his mouth and smiled as he chewed. "Heaven. That's what that is."

She took a more measured bite, but had to agree with him. The pizza was delicious. She didn't indulge often, but she never regretted it when she did.

"I know this is hard for you," he said after swallowing. "I'm sorry."

She shook her head. "We never were very good at being patient with each other."

"We were always good at fighting, though."

"Yes. We were always good at that."

"And making up." He wriggled his brows at her.

She shook her head in response. She dropped her pizza onto her plate and wiped her hands. "We fought too much. Katie shouldn't have had to live like that."

"We never fought in front of her."

"She was never far away. She heard too much. She broke up our fights far too often."

He dropped his pizza, too. "We were—"

"Young?" she finished for him.

"Do you think we were bad parents?"

"No. I think we were...struggling and we let that reach her. We shouldn't have let it reach her. We should have protected her from our truth a little bit more."

"What truth?"

She met his gaze. "That we were miserable."

"*You* were miserable," he stated.

"Fine. I was miserable. You were drunk."

He focused on his dinner. "Didn't you tell me that we didn't need to rehash all this?"

She bit her lip. "Yeah, I did. Sorry. I'm going to go find the gym."

"You didn't eat. Caroline," he said when she stood. "You didn't eat."

"Shouldn't exercise on a full stomach, right?"

"Don't go." His plea stopped her. He gestured toward her seat. "Please. I'm sorry. For once, let's not take our stress out on each other. Please."

Carol hesitated before sitting. When she did, she paused again before picking up her pizza. They ate in silence for a few minutes before John exhaled loudly.

"Tell me about something."

"What?"

"Anything. I don't like all this quiet."

She picked at her crust. "I've been thinking about what to do with the house. How would you feel about me donating it to the children's hospital?"

"What would a hospital do with a house?"

"They'd let families stay there for free while their kids are getting treatment. Makes the experience a little less stressful."

"Like a Ronald McDonald house?"

"Yeah. Something like that."

Though his eyes looked sad, he seemed pleased with the idea. "That'd be good. Yeah. I'd like that. Katie would, too."

She nodded. "I think so."

"You can do that, huh? Give them a house?"

"Mm-hmm."

He smiled. "Maybe you could put a swing set in the backyard. Make sure Katie's room has a bed and a crib in case the family has little ones."

"I can do that."

The curve of his lips faded a bit. "I've got some money left. You should use that to fix the place up a bit. I want it to be nice. But, um..." He grinned that lopsided mischievous smirk of his. "I saw your house, Caroline. You should hire a decorator."

She opened her mouth and gasped. "Screw you."

He laughed as she wadded up her napkin and bounced it off his forehead. The mood between them lightened, making the rest of dinner more tolerable.

"Think you can shower on your own?" Carol asked as she closed the box on what remained of the pizza. Thus far, she'd been able to avoid bathing John, but she didn't think that would be the case for much longer. His mobility was fading by the day. The wheelchair had been helpful for longer distances, but she'd give him a few more days before it became a necessity for him to get around.

"I'll be okay," he said.

As he shuffled off to the bathroom, she grabbed her laptop bag and caught up on e-mails, including responding to a frantic plea from Tiana asking how much longer she'd be gone. She looked at the door where John had disappeared.

Probably no more than a week or two, she typed, and hit send. Her answer nagged at her as she skimmed the rest of her e-mails.

Probably no more than a week or two.

John probably wasn't going to live more than a week or

two. Sitting back, she stared at the screen, but she didn't really see the words in front of her.

"Working again?"

She looked up at John. His hair was slicked back, and he'd changed into the fresh sweats and a T-shirt she'd gotten from the RV.

"One of us has to pay the bills."

He ignored her comment as he headed for the bed. "I need to take my meds. I'm wiped out."

She closed her laptop and followed him to the bed, where he dropped down. Even though he could pry the tops off the easy-open bottles, he struggled to get the right number of pills out. She tapped out the pills for his evening dosage, then snagged his water bottle from the table.

She held her hand out as he worked to pick up and swallow each pill. The little bits of medicine slipped from his grasp, bouncing out of his reach. He tried again. Then again. His fingers clearly didn't work as well as they had even the night before when they had gone through this routine, but she stifled the urge to offer to help. He'd tell her if he wanted her to take over putting the pills in his mouth. She'd wait for that to happen before stripping him of the dignity of taking his own medications. After some effort, he swallowed down the last pill.

She set what was left of the water aside. "Ready to lie down?"

He nodded, and she stepped back, there to assist if needed but letting him take care of himself as much as he could. He managed to get the blankets pulled back and stretched out on his own, but she did grab the blanket when he couldn't get the soft material to cover his legs. She tucked him in and started to straighten up, but he grabbed her wrist.

"Come here," he said.

She sat on the edge of the mattress by his hip, but he shook his head.

"Come here."

"John."

"Caroline. Please."

Frowning at him, she gave in and lay down beside him, resting her head on his shoulder.

He wrapped his arms around her and kissed her head. "Do you remember when we used to lie like this?"

"Yeah." When they'd first started dating, he would hold her like that and talk about their future. Things had been perfect back then, back when she'd believed she could have everything. Before life had opened her eyes to how truly mismatched they were.

"You always left when I started snoring."

"Which never took very long," she said, giving him a teasing poke to the arm.

"You fit perfectly in my arms. Still do."

She pushed her breath out between parted lips when he hugged her closer to him. She wanted to remind him that she was a perfect fit for Tobias, but now wasn't the time. Besides, he knew. John knew where her heart was. He didn't need reminding.

He ran his palm over her arm and entwined his fingers with hers. "Thank you for taking care of me."

"You're welcome."

"Not just the last two weeks. Back then, too. You always took care of me."

Her heart tripped in her chest as his words and actions started to come together and paint a clearer picture for her. He was saying goodbye to her. He'd said goodbye to Katie. Now he was saying his farewell to Caroline. Squeezing his hand, she said, "You took care of me, too. In ways I never really understood until I was gone."

He kissed her head again. "We were a good team. I know we crashed and burned, but when it was good, it was damn good."

"It was great."

"Katie was the best."

"Yes. She was."

Stroking his thumb over her hand, he said, "I know going home won't be easy for you. I'm sorry I was impatient."

She sighed. "I'm sorry I wasn't ready today. I will be tomorrow."

"It'll be nice to have you there with me. I've missed having you there." He was quiet for a few moments before giving her one more light squeeze. "You should go to bed, Caroline. I know you're tired."

She hesitated before sitting up. As she did, she looked into his eyes, wanting to make sure he heard her. "I'm glad you found me when you did. I didn't realize how much I needed to make peace with you. Thank you for helping me do that. I love you, John. Despite all that we've put each other through. Despite all the anger I held on to. I love you."

His eyes filled with tears as he smiled. "I love you too, Sweet Caroline."

The only other time he'd called her that was when he'd asked her out on their first date. She hadn't chastised him then, and she wouldn't now. Resting her hand on his chest, she took a moment to memorize his face before putting a soft kiss on his forehead. "Sleep well."

She glanced back before flipping off the light above his bed. He was watching her. He always watched her. From the day they'd first caught each other's eye in a coffee shop not too far from where they were now. Taking a breath, she went into the bathroom and started the shower as a cloud of depression moved over her.

The end was no longer a distant thing that she could pretend not to see. Death was close, so close she could sense it. John could, too. His eyes had changed. He had accepted what was coming. He hadn't lied when he said he was ready for it. Every word that came out of his mouth now was a goodbye.

She wasn't ready for another goodbye.

Once steam started rolling from the shower, Carol tested the water temperature before climbing in. Alone behind the privacy of the thick white curtain, she pressed her hands to the wall and tried to brace herself for the pain she knew was coming.

She'd spent the last two weeks facing Katie's death. When John had shown up in her office the day before Katie's birthday, she never would have imagined that she'd be back at this place for the anniversary of her death.

Fate seemed to be mocking her. The universe seemed to be saying, *You didn't think you could run from this forever, did you?*

And the house... The house was equally cruel in its mockery of her predicament. *Welcome back, Caroline*, it seemed to say. *I've been waiting for you.*

She swallowed the urge to vomit at the knowledge that

she would take John home in the morning. Twenty-four years ago to the day, to the very day, she'd pulled into that driveway and her world had come crashing down on her.

———

Caroline scowled as she pushed the front door open. "John?" Lugging in three grocery bags as her purse strap slid from her shoulder, she kicked the door closed behind her. "I need help with groceries!" Stomping loudly, she headed right for the kitchen and set the bags on the counter next to the open cereal box. Frowning at the half dozen or more empty beer cans on the counter, she jerked her purse the rest of the way down her arm and let it fall to the floor.

The empty cans hadn't been there when she'd left for work. Which meant that, despite his promise, he'd spent the evening drinking while he was supposed to be responsible for Katie. That son of a bitch. The night she sat him down and told him she was this close *to leaving, he had promised he wouldn't drink when he was the only responsible adult around. She knew it wouldn't last. To be honest, she was surprised he'd made it this long.*

She walked to the bedroom and pushed the door open to find him sprawled on his stomach, snoring. She was tempted to wake him and give him hell, but with him passed out, she'd get a few hours of quiet time with Katie. That was worth letting him sleep it off.

"Hey, kitty cat," she whispered as she entered Katie's room. "Mommy bought some waffles. You hungry, baby?" She crossed the room and tugged the blankets back. The only thing there was a pillow and Katie's bear. The television hadn't been on when she'd come in and Katie hadn't been in the kitchen. She checked

the bathroom. The room was a mess—toothpaste on the counter and clothes only halfway inside the laundry basket—but there was no sign of Katie. She did a quick cleanup of the room before going back to the living room. None of Katie's toys were spread across the old, ragged carpeting.

Suddenly her heart dropped to her stomach as her mother's intuition kicked into high alert. Something was wrong. Something was terribly wrong. The silence of the house was unsettling. The stillness oppressive.

Caroline turned her gaze toward the sliding glass door. She focused on the pool and her breath stuck in her lungs at the sight of two little red rain boots sitting next to the ladder. "Katie!" She ran outside, not closing the door despite her constant reminders to her daughter to do so. The water in the pool was flat. Calm. Inviting. Tempting.

Coaxing someone to climb in.

There was no sign that anyone had given in to the urge to enter the pool, but Caroline knew her daughter. Katie was daring. Katie thought she was invincible. She didn't understand why she couldn't use the pool anytime she wanted. It was her pool. Grandma and Grandpa had said so.

Even if Caroline had doubted Katie would be so brave as to climb into the pool alone, she didn't doubt that she'd never have left her boots outside. The only times she ever took her boots off were to sleep, bathe, and swim.

Caroline knew her daughter, and she knew, in that instant, why she wasn't in the house.

Because she was in the pool.

Calling out to Katie, she ran to the edge and a panic-filled scream burned her throat.

There she was. On the bottom. Beneath the calm water.

The only thing moving was her long sandy-brown hair floating around her face. Her arms drifted over her head. Her eyes were open wide and her little mouth sagged from what would have been her last attempt at taking a breath.

"No!" The plea ripped from Caroline as she climbed the ladder and jumped into the waist-deep cold water. She'd just made it to Katie when another body splashed into the water behind her.

Grabbing Katie's arms, Caroline pulled her to the surface, but the girl didn't gasp for air like she should have.

Caroline didn't breathe either. She couldn't.

John grabbed Katie and dragged her limp body to the edge. By the time Caroline reached the ladder, he had Katie over his shoulder and was climbing out of the pool. He eased her to the grass, cradling her head to stop it from hitting the ground too hard, but it didn't matter. Katie didn't wince. Didn't move. Didn't feel any pain.

Caroline sank to her knees next to her daughter.

Katie's blue eyes were open but unmoving. Unseeing. Lifeless. Her skin was a sickening shade of gray. She didn't respond as John pushed on her chest, counting out compressions.

"Help me." He wasn't exactly calm, but he wasn't frozen like Caroline seemed to be.

All she could do was look at Katie, not quite believing what she was seeing, but knowing it was true. Katie had drowned. While Caroline was at the grocery store buying waffles and strawberry-scented shampoo and grape popsicles, her baby had drowned.

"Caroline. Help me."

She was too late. She'd gotten there too late.

John bent down and forced air into Katie's mouth.

But it didn't matter. Wouldn't matter.

No matter how many times he compressed her chest or blew into her mouth, Katie would never take another breath.

John grabbed Caroline by the shoulders and shook her hard. His desperate gaze held hers. "Help me! Please!"

Snapping out of her shock, she bent down and started breathing for Katie while John made her heart beat. Someone, a neighbor, called out that they'd called an ambulance, but Caroline had known it was too late the moment she saw Katie in the pool.

She'd been there, sitting under the water, for too long to find her way back to them.

Everything seemed to speed up and slow down at the same time. Caroline was stuck in some insane matrix where the world was spinning around her, she was moving like a robot—blow, blow, blow, rest—until someone pulled her aside. Hadn't she just gotten home, just found her daughter at the bottom of the pool, and now the medics were there to take over? Hadn't it only been a few seconds?

John pulled her back enough that the EMTs could get to work on Katie. They shoved a mask over her face and one pumped oxygen while the other straddled her little body and pressed on her chest. He counted rhythmically while the gurney was rushed from the backyard. Then they were in the car and John was following the ambulance saying, "She'll be okay," over and over as if Caroline hadn't seen this very scene play out a hundred times.

Even if Katie lived, which she wouldn't, she'd been without oxygen for too long. Her brain was too damaged to ever recover. She'd be brain-dead. What kind of life was that for her little girl?

No. No. She wouldn't be okay.

Caroline knew that. She'd known that the moment she had allowed that damned pool into her backyard. She should have stood her ground—told her in-laws no. She should have made John get sober. She should have hired a babysitter. She should have done all the things she'd wanted to do but didn't because she hadn't had the strength to fight for them.

She hadn't had the strength to fight for herself. For Katie.

And now she'd lost everything.

———

Carol sat in the driveway of their old house, reliving that day, until John put his hand on her arm.

"Breathe, Caroline."

She inhaled, swallowed hard, and exhaled. The front yard, the house, the tree that had grown, and grown, and was now overgrown. "Jesus, John. Have you done any upkeep?"

He shrugged and answered with his usual lack of concern. "Some."

"The neighbors must love you."

"I've never really been too concerned with what those assholes think. Are you done judging me, so we can go in?"

She dragged her fingers under her eyes. "No, but I guess I can't run forever, right?" She unbuckled and turned her seat to open the side door and get his chair out.

"I want to walk," he said.

She didn't argue. That actually gave her one more thing to focus on instead of thinking about where she was. What day it was. What being here was doing to her heart and soul. She managed to keep herself together pretty well until they made it to the front door. John struggled with his keys and finally gave up, holding his hand open and allowing her to take them.

She didn't do much better. His fingers might not have been working right, but hers wouldn't stop trembling. She almost dropped the keys, but managed to catch them before they fell. Closing her eyes, she mentally braced herself as John put his hand on her shoulder. "I got it," she whispered.

She slid the key into the lock and eased the door open. The past reached out and punched her in the gut before she even crossed the threshold.

"Look at me," John whispered. "Caroline. Look at me." He put his arm around her shoulder, using her for support as much as he was offering it. "We had good times here, too. Birthdays and Christmases. Anniversaries. Parties. Focus on the good times."

She did. She tried to use the memories of laughter to cover the sound of her screaming. She tried to think of walking into this house beaming with pride after Katie's first gymnastics class. She tried to focus on opening presents. Stuffing stockings. Filling Easter baskets.

There had been good times here. She had good memories here.

But when she looked up, she was standing in the living room and her knees grew weak. He hadn't changed a thing. The furniture was newer, but the couch and recliner sat in the exact places they had the last time she was here. The photos that she'd hung on the walls over two decades ago remained. She stopped scanning the room as her gaze landed on the sliding glass door.

She saw the pool as clear now as she had twenty-four

years ago. She saw John grabbing her, shaking her, both of them soaking wet as they kneeled over Katie's limp body.

Caroline. Help me.

Putting her hand to her mouth, she tried to stop the fruit she'd had for breakfast from rising, but the acidic burn was too far up her throat. She ran to the kitchen, leaned over the sink, and vomited. When the fruit had left her, she dry-heaved for several minutes before she was able to rinse the sink and her mouth.

When she stood, John was beside her, his eyes filled with sympathy.

"Better?"

She swallowed but the tightness of her throat nearly made her gag. "How can you still live here?"

"You may have had her ashes, but I had her spirit here in this house with me."

She lowered her face as a sob left her. "I guess you won, huh?"

He filled a glass with water and held it out to her. "I don't know. You managed to have a life after leaving. I never did. I was stuck in the past. Doesn't seem like much of a win now that I think about it."

"Everything's the same, John," she whispered, ignoring the glass in his hand.

"For the most part."

Carol's voice cracked as she asked, "Her room?"

"The same."

She couldn't stop herself from moving around him and deeper into the house until she stood outside the room where she'd spent hours playing and reading with her daughter.

Standing there, she could almost hear Katie's laugh and her voice as she spoke for her dolls.

"Time for bed, Mr. Bear," she'd say. And then she'd deepen her voice and respond, "Just one more story. Please." Because that was what she said every night before bed. "One more story, Mama. *Please.*"

Carol's entire body started to tremble as she reached for the knob. The door creaked as she eased it open, and once again the air was sucked from her lungs.

The room hadn't changed. Not one thing had been moved. Katie's bed still sat against the far wall. Her pile of stuffed animals still filled a corner of the room. There was still a pair of shoes tossed carelessly next to her dresser. And there, by the foot of the bed, sat two red rain boots. To think he'd lectured her about leaving an urn to collect dust. This room was a museum.

The only thing that had changed was the rocker that used to sit in their bedroom, the one Carol had used to rock Katie to sleep in, now sat in the middle of the room. Carol eased down into the chair where John obviously sat and stared at the empty bed.

The last time she had been in this room was the night she'd left. She had grabbed a few of Katie's things—her bear, the tooth she'd put under her pillow for the tooth fairy, her baby book, and a few other knickknacks—before disappearing into the night. She couldn't believe he had never...after all these years...he'd never emptied Katie's room.

"I spend more time in here than is probably healthy," he said from the door. "I feel like she's here. In this room."

"This is why you couldn't move on, John. This house is holding you prisoner."

"Or am I holding it prisoner? Either way, I'll be free soon."

She lifted her head to look up at him. Something in his voice was more resolute, more accepting of his imminent fate.

"You're going to have to update the house when I'm gone. What will you do in here?"

"I'll probably do hardwood throughout. It's easier to clean. New paint. New furniture."

"But here. Katie's room."

She looked around. "Yellow paint would be nice. Then it wouldn't be geared toward boys or girls. Put a crib along that wall, like you said. And a new twin bed." She gestured toward Katie's old frame that hadn't moved since she was old enough to sleep in a big-girl bed. "A shelf with books for all ages. Some games. New toys." She blinked away the tears that were threatening to spill down her cheeks. "I think we should leave her picture on the living room wall. Maybe a plaque to let families know why we donated the house."

"That'd be nice. Everyone who stays in her house should know about her."

Carol smiled slightly. "Katie's House. That's what we should call it. Hmm? Welcome to Katie's House."

John squeezed her shoulder. "Do that, okay? Make sure they remember her."

"I will," she said, putting her hand over his.

He moved slowly, holding her shoulders as he bent forward and put a kiss on the top of her head. "I'm tired. I'm going to rest."

"Need help?"

"No. Don't stay in here too long. You'll go a little mad. Trust me, I know."

She didn't doubt that he did. Gripping his hand before he

stepped away, she looked up at him. "It wasn't all bad, John. I remember that now. We had a lot of good times here. We really did."

"I'm glad you remember, Caroline." Putting his hand to her cheek, he rubbed his thumb over her skin and smiled. "I'm very glad."

She rocked for a few minutes, remembering. Always remembering. That was all her life seemed to be since Tobias's death. Reliving the past. Crying for the present. Dreading the future.

That must have been the cycle John found himself stuck in for the last twenty-four years. How sad for him. To never take a step forward.

Eventually she pushed herself up and walked down the hall to the master bedroom. The door opened without a sound and she frowned.

Just like Katie's room, this room hadn't changed since she'd gone. She expected to see John there. He'd said he wanted to rest, but the bed was empty. "John?"

He didn't answer as she ventured into the room toward the bathroom. He wasn't there either.

That feeling—the one she'd felt twenty-four years ago to the day—gripped her stomach. Something was wrong.

Just like Katie, a voice whispered in her mind.

She trotted through the bedroom, down the hall, and into the living area. There on the kitchen counter, next to the sink where she'd vomited earlier, was a prescription bottle. That hadn't been there before. She hadn't brought his meds in.

Standing there, staring at it, she recalled this morning. How strange he'd been acting when she'd emerged from the bathroom. How...at peace he'd seemed all day. She attributed it to finally agreeing to take him home. But, thinking back, she hadn't put his medications away after his morning dose. She'd left them on the table and gone to the bathroom. When she returned, John was packing the overnight bag. Including his prescriptions.

He must have tucked this bottle in his pocket. She looked at the label and a hot poker stabbed at her heart.

"If you were to accidentally ingest...that would be fatal."

That was what she'd told him. Followed up by a request that he not overdose in her RV.

Jesus. While she'd been in the hotel bathroom, bracing herself for facing Katie's death, he'd been plotting his own.

Looking at the glass door, as she'd done years ago, the same knowing dread hit her. She knew exactly what she was going to find when she opened that door.

"John," she whispered.

She crossed the living room. Staring out at the yard, she found him precisely where her instinct told her he'd be, lying on the grass in the same spot where he'd put Katie after pulling her from the water. The same spot where he'd pressed on her little chest, desperate to force life back into her body. The same spot where they'd both known, even if they hadn't said the words, that she was gone.

"John!" Carol had to force herself to move, but she ran out and eased down beside his unresponsive body. Swallowing hard, she checked for any sign of life. Finally he gasped and opened his eyes. She offered as much of a smile as she could muster for him, but a quiver rushed through her chin as she tried.

His lips curled into that lopsided grin. "Sorry, Caroline. I just couldn't do this anymore."

Brushing his hair back, she hushed him. "I know. It's okay."

"She's here. Katie's here. Do you feel her?"

Carol held her breath, stilled her mind, as a strange sensation filled her—a fluttering that made her think maybe they weren't alone. "Yeah. She's here."

"She's waiting for me."

Choking back a sob, Carol ran her hand over his arm, stopping at his wrist to check his pulse. Weak wasn't quite the word. The beats were so faint and far between, she wasn't quite sure how he was still conscious.

John touched her hand, and she held his tight. His eyes no longer looked as if he was lost somewhere between the past and the present. His smile wavered a bit, relaxed around the edges, but didn't fade completely. "The best thing that ever happened to me was you, Caroline. It's okay. I know you can't say the same."

She shook her head. "I wouldn't have had her without you, John. So, yes, I can. You're the best thing because you gave me Katie."

He cupped her face. "Forgive me?"

"Yes. I forgive you. I'm sorry it took this long."

"It's okay." Serenity filled his eyes. "It's okay. You're here. We're all here."

She nodded. "I'm right here. I'm with you. It's okay." She brushed her hand over his chest, the way she'd always done to soothe him. "I'm right here. It's okay."

He smiled as his eyes swam out of focus. "Hey, kitty cat," he whispered. "Daddy's home."

Carol choked on her cry as his body relaxed. Air

whispered from his lips as his eyes lost their light. But the little smile on his lips remained.

Kissing his forehead, she swallowed the need to scream out for him. This wasn't like Katie or Tobias. John hadn't been ruthlessly ripped from her life. John had made his peace and exited on his terms. There was no other way she could imagine his life ending. Instead of screaming and collapsing and cursing his loss, she closed his eyes, kissed his head again, and whispered, *"Guh-night*, Daddy. We love you."

EPILOGUE

CAROL SIPPED her wine as she stared at the box on the counter. The postal service had affixed a sticker to the front telling her and anyone who encountered the package exactly what was inside.

Human remains.

She'd signed for the box and went about her day as if it wasn't there taunting her throughout the afternoon and into the evening.

After setting her glass down, she tore off the tape, pulled the sides apart, and removed the bubble-wrapped urn. She meticulously unwrapped it, then traced her fingers over the lettering.

JOHNATHAN ROBERT BOWMAN
SEPTEMBER 3, 1961
JUNE 22, 2019

She recalled her threat to flush him down the toilet and smiled. "I should do it, you know," she said to the urn.

Twenty-five years ago, she probably wouldn't have hesitated, but after their road trip, she knew he deserved more. He deserved to be with Katie in all the places they never got to see.

She heaved a sigh as she pushed herself up and walked across the bare living room. She set his remains on the mantle between Katie's urn and Tobias's picture. Taking a moment to look around the near-empty room, she realized this was it. She'd been waiting for John. She had no more excuses now.

With two bidders warring over her house, what was left of the furniture would be auctioned by her real estate agent when she left. Elijah and Mary had flown down and driven back to St. Louis in Tobias's car, taking with them the few items—photos and some keepsakes—Carol intended to keep. Everything else had been sold.

Her co-workers had held a lovely retirement luncheon for her the week before. She had nothing left to do but put a few bags and two urns into her RV.

Oh, and the map sprawled across the kitchen counter.

Standing at the counter, she looked over the list again.

New Orleans. Disney World. Everglades National Park. Biltmore Estate. Shenandoah Caverns. Washington, D.C. Statue of Liberty. Niagara Falls.

From there... Well, she'd figure out where to go from there.

Twisting the wedding ring on her finger, she looked out at Tobias's garden. Her next list would be for him. She'd take John and Katie, too, but the next list would be for Tobias. He'd want to see mountains and glaciers and go white-water rafting down the Colorado River.

Yeah. The next list was for Tobias.

Until then, she needed to get some rest. She wanted to get up and get on the road first thing in the morning. She could easily make New Orleans, but it was the next leg of her journey she was bracing herself for. Once she headed toward Florida, she'd feel obligated to see her mother. Considering all the things she'd faced in the last few weeks, she had no doubt she wouldn't be able to smile and fake her way through a visit. She had some things to say about the way her mother had always treated her, and she was finally ready to say them. That wasn't going to be an easy conversation and, as much as it needed to be had, she was dreading it. While Carol's anger at John could become an all-consuming tsunami at times, the rage toward her mother was more like an undertow—never quite overcoming her, but never letting her go either. She was ready to free herself, and her mother, from that trap.

She'd deal with that when she got to Florida, though. She was learning not to worry about what was ahead and to go with life's natural ebbs and flows. She had promised John she'd do better, be better, live more for today. That was what she planned to do. He'd wanted that for her. Katie would have wanted that for her. As would Tobias.

She had a lot of living to make up for, too. She'd spent too much of her life hiding. It was time to live. For her and for them.

"Okay," she said to the empty room. "One more night. Then... Then I'm a retired woman living in an RV." That sounded terrifying, but she was learning to embrace that life was terrifying. Tobias had spent the entirety of their marriage dragging her from her comfort zone, but John had made her accept that she was going to have to do that for herself now. If she didn't, she really would sit in her office for the rest of her life. The idea of living without Tobias by her side was terrifying, but she could do this. She could visit these places. Sprinkle John's and the rest of Katie's ashes. Let them go and heal. She could even learn to live on her own. Not that she was alone. She had her family with her.

Tobias. Katie. And John.

Heading up the stairs to spend her final night in the room she'd shared with Tobias for nearly fifteen years, she stopped halfway up and turned around. She didn't hear the words so much as she felt them. Looking at the two urns and the photo on the mantle, she froze and listened with her heart.

Guh-night, Mommy, the room seemed to say. *We love you.*

Carol smiled at the tranquility that rolled through her and seemed to hug her slowly mending soul. "*Guh-night*. I love you, too."

Carol Denman's journey continues in A Life Without Flowers, the much anticipated sequel to A Life Without Water.

A LIFE WITHOUT FLOWERS

a novel

MARCI BOLDEN

EXCERPT FOR A LIFE WITHOUT FLOWERS

Though the late August sun warmed Carol Denman's shoulders as she strolled down a well-kept sidewalk, a chill settled in her gut. She'd taken her time hooking up her RV in a nearby campground before walking the short distance to the townhome her mom and aunt had bought after moving to Florida. The closer she got to the picture-perfect retirement community, the more disconsolate she felt.

Visiting her mother was never high on her list of things to do. The two of them butted heads incessantly. No issue was too insignificant. They could, and usually did, fight over anything. However, Carol's outlook on life had changed recently, and she'd made this trip to the suburbs of Orlando hoping they could find common ground. If she was ever going to have a relationship with the woman who had brought her into the world, Carol was going to have to make the effort. Judith never would.

As Carol approached the porch to a smoky-blue townhome, her aunt yanked the door open and gasped as if she wasn't expecting company, even though Carol had texted when she'd left the RV park. Ellen spread her arms wide, causing her teal and pink kaftan to flow like a kite flying above the beach. Carol had bought the dress for her aunt in Honolulu. Carol and her husband Tobias had vacationed in Hawaii a few summers before his death. Though they hadn't set foot on a beach due to Carol's aversion to water, they'd had an amazing time hiking the volcanoes and rain forest in between visiting museums.

Feeling happiness for the first time since arriving in Florida, Carol stepped into one of her favorite hugs ever. Aunt Ellen had always made Carol feel as if there was a special connection between them. Her aunt had been a ray of sunshine Carol would have spent her life basking in if Ellen hadn't lived so far away.

"How's my girl?" Ellen asked, squeezing her niece.

"I'm tired from packing up the house, but I'll survive. How are you?" Carol leaned back and her heart grew heavy.

The last time she'd seen her aunt and mom was at Tobias's funeral almost a year ago. The energy that had always radiated from Ellen seemed dimmer now. Age was taking a toll on her, as it was Carol's mother, reaffirming how necessary this trip was.

Ellen pressed her fingertips under Carol's chin as she looked her over. "You look like hell."

"Thanks."

"Are you sleeping?"

"As much as I can." Carol stepped into the cool air of the open living area. The chill she'd felt earlier rolled through her again, but not because of the change in temperature. Being in the same house as her mother set her on edge.

Knowing she'd come to confront a lifetime of emotional neglect made her blood run cold.

A painting on the wall caught Carol's eye, and a smile lit her face. The bright colors created an abstract image of mountains made of checkerboards and a waterfall filling a teapot. The last time she'd been in this house, her mother's bland taste had dominated. She was glad to see her aunt making room for her more eccentric style. "That's a great piece. When did you paint it?"

Ellen moved between Carol and the art. "Don't change the subject."

"What subject?"

"*You*. You're the subject. I was surprised when Judith said you were coming to visit, but now I have to wonder if there's more to it than you passing through. Are you okay?"

Carol nodded to reassure her aunt. "I've spent the last few weeks getting ready to live on the road. Like I said, I'm a little tired, but I'll catch up on sleep."

The way Ellen pursed her lips and cocked one brow suggested she hadn't believed Carol's excuse. Ellen always could see through her. "There's more."

There *was* more. Carol hadn't slept for days knowing she was on her way to visit her mom. She hoped to find a way to mend their relationship, though she wasn't foolish enough to think doing so would be easy. She was dreading the days ahead. "Where's Mom?"

"It's Sunday. Where do you think she is?"

Every Sunday for as long as Carol could remember, Judith made enough chicken and dumpling soup for Carol's father to eat leftovers for the week. That habit had remained, even though her dad had been gone almost four years. Carol followed the familiar scents to the kitchen, where she found her mom standing over a big silver pot, staring intently. Unlike the living area, Ellen's spunk hadn't migrated to the kitchen.

This was her mother's domain, and the neutral colors and clean, bare counters proved as much. Ellen tended to leave a mess in her wake, whereas Judith cleaned while she went. Despite making a homemade meal, Judith had left not even a trace of flour on the counter. The room was pristine. Sterile.

She hated to admit she'd kept her home closer to Judith's style than Ellen's. Carol had inherited her mother's need for cleanliness and order. She'd always hated that about herself but had never been able to change. Maybe now that her living quarters were barely bigger than a van, she could finally learn to live with signs of disorder. She doubted that, though.

"Hey, Mom," Carol said with a forced smile and more excitement than she felt.

Judith lifted her face and smiled, too, but the corners of her mouth wavered as a crease formed between her brows. Even though her mom was in her midseventies now, Carol could easily picture how she looked years ago with their piercing blue eyes, full lips, and narrow nose. Her age hadn't softened her heart or her sharp appearance. She still wore her long hair pulled back in a bun, though the strands were white now instead of the light brown she'd shared with her daughter.

"You're not sick, are you?" Judith asked.

And *that* was the extent of the warm welcome, which really was about as much as Carol was expecting. "No."

"You shouldn't be here if you're sick."

"I'm not sick. I'm tired. I've been on the road." She stepped closer, but the way Judith reared back caused Carol to stop. Her obvious aversion to embracing her daughter stung.

"Wash, please," Judith said.

Carol let the request sink in for a few seconds before turning toward the restroom. This wasn't anything new. Judith had never been warm and affectionate. Ever. In fact, if she *had* smiled and opened her arms like Ellen, Carol would have been the one pulling away with hesitation.

As she washed, Carol pictured the one thing she was counting on to keep her grounded over the next few weeks.

Tobias had filled their backyard in Houston with a variety of flowers. He would spend hours trimming and pruning and talking to the plants as she sat at the little wrought-iron table reading and sipping wine. If Carol cleared her mind enough, she could take herself back there. As a warm breeze brushed her cheeks, she could hear his deep, soothing voice and smell the sweetness of *Salvia dorisiana*, one of the varieties of fruit-scented sage he'd loved so much.

Those were some of the happiest moments Carol could recall, and she clung to them like the lifeline they'd become. She was going to need that lifeline to get her through forcing her apathetic mother to face their broken relationship.

"What the hell am I doing?" she muttered, grabbing the pristine white hand towel embellished with her mom's signature needlework. Carol took her time wiping the water from her hands and face before staring at her reflection.

Part of her wanted to walk out there and announce she'd changed her mind about how long she intended to stay. She'd hang out for a day, maybe two, and then be on her way. But she was here with a purpose, one she couldn't walk away from. Facing the chasm between them was the only way to cross it. She couldn't run from her past forever.

The last few months had taught her a brutal lesson—the past *always* came back to be resolved. She had to work this out while she could. Life had shown her time and time again that people could be ripped away without warning. Her mother was older—time was running out.

"You can do this," she told herself before folding and rehanging the cloth precisely how it'd been before she'd dried her hands and face.

Back in the kitchen, Carol stopped at her mom's side. "It's nice to see you."

"You too," Judith said, though her attention remained on the soup.

"So you're one of us old retirees now," Ellen said, busying herself with fixing a pot of coffee. Though she hadn't looked at Carol as she'd spoken either, her lack of eye contact didn't feel nearly as deliberate as Judith's.

"I am." Carol tried to not overanalyze the slight she felt, but her mother's cold shoulder was already irritating her. She hadn't been in the house for five minutes yet, not nearly enough time to start reading too much into her mother's behavior.

"And living in an RV," Judith stated.

Then again, the clipped tone illuminated everything Carol needed to know. She was getting a frigid greeting because her mother disagreed with her choices. As usual.

"For now," Carol said. "That will grow old eventually, and I'll settle down somewhere."

"Where, Carol? You're selling your house."

Carol cast a glance at her aunt, who diverted her eyes like a child trying to avoid trouble. From the moment Carol had filled her mom in on her plans, Ellen had likely been listening to all the ways Carol was messing up her life *this* time.

Judith turned and stared Carol down. "And what about your belongings?"

"I've sold most of them." She stood a bit taller—a matador bracing for the bull to attack. "Mary took the rest to St. Louis."

Her mom scowled as if she were already fed up with Carol's foolishness. "You burdened your mother-in-law so you could roam the country without a care?"

"I'm sure Mary didn't mind," Ellen offered. She was well-practiced at diffusing the tension between Carol and Judith before things erupted. For years, whenever Ellen was visiting, she would wade into turbulent waters in an attempt to calm them. She was rarely successful.

"No, she didn't mind." Carol's words were almost as sharp as her mother's. "I didn't send her home with anything larger than a few boxes of framed photos. Mary was happy to take them."

"You told me she drove home in Tobias's car." The slight smirk on Judith's lips seemed to imply that she'd caught Carol in a lie. "That's a bit larger than a box."

Carol bit the inside of her lip. Pictured flowers in the wind. Heard Tobias's voice in her mind.

Don't take the bait, she imagined him telling her.

"I gave Tobias's car to his mother," Carol said calmly. "She's not storing it for me. I *gave* it to her after *I* paid off the loan. All we had to do was switch the title. There was no burden passed to her. Thank you for being concerned, though." The last bit came out dripping with sarcasm, but Carol didn't care. For Judith to suggest Mary viewed Carol as the inconvenience her parents always had enraged her. She would never place undue stress on Tobias's family. They were the best thing in her life.

Judith narrowed her eyes into an accusatory stare. "Is this some kind of midlife crisis or...or...some kind of mental breakdown?"

Ellen carefully set three bowls on the counter before turning toward Carol. Where her mother had been direct and borderline harsh, her aunt offered Carol a concerned look and soft smile. "Honey, did something happen at that conference?"

Carol creased her brow with confusion. "What conference?"

"You went to a conference, and then, out of nowhere, you decided to retire and sell everything to live in your camper," Ellen said. "Why? What happened?"

John. John had happened. Her ex-husband had shown up and turned Carol's life upside down, as he'd always done.

Carol had loved being an executive at a pharmaceutical company. However, she'd clung to the monotony like a life preserver after Tobias's death. She'd stopped living— socializing was limited to work; her home became an extension of her office. When John resurfaced, he'd forced her to face that she'd put herself on autopilot and was in danger of never coming out. He had woken her from a daze and made her promise she wouldn't spend her life hiding behind her desk. She had the money and the means to travel. She only had to find the courage to leave the security of her self-inflicted prison—which she'd done without much of an explanation to her mom and aunt.

Though it pained her to concede so soon into her visit, she had to give this one to her mom. From Judith's point of view, Carol's abrupt redirection came out of nowhere. She didn't know where Carol had been or what she'd been going through because Carol had constructed a story about going to a conference rather than dealing with the fallout of her mother's reaction to her taking a trip with John.

Explaining to her mom and aunt where she'd been, as well as what she was planning to do after her visit, was one of the many reasons for needing to see them in person. This wasn't something she'd wanted to discuss over the phone.

"I wasn't at a conference," Carol said calmly as she sat at the small round table in the corner of the kitchen. "I was on the road, but I didn't want you to worry about me."

Judith slammed down the wooden spoon she'd been using. Droplets of soup landed on her apron. "So you *lied*?"

Ellen waved a hand at Judith, as if to dismiss her anger, and stepped closer to Carol. "Why would we worry, sweetheart? Where were you?"

Carol took a second to brace herself, knowing the reaction from her mother was going to be over the top. "I was with John."

Judith visibly stiffened, straightening her shoulders and lifting her chin as she widened her eyes. "*John Bowman*?" She spit out his name as if the words tasted bitter on her tongue.

Carol supposed they probably did to Judith. Her parents never forgave her for falling in love with a man they hadn't deemed good enough. When she'd gotten pregnant and switched from premed to nursing, John became the bane of their existence. Though Carol and John's daughter, Katie, had been the best thing in Carol's life, her parents had never come to accept John.

On one hand, Carol didn't blame them. John's devil-may-care attitude had been an affront to everything they stood for. They'd warned her he was going to drag her down. They'd been right. He'd distracted her from her studies, seduced her into his bed, and spent the next eight years undermining every attempt she'd made to get her life back on track.

However, her parents had made things so much worse than they should have been. If they'd been kinder and more supportive, she might have felt she'd had the support system she needed to leave John long before she did. Long before staying with him had cost her everything.

Katie had died in a horrible accident weeks after her sixth birthday. An accident that everyone, including Carol, had blamed on John. She'd hated him for decades. She hadn't forgiven him until he'd reappeared out of nowhere and she finally came to understand he hadn't been the only one to blame. Something her mother would never comprehend.

"Oh, God," Ellen moaned. "Why?"

"He found me in Houston about two months ago and wanted to take that trip we'd planned for Katie."

Though Ellen was the calmer of the two sisters, her voice came out shrill, somewhere between disbelief and accusation. "And you went?"

Carol hadn't wanted to take that trip, but she didn't regret going. If she hadn't, she never would have found a way to forgive John and let go of the anger that had been holding her back. "He was sick." Her voice came out tense. John had so quickly gone from her archenemy to someone she could admit she had always cared for in some way. Losing him hurt. "He needed to make peace with the past before he died. So, yes, I went."

"*Carol*," her aunt said, sounding as if she'd been the one encumbered with nursing John for weeks. "No wonder you look so exhausted. Honey, are you okay?"

"I'm fine," she stated without hesitation. "Seeing him again was one of the hardest things I've ever done. I'd been hanging on to *a lot* of anger and resentment for so long, but he helped me realize I needed to make peace with the past too." She smiled as warmth filled her chest. "We went to all the places Katie had wanted to see."

"Mount *Hushmore*?" Judith asked softly.

Carol laughed at the reminder of the way Katie always mispronounced the national monument. "Yes. We went to Mount *Hushmore* and Yellowstone. Everywhere she wanted to go. He met Tobias's family when we went to the Gateway Arch. That was...interesting." Her smile softened. "He died the day after I got him home to Dayton. On the anniversary of when we lost Katie."

Ellen gasped. "Were you with him?"

An unexpected prick of tears stung the back of Carol's eyes. "Yeah, I was holding his hand. He said Katie was there too. I believe him because I swear, I felt her waiting to take him...wherever. It was very serene, and I'm glad I was there for him."

Carol was pulled from her moment of recollection when Judith let out a bitter half laugh. She glared at Carol, her eyes burning bright and hot with anger. The way she stood taller, shook her head, and pressed her lips tight let Carol know she was having an internal debate. If history proved true, she'd say what she was thinking, no matter how hurtful her words might be.

Judith's voice came out strained, as if saying the words cut at her throat. "He didn't deserve to die in peace after everything he did."

"Don't say that," Ellen chastised.

Judith didn't seem to hear her sister's warning. "Why in God's name would you let him back into your life after all these years?"

Tightening her jaw, Carol waited until the urge to lash out eased. "I spent a good deal of the time reminding him of the role he played in Katie's death." Carol still felt shame over that, even though John had assured her he understood her anger. "He made so many mistakes, and I rubbed his nose in every one of them until..."

"Until what?" Ellen coaxed.

Twisting her wedding band, drawing on Tobias for strength, Carol said, "When John first showed up, all that anger boiled over. Everything he said gave me an opening to throw the past in his face. Then, one day I was lashing out at him, and I realized a very ugly truth."

"What truth?" Judith narrowed her eyes, as if daring her daughter to defend John.

Carol hesitated. "I carry as much responsibility for what happened to Katie as he did."

"No," Ellen stated firmly, "you do not."

"I knew his drinking was out of control, but I trusted him with our daughter anyway. I was wrong to think he could take care of her."

Ellen crossed the kitchen and put her fingers under Carol's chin, gently forcing her to look up. "You listen to me.

You are *not* responsible for what happened to your little girl. You weren't even home."

Carol appreciated Ellen's attempt at easing her guilt, but she'd already come to terms with the truth. Katie's death was an accident. One that could have been avoided if she and John hadn't been too young and naïve to face their problems head on. They'd both fallen into a cycle of denial about his addiction that contributed to a horrible outcome.

Clutching Ellen's hands, Carol said, "I knew John was an alcoholic, and I ignored it. I could have done things differently. I could have been stronger. I could have forced him to get help. But I never put my foot down because I was tired of always being the bad guy. I didn't fight when I should have."

Ellen shook her head. "*He* was the addict."

"And I was the enabler."

"You were a wonderful mother," Ellen said. "Don't you ever forget that."

Carol offered her a soft smile. "I haven't forgotten. But being a good mother doesn't make me blameless."

Judith interrupted the sweet moment with the same frigid voice she'd used before. "You always did let that man get into your head and twist you around."

As if reminded they weren't alone, Ellen stepped back, clearing the way for Carol to look at her mother.

The fire in Judith's eyes hadn't died, but she'd clearly put up the wall she was so good at hiding behind. She used that mechanism to keep the world, including her daughter, on the outside of her emotions. Carol had learned how to do the same. She'd hidden behind her walls for far too long.

The muscles in Judith's jaw flexed several times before

she spoke. "God knows your father and I tried to talk sense into you. You wouldn't listen."

"You may not have liked John," Carol said calmly, "but without him, I wouldn't have had Katie. I wouldn't change that for anything. Would you?"

Her words hit her mother's heart. Carol knew by the slight jolt that caused her to sway.

Judith threw up her hands before walking away.

Ellen frowned at Carol. "That wasn't called for, Carol. You know she loved Katie."

Shame made her lower her face. "I know. I'll apologize."

Carol pushed herself up and went in search of her mother. She found her in the living room, staring out the window, shutting out the world around her as she tended to do when she was frustrated with her daughter, which was most of the time.

Continue Reading A Life Without Flowers

ALSO BY MARCI BOLDEN

A Life Without Water Series:

A Life Without Water

A Life Without Flowers

A Life Without Regrets (Coming Soon)

Stonehill Series:

The Road Leads Back

Friends Without Benefits

The Forgotten Path

Jessica's Wish

This Old Cafe

Forever Yours

The Women of Hearts Series:

Hidden Hearts

Burning Hearts

Stolen Hearts

Secret Hearts

Other Titles:

California Can Wait

Seducing Kate

The Rebound

ACKNOWLEDGMENTS

A huge thank you to Shelly Stinchcomb for your endless encouragement and to Shelley Denman for letting me "borrow" your name. I hope this book has made you both proud of your involvement in making it a reality.

ABOUT THE AUTHOR

As a teen, Marci Bolden skipped over young adult books and jumped right into reading romance novels. She never left.

Marci lives in the Midwest with her husband, kiddos, and numerous rescue pets. If she had an ounce of willpower, Marci would embrace healthy living, but until cupcakes and wine are no longer available at the local market, she will appease her guilt by reading self-help books and promising to join a gym "soon."

Visit her here:
www.marcibolden.com

facebook.com/MarciBoldenAuthor
twitter.com/BoldenMarci
instagram.com/marciboldenauthor

Printed in the USA
CPSIA information can be obtained
at www.ICGtesting.com
LVHW041049010923
756940LV00001B/103

9 781950 348206